CHAPTER

1

"Snowball hot chocolate for me." Grace hopped down the cafe steps, narrowly avoiding a life-sized light-up penguin. "And a tea for you. Unless…" She wafted the red cup under my nose. *Yes*, it did smell of melted toffee, and *yes*, it did have tiny Rolos floating on the top, and *yes*, I'd normally do bad, bad things to get my hands on anything-very-tiny-that-should-be-normal-sized, but my best friend knew my rule…

"Tea for ever." Aka, there was no way I was having a Christmas drink. It was a slippery slope. One minute I'd be developing a taste for candy-cane cream, and two weeks later I'd be wearing a light-up jumper and singing along to Mariah. "Thanks though."

"Well, you know what they say…" Grace looked around at the festoon lights strung up along the ramshackle black-and-white shops on the high street. At the Christmas tree twinkling outside the big Marks and Spencer. At the light-up crackers that had been weaved into the streetlights, ready to be lit up. "... definitely not the most wonderful time of the year or anything..."

I ignored the hard prod she gave me in the ribs. What was it about lightbulbs that made everyone act weird? No one got emotional about torches?!

But Grace was resting her chin on her hands and smiling innocently in her way that couldn't not make me laugh.

"See also..." I struggled to keep my face straight. "'I wish it wasn't Christmas *any* day'." But my mistake was singing it to the correct tune. Grace waggled her finger at me in excitement.

"Seeeee!! Even Grinchy McGrinch-face has got some Christmas spirit buried in there." I raised an eyebrow. "OK, OK." She laughed. "Too soon." But my eyebrow gave up, and instead I smiled. Grace would happily make tinsel a year-round house decoration if she could, so I needed to rein in my Scroogey vibes. Especially this year. "But be warned, I'm never giving up ho-ho-hope."

Grace was the only one who knew my secret. The real reason why I hated everything red, gold, green – or

2

ALL THE JINGLE LADIES

BETH GARROD

SCHOLASTIC

Published in the UK by Scholastic, 2022
1 London Bridge, London, SE1 9BA
Scholastic Ireland, 89E Lagan Road, Dublin Industrial Estate,
Glasnevin, Dublin, D11 HP5F

SCHOLASTIC and associated logos are trademarks and/or
registered trademarks of Scholastic Inc.

Text © Beth Garrod, 2022
Cover image © AdobeStock

ISBN 978 0702 31416 2

A CIP catalogue record for this book
is available from the British Library.

Printed by CPI Group (UK) Ltd, Croydon, CR0 4YY
Paper made from wood grown in sustainable forests
and other controlled sources.

1 3 5 7 9 10 8 6 4 2

This
and di
ficti

anything even remotely gingerbread flavoured. The real reason I went into hibernation in November and didn't come out till January.

When I was little, Christmas had been my favourite time of year. Right up until my parents, with their nice normal jobs in a nice normal library and something to do with nice normal pet insurance, decided to not just play music for a hobby but to release a song. And not just any song. "Love Your Elf!" – the world's worst Christmas song *ever*. Cheesy lyrics? Tick. Sleigh bells? Jingly tick. Totally cringe music video with the final line delivered by an annoying child painted green, with curly bright red hair pulled up in high plaits, and dressed up as a Christmas elf EVEN THOUGH CHRISTMAS ELVES AREN'T EVEN GREEN? A massive, flashing, factually inaccurate big green-and-red tick.

And if anyone knew just how annoying the child was, it was me. Because I *was* the child. Annoying Green Christmas Elf was me. And every Christmas that stupid lyric haunted me.

"Happy holidays from the cutest little elf in the whole wide world!"

I'd delivered it with such enthusiasm too. And I really shouldn't have. My wobbly front tooth meant I whistled my way through the Ws.

My six-year-old self had thought being on a set with fake snow in the summer was the coolest thing ever. Which it was, until after a few years of being a slow burn, the song started to get popular. And as the world discovered "Love Your Elf!", they also discovered the video and the "cutest little elf", and for the next few years, as Christmas rolled round, so did the shouts across the playground about my "elf-esteem" and strangers asking "was it easy being green". Having the surname Bell really didn't help either. And every year, as we got closer to December, the more I started to panic.

Eurgh. The only thing that had made it any better was moving to Bromster five years ago and keeping my elf identity a secret. Since being here I'd managed to avoid all things Christmas, and done everything I could to prevent raising any elfy suspicions, including not being seen out with my parents, just in case someone recognized us. But the hard work had been worth it. Now I was fifteen, I'd finally managed to get back to being normal Molly, and I hadn't been the butt of a joke about "elf and safety" in years. Just the way I liked it.

Grace looped her arm through mine. "Soooo, if we're not talking about Christmas, which judging by that face we're not." Oops. Time to shake off the elf-rage and get back to being better company. "Any news back from

Zaiynab?" She said it even more cheerfully than normal. "Cos I'm ready to bail on the whole dancing thing and become a full-time POWR-nat-or..." She trailed off. "POWR-natic?" She shrugged. "Or whatever their fans are called."

I wasn't sure The POWR had a fandom yet – even if they were my favourite band of all time. Zaiynab and Matt went to our school and were two years above – and together they made the kind of indie-retro music I loved. Which is why, even though I was too intimidated to even look at them at school, when they'd said they were looking for someone to help behind the scenes on production, I'd sent them some of my lyrics and beats (well, Grace had been the one to actually press send, but teamwork makes the dream work). Behind the scenes was *exactly* where I wanted to be! But I hadn't heard anything since.

"No news."

"*Yet*." Grace jumped right in. She always had my back.

"Yet. And remember when you see them, my parents know NOTHING."

The less they, or anyone else, knew about me and my life the better. Grace was my only safe space.

"Sure thing, Mol." We turned down to the path by the river. It was freezing, but I always went this way as no one else from school did, so it was easier to get home without any unwanted conversations. "Although..." Grace stopped. "You know what works *wonders* for de-stressing when waiting to find out if you got a place in the best band in St Augustine's?" I coughed. "Sorry, the world..." *Better*.

Grace reached into her back pocket and pulled out ... nothing. She waved the nothing in the air. "Two tickets to see *Sleigh Another Day. With me! Next weekend!*"

Face – be kind! Do NOT look horrified. It's so nice seeing Grace happy for a change, do NOT ruin it! "The ... *Christmas* romcom?"

"*Mrghhhhhh.*" Grace made a noise like a melting horse, a soppy grin on her face. "*THE* Christmas romcom, with that guy I was telling you about. God's gift to eyes." Grace loved all things film and had filled me in – it was the first major movie for this new actor, and by the way Grace had gone on, I was expecting big things. Big, super-hot, great hair, perfect smile, weirdly alluring forearms kind of things. "And Maeve Murphy. Style icon. Legend. All-round goddess." Even I, who knew nothing about movies, knew who Maeve was. She was a few years older than us, and a total badass who took no nonsense from anyone. "Apparently their chemistry is a-maaaa-zing."

"Are we talking Grace and Simon amazing?" I asked, knowing it would make Grace smile even more. Yup, there it was. The big dreamy smile. Happy-dazed blinking (resulting in me emergency-manhandling her out of the way of a bin). "Doesn't Si want to see it with you?"

Grace shrugged.

"Simon said it's not his thing…" Why was this making her smile even more? "Have I ever told you, he looks really cute when he's disinterested."

"You *may* have mentioned it." She really had. And done a photo presentation as "evidence". See also Simon looking cute when he a) used a vending machine, b) took off shoes and c) sneezed. "What about your dad? He loves cinema trips with you…" I trailed off. "Even if he thinks carrot sticks are a legit snack."

I loved Mr W but claiming they were as good as popcorn was just factually wrong.

Grace's smile disappeared. "Don't think he'd be up for it this year. You know he said we shouldn't do presents for the first time ever?" I nodded. "And our Christmas party is off too?" I didn't know that bit. They had a friends and family party every year, and it was the only festive thing I actually enjoyed going to. Or went to at all. She sighed. "Last night he said we aren't even getting a tree." Ouch.

I instantly felt rubbish for not just saying yes to the film. Terrible friending. Grace's house, Grace's family, normally rivalled Father Christmas and his grotto when it came to going all out for Christmas. Grace lived with her dad and granddad, Grampy G, who loved Christmas more than anyone I'd ever met. Grampy G normally decorated every inch of their house – even the loo had a Santa hat – dressed up as Father Christmas and had a tradition for every single day in December. Some for November too.

Grampy G was the one who made their Christmas cake. The one who made sure the Christmas tree farm always picked out the best tree for them. The one who made sure Grace and her dad still hung up stockings every single year. The one who organized our local primary school to design Christmas lights for our village, which were guaranteed hilarious and made drivers come from all over the country just to take photos. Grampy G was even the one who first got me into baking, with all his Christmas biscuit recipes.

And last year, he was the one who cheered up all the residents in his care home, Holly Hospice, by organizing a huge Secret Santa with presents for every single one of them.

But … and it still hurt so much to think about it. Last year, Grampy G had passed away a few days before

Christmas. December 22nd.

I looked back at Grace – she was twiddling the silver bracelet he'd given her when she was little. We'd all known it was coming, and the staff at Holly Hospice had been amazing, but it was so awful. So, so awful. And Christmas had passed by like a gloomy Monday in January.

And I realized right then, that this year, how I felt about Christmas could take a serious break. As much as I'd hate it, it was time for me to channel my inner Grampy G. Be the Christmas buddy Grace needed, and un-cancel Christmas just for a few weeks.

"Count me in. For the film." Grace looked at me like I'd just been body-snatched. "Sounds great."

"Count you in for … the super Christmassy romcom?"

I nodded. Luckily Grace was too busy whooping and hugging me to see the fear in my eyes. I was just going to have to lie very low at the cinema. So low I was horizontal. Anything festive was a high-risk zone. "And maybe I can try your hot chocolate after all. It smells TOO good."

"Yes, Mol! We love to see it!" Grace grinned as she watched me take a sip. "Who knows. You might love the film?" A cheesy Christmas film where everyone lived happy ever after? All signs were pointing towards no. "It's got *everything*. Giant snow globes. A high-speed snowy sleigh chase through the snow in Lapland. A hot snog by Edinburgh Castle in the snow."

So lots of snow then. If there was one thing Grace loved more than Christmas, it was films. Well, that and Simon. If there was a movie about Simon at Christmas in the snow, she might actually explode. She'd been counting down to watching *Sleigh Another Day* ever since it was announced. I'd only been half-listening, as I assumed I'd never see it in a million years, but had picked up that it was this year's big British festive romcom. Something to do with a guy who hated Christmas, but who moved in next door to a girl whose family made festive decorations for a living. So *of course* they were going to fall in love. *Of course* it was going to be super cheesy and full of sleigh bells and perfect snow. And *of course* they were going to live happily ever after. Had anyone in real life ever had a snowball fight and ended up more in love? No, they ended up soggy, with wet gloves, numb hands and socks full of snow … and regret.

But Grace was rewatching the trailer on her phone. She held out a reindeer-shaped earbud.

"Honestly, this bit where Joseph D Chambers dresses up as Santa…" She trailed off. "Is it OK to fancy Father Christmas? Asking for a friend."

"Well, tell your friend, who is one hundred per cent definitely you, it's probably illegal in ten countries but I'm not judging."

I left her to it and flicked through social media. I never posted, just lurked. Today's clip that was everywhere was Daisy, a girl I played netball with, chatting to a friend as a seagull lands on her head and she shrieks. It already had its own dubstep remix, over 3,000 likes, and the top comment said Daisy should now be known as Cliff.

And *that* was why no one could ever, EVER know about Elf Girl. I shoved my phone in my pocket. Grace was watching a dog in a snowman costume trot past, the sad look in her eyes back again. Animals in festive costumes were Grampy G's fave.

Right, time to step up Mission Cheer Grace Up.

"Grace, just a thought… If you and your dad aren't doing presents how about I ask for donations to Grampy G's fundraiser too? Instead of any for me?" I paused. "We can just borrow my sister's stuff and pretend it's ours? Win win."

But it worked. Grace stopped getting teary-eyed at the snowdog. "You'd really do that? Aren't you holding out for that art subscription box?"

I grinned. "And *that's* why having a February birthday can be very useful."

She gave me the biggest hug, my puffy coat taking the impact. "You are the absolute best, you know that?" But this could be the perfect way of giving our fundraiser a boost. All year we'd been trying to raise £500 for a Christmas party fund for the residents of Holly Hospice, to help Grampy G's legacy live on. But despite putting everything into it, we'd only got to £326 and things had completely stalled.

"WELL. HELLOOOO THERE BROMSTER CHRISTMAS LIGHTS FANS!" A man's voice wafted down the path from the cathedral. "IT'S TIME TO GET ON DOWN TO SOME SANTA-TASTIC CHRISTMAS CHOOOONS!"

Oh no. Oh no, oh no?! I knew *just* what this was.

Normally not much happened in Bromster except the time we hit the news for being the only place in the UK to run out of gherkins in McDonald's. But at Christmas they threw a huge street party to turn on the lights. Complete with cheesy Christmas karaoke.

I normally avoided it like a herd of stampeding reindeer. But Grace was full meerkating, trying to work out where the voice was coming from. With a roar from the crowd the band launched into "I Wish It Could Be Christmas Every Day". Did anyone ask for a banjo cover of it? No. Were they getting it anyway? Absolutely.

And Grace was … walking towards it?! Had she not realized what this was?!

Yes, I was going to try for some Christmas cheer, but this was too much! Too soon! She was walking towards the ultimate danger zone.

"Grace?! It's…" I nodded to the huge crowd dancing around the stage. *"You know what!"*

The second to last Friday in November, aka Bromster's annual Christmas lights switch-on. Complete with most embarrassing band in the world, The Rocking Stockings, doing their one performance of the year. And there they were: a giant six-foot-seven parsnip on guitar and a very enthusiastic Christmas turkey on banjo. Last year the local paper had described it as "an eaten-a-whole-Toblerone-on-Christmas-Day hallucinogenic experience" and that was being polite.

Who wants to see giant man-parsnip crooning? *Ew.* Even the phrase "man-parsnip" made me shudder.

"C'mon, Mols?" Grace was hopping around. "We've never been. And there's space at the back to hide…"

Every bit of me wanted to run away. But Grace was doing some kind of Christmas bop, and a picture of Grampy G giving me one of his looks flashed into my brain.

"The very back?" I asked, optimistically. Too late.

Grace was already dragging me down the cobbled street. I spotted some lads from school and pulled my hoodie up. I already regretted this. Oh and great, there were my netball team, filming The Rocking Stockings, laughing their heads off, and not in a good way. I, however, found it less funny.

Because The Rocking Stockings were my mum and dad. Which was why my life was one big carefully constructed plan to make sure no one knew we were related. The Rocking Stockings, who were now kissing under some fake mistletoe, were the reason I always walked the long way home. That I said "no" whenever my parents offered to pick me up from school. Or town. Why I'd told them our netball matches didn't allow supporters.

My only small victory was that when we moved, I'd got them to agree to switch the name of their band from The Brussel Shouts to The Rocking Stockings, so no one knew they were behind "Love Your Elf!"

I grabbed Grace's bobble hat and pulled it on.

"No eye contact. No waving. And absolutely no talking to them afterwards."

"I know the drill, Mol … though the offer to be a dancing roast potato for them still stands." I flared my nostrils. "Tell me they don't look amazing up there?!"

She'd never seen them in action before.

"They do not look amazing up there." I felt a bit bad. I did actually love my parents to bits. I just wished they could be more … less. I crossed my fingers and willed them to remember our deal. That if they ever saw me when they were like this, they HAD to ignore me. One forgetful wave and the last five years of carefully getting back in control of my life could be over.

"SO, WHO IS READY FOR…" My breathless dad drummed the mic on his knee. "REQUEST TIME?!"

The crowd cheered and started shouting out suggestions. "'Love Your Elf'!" someone screamed. And again. I glared at Dad. There was NO way. They'd agreed NEVER to play it in public ever again!

But the crowd were clapping and chanting it over and over. "ELF! ELF! ELF!"

Mum and Dad scanned the crowd. Were they looking for me? They KNEW the rule?!

"Grace," I panicked. "Can we go?" But she'd disappeared to hunt for some free churros.

And like a giant out-of-control sleigh careering towards me, my nightmare smacked me in the face. The Rocking Stockings were playing "Love Your Elf!". The crowd were singing. And … was my mum trying to prove a turkey could twerk?!

"OK, *THAT*…" Zaiynab appeared out of nowhere, her

perfect black bob swinging under her chin. What was she doing here? And why was she talking to me?! And why was Matt with her? And could Grace please come back?! "... is exactly NOT what our band is looking for." She laughed.

"Hahahahaha!" I panic-howled like I'd never heard anything funnier. "Yes, absolutely. *Awful*," I said in a total flap. This could not be happening?! *Graaaaace*. I tried to summon her with my mind.

"And this song?" Zaiynab looked like she was personally insulted by it.

Were my toes sweating? My toes were sweating.

"Yes. Absolutely. Awful," I said. I needed some more words. But it was hard to think when Matt was flinching at Mum and Dad harmonizing "we think you're really swell".

"Who could write lyrics like that?!" Zaiynab grinned. But ... I knew all too well. My closest genetic relatives. And Mum was now yelling, "Let's put the rock into root vegetables!" "Novelty music is The Worst, right, Matt?" He nodded as Zaiynab sighed. "And that cute little elf line?" My parents had got a child up onstage to sing it. "Poor girl."

Matt stared at the stage, in what looked like shock. "If we *ever* do that onstage ... permission to kill me."

Dad was giving Mum a piggyback as she swung the mic around her head.

"Yeah." Think of something insightful to say, Molly. "Absolutely. Awful." OK, this time Zaiynab definitely noticed.

I HAD to get out of here. What if my parents waved? Or said hello? Zaiynab and Matt would never speak to me again, let alone consider me for The POWR. "Anyway, I need to go and..." I looked around for an urgent excuse. "Get some Christmas churros. Urgently."

"Sure," Zaiynab said politely, like a churros emergency might actually be a thing. "We just came to say thanks for sending your stuff. We need a bit more time, though, so watch this space."

Watch this space? Did that mean there was hope after all?

And, as I scurried towards a man dressed as a giant churro, I wondered: was it finally my turn for a Christmas miracle?

CHAPTER

2

I swear even Mr W – who once accidentally blended his own finger and just said, "I see" – gasped.

This *had* to be a joke? A flashing green-and-white laser beam joke.

"Mols." Grace shook my shoulders. "You OK?"

I blinked. But the outline of a snowman brandishing a carrot was already burnt into my retinas.

"You look like a zombie," Grace said quietly. "A Christmas zombie, and … well, that's not a thing." But even Grace couldn't take her eyes off what was in front of us. It was like Times Square had landed in our village – if Times Square mainly displayed flashing reindeers.

Mum and Dad had mentioned they were going to "commit to Christmas" this year, but for some naïve reason I thought they'd listened when I'd said words like "subtle" and "tasteful".

A full-sized sleigh on the roof.

A snowwoman climbing the only tree in our garden.

And was that a fake reindeer putting its head in and out of our kitchen window pretending to eat a light-up carrot?

HOW WAS ANY OF THIS SUBTLE AND TASTEFUL?!

And did some fake snow just land on my nose? Brilliant.

Not content with lighting up our little cul-de-sac enough to be seen from space, they'd sprayed it with fake snow too. Thank goodness our little village consisted mainly of old people and cats.

I pulled Grace's bobble hat down even further, as if somehow it could double up as an invisibility cloak.

"I really have never seen an elf as big as this," Mr W said calmly, looking up at a flashing green-and-red stripy pair of shorts towering above him. Wasn't the key word for Santa's little helpers, *little*? Not nine foot!

And my parents nagged me for wasting money leaving the TV on standby. Make it make sense.

I buried my head in my hands. If anyone found out this was my house, my life would be a nightmare. Grace grabbed me, pulling me out of the way of a cracker-wielding snowman which had started to robotically wheel around the grass.

"I'm s-sorry, Grace." My voice spluttered. "I should have warned you…" Of what I didn't know. My parents being out of Christmas control? Having an eye poked out by a mechanical cracker? Grace wasn't even getting a tree, and yet I'd brought her here, to enough festive illuminations for an Olympic opening ceremony.

"Warned me?" Grace ran on to the small patch of front lawn and grabbed a handful of snow. I *think* it was shredded old plastic carrier bags, but if Grace was going with it, I wasn't going to burst her bubble. "This is the highlight of the week." She stopped dead. "Maybe actually YEAR." She did actually look happier than she had done in ages. She grabbed her dad's hand and pulled him over to our fence. "Dad, c'mon, tell me a dreamy singing robin" – she pointed to the mechanical mutant-sized robin chirping quite a threatening version of "Merry Christmas Everyone" – "doesn't get you in the festive spirit?"

But Mr W put a gentle hand on her arm. "Grace, please don't do this. I thought we'd talked about it…"

"Du-du-du-daaaaaa!" Mum flung open the front door, her red-and-white dressing gown that said 'Mrs

Christmas' on the back billowing behind her. She'd sewn lights into the sleeves – did she know they were flashing orange? She looked like a road sign. "Whaddya think?"

Dad stepped out in a matching Mr Christmas dressing gown and light-up Christmas pudding slippers, clutching a very confused Sosig, who was wearing a fluffy owl dog-hoodie. Of course. How traditional. Two Christmas roadworks and their trusty dog-owl. My poor traumatized Pomsky gave me a look of pure despair. Sorry, Sosig – if I had any idea how to rein Mum and Dad in there wouldn't be a mechanical snowman yelling "happy holidays" to a confused food delivery driver next door.

I counted down ... forty-nine days till Christmas decorations could come down. Forty-nine days to do whatever it took to stop anyone discovering that Father Christmas had sneezed all over my house. And lawn. Oh yep ... Cara too. Who knew you could get a red nose and antlers for a camper van?

"The whole thing's epic," Grace said, taking a photo of Sosig, who had tilted his head, his tongue lolloping down past his chin. Honestly, how many dogs know how to work their angles?

"It's a health hazard," I grumbled to myself, almost tripping over a herd of miniature reindeer. They were at the end of the path to our little garden gate and Mum was happily explaining that once December started, we'd move them one step nearer every day until Christmas day until they reached our chimney. Inside our house. Which made falling over when trying to watch TV a guaranteed activity.

But I could hear a car coming down the little high street, so ran inside before the headlights picked me up. Oof, my heart sank – inside was no better, every single surface was covered in Christmas. Or glitter. Or both. I hurdled a row of mini snowmen just to get to the stairs.

Dad closed the front door and whipped out his face mask. "Masks on, guys. Don't want anyone catching tinsel-itis." He laughed so much he didn't notice my groan. At least Grace looked happy and Grampy G would definitely approve. "Isn't it mesmerizing?" Dad stared lovingly at a dancing Christmas pudding doorstop. "Now, seeing as it's a Grolly evening tonight" – that's what he called "Grace and Molly time". He nudged my elbow. "Girls together. We love to see it!" I needed to get him off the internet. *Immediately.* "And seeing as we're celebrating." We were? "We thought we could have pizza. Samuel's fave, if I'm not mistaken?" He waggled his eyebrows at Mr W.

Suspicious. This all seemed worryingly normal. And what celebration?

"Piiiiiiiiizza?!" A blur of long brown hair and fluffy horse onesie bump-slid down the stairs right on to my feet. If my little sister Billy wasn't riding a horse, near a horse, watching videos about a horse, then she was dressed like one. It had been just me and Tess until I was ten, but then along came Billy. My parents were good at surprises. "I love pizza!!!!" She threw her hands around my waist. I patted her head. She neighed. Yup, my family was totally normal.

"Great. *Christmas* pizza it is." Dad rubbed his hands together. "Brussels, carrots in cardis" – it's what he called veggie pigs in blankets – "potatoes, the works. Oooh, does cranberry sauce go with cheese...?"

Why was nothing about my life ever normal? I looked up at the big gold disc on the wall.

I swear that stupid song was when it had all gone wrong. How could three mins twenty-two seconds cause so much havoc?

"Someone say pizza?" My big sister Tess leant over the banister at the top of the stairs. Why was she home from uni? Probably making sure Mum and Dad didn't give her room to me. Or maybe it was to enjoy my despair at the Christmasification of the house. She loved laughing at my pain. "Oh, hi, Grace!" She caught me looking at the gold disc. "You're not still going on about that, are you?"

I wasn't sure one small sigh to myself counted as "going on", but it was impossible to argue with my sister.

"Oh, hi, Tess. I'm fine, thanks – thank you for asking." I walked up the stairs. "And before you check, I'm completely and utterly totally OK with the very tasteful and subtle Christmas decorations that are literally ..." I noticed the hallway lampshade which had been replaced by a giant bauble. "... everywhere." My house looked like a photo of "You Won't Believe What One Family Do For Christmas".

"Great, isn't it?" With a smug smirk, Tess threw a piece of tinsel round her neck like a scarf. "Oh, and you officially *have* to be nice to me." She stood firmly in my way. "I'm currently heartbroken."

"Is that right?" She mainly looked delighted at how miserable I was about living in The Grotto, Grotto Street, United Grottoland.

"It is right. Eva split up with me." Oh, that was actually bad news. They'd been together all term, a record for my sister. "So I'm going to have to throw myself into being single and ready to mingle." She shook a Christmas squirrel ornament with a tiny bell on it. "...and jingle." She cackled in a way that made me feel deeply uncomfortable – like when *Naked Attraction* came on when we were watching TV with Mum and Dad.

"Is that why you're back?" I squeezed past her and

headed into my and Billy's room. Thank goodness. Not a decoration in sight. I collapsed on to my bed with relief.

Tess leant in the doorway. "Nah, Mum and Dad asked. Said it was urgent…"

"Worrying," I said. Tess nodded. The calamity of being in this family was something we both agreed on. Annoying as my big sister was, it was good having another human in the world to experience being the offspring of my parents with. Billy didn't count, as she would rather be the offspring of a horse. But Billy was calling Tess, and Grace popped her head in to ask me to plug in her phone while she grabbed some drinks.

I fumbled under my bed for my charger, but my hand found something else. The one Christmas thing I'd kept – the card Grampy G had sent me last year. He'd been so ill but had been determined to write them for everyone – Grace and I had hand delivered the lot.

I shuffled back on to my pillow and opened it up.

To the marvellous Molly-Moo

Just seeing his shaky handwriting felt like a punch. I hadn't had any grandparents growing up and Grampy G used to say he'd filled in the paperwork to make me a granddaughter-in-friend-in-law.

*oh oh oh!**

*Have the merriest of Christmases, and may all
of your new years be merry and bright.*

I could say it word for word without even looking at
the card.

*Keep shining, Mol. You're a Christmas star, and
the best gift you could ever give me is a promise
to make sure Grace always celebrates Christmas
with the magic it deserves. You too.*

*It really is the most wonderful time of the
year.*

All my love,

GG xx

*PS Don't forget to send Gracey pics of Sosig in his
outfits!!!*

**That's what Santa Claus says when he walks
backwards.*

Ouch. My eyes prickled. I stuffed it away. Grace didn't
need to see me upset – that wouldn't bring Christmas
cheer, and that's exactly what I'd promised Grampy G

I'd do. And I really did want to bring Grace some cheer. So if her dad was cancelling Christmas, what else could I do? I plugged her phone in and I noticed she'd updated her wallpaper – a picture of her, Grampy G and Mr W. All big smiles, all wearing paper crowns, at the Holly Hospice Christmas party; the staff pulling party poppers around them. An idea pinged into my head. And by the time Grace came back with the drinks, it had escalated into something way bigger.

"Grace. You know you said this is the first year you're not having your Christmas party? Well …" Was I going to regret this? Probably. If it wasn't such a sure-fire way to give Grace's Christmas a boost, there was no way I'd even suggest it. "… what if we could celebrate Grampy G *and* raise money for Holly Hospice?" And maybe even help her dad find some of the Christmas joy he used to have so much of?

Grace bent forward and put her head on her knee, like it was totally normal to bend like a pretzel.

"Go on…"

"Well … if your dad doesn't want to throw your Christmas party. How about … *we* do? In Grampy G's honour?" Grace tilted her head. "Just something little for our families, Simon, whoever." Only people that I could trust to be seen out in public with my parents. "We could have music, maybe a secret Santa, and things to raise money? Like an auction? Or a bake sale…" Yes, I was seeing it already. I could design a totalizer, and Grace could run the show while I helped out behind the scenes. "Oooooh, and you could do your *Nutcracker* dance?" The one she'd had to pull out of last December that her dad had never got to see. "Imagine. We might finally hit that five-hundred-pound target?"

But I didn't need to say anything else. Because Grace had jumped on to the bed. Well, more specifically, on to me.

"Molly, you're a genius! BEST. IDEA. EVERRRR!!" She gave me a massive cuddle, Grampy G style. "We'll totally hit our target! And Grampy G would LOVE it." She bounced off the bed and walked to the window. "The first ever … Grampy G's Grotto…" She was grinning as she looked out. "We've even got the decorations already. AND WE CAN ASK SIMON TO HAVE IT AT HIS FAMILY'S RESTAURANT!" Grace did hear me say "little", right? But she'd collapsed back on the floor and was fanning herself. "Sorry, too many good ideas all at once."

She messaged Simon immediately and then started recording an audio note of a steady stream of ideas. Sosig-shaped gingerbread! Pin the tinsel on the Christmas tree! Hook a Christmas turkey!

And I loved it. I hadn't seen her this happy in ages. And it was the first time I'd seen her look forward to Christmas all year. Yup. This was going to be fine. Wasn't it?

Grace suddenly sat up.

"We can tell everyone at dinner!" She rubbed her hands together.

"Sure. I can start working on the invites tomorrow..." I could already see how I wanted it to look. A cute minimal Christmas house, the Holly Hospice logo strung across in lights. Ooh, and we could use that picture of Grampy G when he dressed up as Santa and climbed on Grace's roof.

Grace's phone lit up. And when she saw who'd messaged, so did she. It had to be Simon.

"Is it a yes?"

"How did you know?" She tried and failed to stop smiling. "He said he'd ask his parents. And I'm sorry, but seriously..." She closed her eyes and pretended to dribble as she turned the screen to face me. He'd sent a changing room selfie of him trying on a posh suit, along with "*approve* 😜. *For date night* ♥ 🔥".

"How am I meant to reply to *that*?" Erm, I wasn't exactly the best person to give her dating advice, since I'd been on a sum total of ... none. And had kissed a sum total of … no people. "'Spose there's only one way…" She dug out the photo of us pulling stupid faces on the walk home and sent it off.

Guess that wasn't for our eyes only then – must remember that next time I do that zero neck pose. What would Si reply with? I'd never seen a funny selfie from him *ever*. He was all broody looks and captions that made no sense. Still, at least he posted on social. I would never. Too much risk of my old life getting jumbled up with this one.

"He's anniversary shopping, isn't he…" Grace zoomed in and out on his picture with a soppy grin. She'd booked a posh meal for them and had been counting down to it for weeks. Around fifty-two of them. "I was just going to wear my gold dress, but if he's looking like *that*, I'm going to have to step it up."

"Oi. As if you need to step up *anything*," I said. She rolled her big brown eyes – taking compliments wasn't one of Grace's many skills. "Anyone who gets to go out with THE Grace Wright is hashtag blessed indeed." I put my hands together and tried to look priest-y and wise. Grace laughed – she never believed me. But she was the best, inside and out. Not only was she the funniest, most optimistic, kindest person I knew, with her huge smile and cheekbone-dimple combo, she had one of those faces that could switch from super friendly to full supermodel vibes, just by looking out the window to see if it was raining. I once took a photo of her reading a cheese packet and she looked like she was on a magazine cover. Not that she thought it for a second. But dinner was ready so we headed downstairs, excited to make our announcement.

In our house, there was one thing more worrying than Mum and Dad wearing matching, flimsy dressing gowns with a tendency to fall open. Or Tess saying she was "pleased" to see me. And that's discovering a big "SURPRISE!" banner in the kitchen.

I looked at Mum. She was holding a glass of wine. PHEW! I loved Billy, but sibling number four I was not ready for.

"Take a seat." Dad gestured to the table. I smiled at Mr W, respecting that he'd stood firm in jeans and jumper when my parents were in their third costume change of the evening. "Or should I say, pull up a polar bear."

Oh yes. Our chairs now had added white ears and tails. Of course. And our serving bowls had been replaced by stocking-shaped dishes. And Sosig's bed was now a glittery gold sleigh. Billy was already tucking into a slice of Christmas pizza. Nothing fazed her.

"Should I be worried?" I sat down slowly. Tess caught my eye, looking just as alarmed.

Mum rubbed my shoulders. "Only if you don't like surprises." Dad bopped her on the nose. "Pretty amazing surprises."

I didn't think I did. Mum and Dad's definition of "amazing" was way too broad. And was that champagne? We normally had supermarket-brand cola. Gulp.

"Are we moving?" Tess folded her arms. "Cos if we are, can I remind you how much I *need* my own room, please. And it better be near enough to still see my friends."

"Nope." Mum offered Mr W the jug of weird white liquid. "Snowball smoothie, Sam?" It looked like milk with white chocolate buttons in. "It's milk. But with white chocolate buttons in."

Grace saw my horrified face and mouthed, "Don't worry". Easy for her to say. Her responsible adults weren't currently dressed as a Christmas tree and a giant cracker.

"Are we getting a pony?" Billy said, her eyes so wide it was like she'd spotted the real Father Christmas.

"No, darling," Dad said softly, but Bil's smile only got bigger.

"TWO PONIES?" She huffed when he shook his head. "Reindeer then. Can you ride a reindeer? I think *I* could ride a reindeer." We'd taken Bil to a city farm last year and she loved the reindeer, whereas the one giving me evils had bitten a hole in my glove. "Did you know they've got really hairy noses. To warm the air that comes in? And hairy feet too. Hairier than Dad's."

Silence.

"It's not that, Bils. And for the record" – Dad shot Mr W a look – "I would say I had very *averagely* hairy feet."

Definitely a thing only someone with very much above average hairy feet would say. Mr W sipped at his smoothie, staring at the table, clearly not ready to engage in furry feet chat.

"So if there are no more guesses…" Dad flicked on the flashing Christmas lights on his costume. "Get ready to crank your Christmas fun up to ten!" Erm, mine was very much on a minus twenty with no intention of shifting. Mum sidestepped next to him.

"Kiddos, you might need to pack your bags!" She shimmied. I'd never seen a cracker shimmy before. "And get ready to take some serious selfies." Or did she say "elfies"? *Argh*. Not even December and my elfxiety was already out of control. "For a weekend away. *Next* weekend."

Finally I relaxed. A trip away? That *was* actually quite cool. We never went anywhere! Although…

"But Grace and I have got tickets for something…" If

I kept Grace away from drooling over Joseph D Thingy, very bad things could happen. "*Sleigh Another Day.*"

Mum grinned. "Well, hopefully Gracey can forgive us. Because she's invited too."

Mr W smiled at his daughter. "Which you're going to need to say a very big thank you for…"

Grace gave me a look. I shrugged back. Zero clue, my friend.

"Shall we?" Mum squeezed Dad's hand. They'd rehearsed this. Dad cleared his throat dramatically.

"Buckle up, Christmas bunnies." I think he was getting confused with Easter. "We're off on a very special family trip to … London!" LONDON?! *Cool!* I'd always wanted to go!

"And don't worry about missing *Sleigh Another Day.*" Mum was bouncing so hard the end of her cracker knocked a fork off the table. "Because we've all got tickets to the PREMIERE!!!"

Grace dropped her burnt pizza crust on to her plate. It bounced off right on to the head of a sleeping Sosig, who woke up looking like his Christmas dream had been answered.

Tess just said "dope".

And Billy neighed.

But me? I didn't know what to do?!

I'd never even been to London. Let alone gone to a star-studded premiere!

How on earth had we got premiere tickets?

What madness was happening?

I pictured us all on the red carpet – Grace (drooling at the cast), Tess (looking as glamorous as one of the stars), Billy (hopefully not dressed as a horse) and Mum and Dad (nope, all bets were off with them) ... And me. Who would be...

Looking awkward. Hating the cameras. Hating the attention. Hating the fact that someone, somewhere might see us together and figure out that I was that stupid little Elf Girl. That my family were The Brussel Shouts.

Nope, this wasn't the greatest idea ever. It was the biggest threat yet to my lovely normal life!

"Erm..." I had to get out of this. But ... I looked over at Grace, who was hugging her dad. Had her eyes welled up? *Had his?!*

Could I really not go? I'd only just promised myself I'd commit to all things Christmas for Grace, just like Grampy G had asked, and they didn't come much more festive than this.

"Sounds great," I lied. "But, is the red-carpet thing up for discussion?"

If I could just swerve that, this could be OK.

"Excellent question, Molly-Moo." Dad ruffled my hair, leaving a chunk dangling right across my eyes. "Because no one's asked us the golden question... *Why.*"

Whatever the answer was, Mum couldn't hold it in any longer. It actually exploded out of her.

"THEY'VE ONLY GONE AND PICKED '*LOVE YOUR ELF!*' AS THE TITLE TRACK FOR THE FILM!" My breath caught in my throat. Was the room spinning? Was I going to be sick? "Looks like us Bells are going to be famous all over again!"

CHAPTER

3

TO DO:

- *Finish invites*
- *Pack hoodie (black)*
- *Pack jeans (black)*
- *Make deal with Tess (bribe with cake???)*
- *Survive and pretend this never happened*

"Names, please!" a man in a sharp suit, wearing a headset and clutching a clipboard like it was a shield, barked at the group in front of us. My worst nightmare was happening.

Mum and Dad hadn't bought a single one of my excuses to avoid the red carpet, not even that I'd "forgotten" to pack my dress, and so here I was. In black jeans, black polo neck and DMs. The invite had said "black tie" not "art thief" and my plan was to pull my hoodie up and power walk so fast I made it into the cinema without a single picture or video being taken that could make its way back home. If worse came to worst, my hope was that any photographers would assume I worked here and ignore me totally. I'd had to bribe Tess hard – agreeing to *never* ask for her room in return for her not posting anything on social that could even give away that we were here. But sharing with Billy till I went to uni was worth no one finding out about Elf Girl. About my family.

"Oh my actual days." Grace grabbed my arm as another huge cheer went up from the crowds packed against the barriers along the red-and-white-striped carpet. Grace legit looked like a goddess in her shimmering gold dress and statement orange lipstick. She'd even got tiny snowflakes pinned into her braided bun, and they were sparkling against her black hair.

"Is that ..." Grace squeaked. Again. She'd been squeaking at two-second intervals ever since we arrived. At least she was loving this. "... Stormy?"

The woman so famous she didn't need a second name? I peered through the crowd and glimpsed a mass of cherry-red curls, with a light-up candy-cane hat perched on top. Definitely her. Stormy was pulling a diamanté lead with a tiny fluffy white dog on the end. No … three dogs … no, *ten*? HOW MANY DOGS DID THIS WOMAN NEED TO GO TO THE CINEMA?!

"Hello-ho-ho-ho!" A man dressed as a nutcracker whizzed over on a hoverboard in the shape of a present. "You guys look like you might be interested in some of these…" He pinged open a stocking-shaped case, and in it was … what looked like an entire branch of Claire's Accessories: Christmas Edition. "Pick what you want and I'll take a photo for the big screen." He glanced up at the giant screen on top of the cinema building, scrolling through pictures of smiling faces.

"I think I've died and gone to Christmas heaven," Grace said, taking a necklace made of tiny Christmas lights. "Mol…?"

But I was already bent down, pretending to do up my lace. "Let me know when he's gone," I hissed. I had to avoid all photos at all costs.

As Grace and Billy posed, I scurried away, risking my first proper look around Leicester Square. I'd spent the last hour staring at my feet, as if avoiding the posters, the signs, might make this all less real. But it was definitely real. Leicester Square was bigger than it looked on TV and it'd had a full *Sleigh Another Day* makeover.

Arches made of candy canes and fir cones, a winter-animal merry-go-round and see-through igloos serving free hot chocolate and cookies. There was even fake snow (not made out of carrier bags), a sleigh pulled by reindeer (the one with big antlers looked suspiciously like the one who bit me) and halfway down the red carpet was a two-storey edible gingerbread house, big enough to walk into. With my back firmly turned to the photographer, I shuffled next to Dad.

"And to check again …" I whisper-hissed over the cheering. I didn't want Grace to know quite how much I was hating every second. "… I can't just meet you inside."

I'd scanned for any other route in, but unless I climbed on the roof of the gingerbread house and leapt into the upstairs window, which didn't exactly feel more discreet, I couldn't see an alternative. Dad put his arm round me.

"C'mon, Mols. What do you really think's going to happen?"

I do something so totally embarrassing on the red carpet I become a meme by the time I've reached the cinema and the world realizes I'm Elf Girl from that stupid song and everyone back home never lets me forget it and The POWR never speak to me again as they were looking for a cool new band member, not an embarrassing elf, and I have to take a one-way trip to space.

I went with "I dunno" instead.

Dad squeezed my shoulder. "Remember what Dilys says." She was the world's oldest skydiver and Dad was obsessed with her. "Feel the fear and do it anyway!" He paused. "And also, no. There's only one way in."

"Well, you remember what I said." As we edged nearer the front of the queue, I felt more and more sick with panic. "I'm heading straight inside. No photos, no posing, no…" I looked at all the cameras flashing, and the TV crews, and shuddered. "No anything."

Dad nodded. "Not as catchy at Dilys, but sure."

At least Mum and Dad were pretending to be normal for the day, wearing matching dark green velvet suits. (Mr W had said the four-armed four-legged onesie for two people they'd ordered might "be impractical for cinema seating". Yet another reason I was grateful for Grace in my life.) We shuffled nearer to the start of the red-and-white carpet, and I zipped up my black hoodie. Grace knew exactly what I was doing.

"Don't worry, Mol. We've got this." I smiled as best I could, even though all I'd actually *got* was stomach cramps and hands that were both freezing and sweating. "It might be better than you think? Maeve in the flesh. Free popcorn." She nudged me. "Free *bottomless* popcorn.

Breathing the actual scent of Joseph D Chambers." She looked at me seriously. "The ONLY man for me other than Simon. Which reminds me…" She held out her phone for me to take a photo of her with Stormy in the background. Simon must have had at least twenty photos already, but Grace didn't want to lie to him about being here, and she didn't want to give away my secret either, so had come up with a cunning plan to sort-of-truth and tell him we were in London for the weekend and had swung by to see the premiere, like other tourists.

"Photos are key." She threw up a peace sign. "It's all about doubling-down. Details to make it believable."

I clicked, then felt a tug at my sleeve. "Do I feel sick because I can see real reindeers and they're the best," Billy said, without taking a breath. "Or because I've eaten three packets of these?" She held up a squashed packet of mini veggie sausage rolls shaped like mittens. "Maybe four."

Bil put another one in her mouth and chewed, really pondering it.

"Probably the reindeer. But maybe stop eating those just in case. You still need room for pick 'n' mix, right?"

"I love pick 'n' mix!" Billy grinned, and she stuffed the rest of the pack into my pocket. She looked so cute in her "I Heart Christmas" sparkly red jumpsuit that she'd made me customize by adding furry red letters, so it also said "and horses". Yup, everyone was looking their most glamorous selves, and I was just a mime artist/glorified pastry carrier.

"Be still my beating heart…" Tess grabbed my arm. "Is that who I think it is?" Even at six foot in heels, my sister had to crane to see the big blacked-out car which had just pulled up. But the biggest roar yet from the crowd confirmed it, as did the swoosh of perfect bright auburn hair.

"Maeve. Actual. Murphy," Grace whispered, flashes exploding in every direction. "Maeve. ACTUAL. MURPHY!!"

Even my dad, who once called Harry Styles "Barry", knew who Maeve was. She'd been in all the biggest, funniest films of the last few years – and now here she was, in real life!

"Do humans really look like that?" I stared as Maeve signed autographs, chatted effortlessly to her fans and pulled silly faces in selfies. In her long sparkly green dress she looked like a mermaid. But even more magical. "I swear she's…"

"Glowing," Grace finished off for me. "Apparently she's having a thing with Joseph, so if you spot ANYTHING tell me. IMMEDIATELY."

But I didn't have time for gossip. I was too busy plummeting into a full-on wallow in my own despair. I yanked my ponytail out and scraped my fingers through my long bob, my wavy hair sticking out where the band had been.

"This was a bad idea, wasn't it?" I mumbled to myself. Instead of feeling invisible in it, I felt like I was sticking out like a sore thumb.

"NEXT!" Clipboard Man yelled. *Wah!* We were at the front?! "I need to see those wristbands. Especially *yours*." He peered at me like I was something that once gave him food poisoning. "We haven't got all day."

I instinctively put my arm around Billy to protect her from his extreme grump. But she wriggled free and stuck her wristband out.

"I'm Billy!" she said, hopping around with such energy her sequins jiggled. "This is my family! And Grace. But she's family really. We wrote the theme song. OF THE WHOLE FILM."

I didn't nod. I wasn't ready to confirm or deny anything.

But like Billy was some kind of horse-loving Christmas witch, the live band started playing "Love Your Elf!". Billy shrieked so loudly Clipboard Man cowered behind his board. Which was an error as Bil spotted the gap, ducked under the barrier and sprinted on to the red carpet. Clipboard Man might be good at stopping burly adults, but he was no match for my little sister. With a heavy huff of disgust, he unclipped the thick black rope.

"Somebody stop that child, please!"

Tess, Mum and Dad hurried off – but my feet wouldn't shift.

"I'll be here every step of the way." Grace took my hand. "… Unless of course Joseph D Chambers turns up, in which case it's every man for himself, but let's cross that bridge when we come to it."

Grace smiled. Her big, warm smile. And I remembered why I was doing this. Because for the first time in almost a year it really felt like Grace was beginning to get some of her happiness back. I was just going to have to dodge every camera and not get too close to my family in case anyone thought we were related. *Easy, right?!*

"Well, in that case…" I pulled my hood up and stepped out. *All I had to do was walk.* Fast. Then watch the film. Go back to the hotel. Go home. And live my life in hermit peace.

"Mol!" Mum yelled. "Over here…" My family had gathered together, protecting Billy from the cameras because she was only six. Oh no, they were clapping as she did a full dance routine to "Love Your Elf!" complete with trotting about on all fours. And was that man thrusting a microphone in Mum's direction?

"Quick question for BTV news?" This was being filmed? "We're going live in thirty."

Thirty seconds?!

Until me, my family and my dancing sister-horse were live ON THE TELEVISION.

I pictured Zaiynab and Matt watching back home.

And then I pictured … everyone else in the world also watching it.

I dropped Grace's hand. And ran. No idea where but I had to get away. Far, far away.

The yells from Mum and Dad blurred into the shouts of the crowd as I sprinted past a line of staff wearing gingerbread outfits. I had to get off this stupid carpet!

I didn't care if I was grounded for life and had to share a room with Billy for eternity! She'd probably be travelling the world doing competitive reindeer jumping anyway.

I had to get out of here!

But the stupid carpet was stretching on and on! I ran even faster. Head down, hoodie up. Past the step and repeat interview area. Past the cameras.

Past the celebs no one recognized hanging around hoping to get interviewed.

Past the crowds leaning over the barriers, waving posters and cheering.

Where was the end?!

I turned the corner (who knew red carpets could have corners?). Phew! There were the cinema doors.

But no. Oh no! There was Dermot Crown – an influencer with millions of followers, who posted funny edits of celebrity fails. There was no WAY I could sprint past him. It could be a fate worse than Elf Girl! There was nothing for it. With a final burst of speed, I swung off the carpet and raced into the doorway of the giant gingerbread house.

But instead of it being empty, it was packed.

OOF.

I ran slap-bang into a guy wearing a *Sleigh Another Day* sweater.

"Are you here for the Maeve meet and greet?" He hugged me. "Maevenators rule! Or are you a Maeseph like me?" I just stared at him. "If I saw Maeve and Joseph together today. Like *together* together. CAN YOU IMAGINE?" He fanned his face. "S-actual-woooon." I swallowed, trying to catch my breath. "Can you hold this while I fix my hair?" What. Was. Happening?! He thrust the handle of a sign into my hand. "Don't want to meet Queen Maeve with this hedge on my head." Was that a bark? And his hair looked fine. Great actually. AND WHAT WAS HAPPENING? "Do you think she'll pose for photos…" But he didn't finish because he broke into a scream. "SHE'S HERE!!!!!!!"

"No cameras!" a gruff security guard shouted as the crowd pushed forward. But I was facing the wrong way. And clinging on to a sign. And losing grip on reality?! My feet hardly touching the floor, I got swept backwards.

But then I saw it. A side door out of the house and into the cinema, next to where a stressed-looking person clutching an iPad was hanging on to Stormy's dogs. If I could squeeze through the crowd, I could slip out and into the safety of the cinema. Finally! A glimmer of hope! Keeping my head down I pushed through the cheering fans, using the massive sign to part them. It worked!

I made my way out into cinema. With no cameras. No fuss. No drama.

Or … not.

What actually happened was, as I pushed through the crowd, something bashed at my pocket, making me spin round … to discover one of Stormy's dogs jumping up at me, growling, its jaw clamped on to my pocket. It was trying to get one of Billy's leftover sausage rolls! Which

would have been OK if the other dogs hadn't joined in –
and so, instead of running out the door, I tripped forward
in a tangled mess of diamanté leads. In a desperate
attempt not to cement my place in history as "girl who
murdered Stormy's dogs by staking it through the head
with a giant wooden sign", I jabbed the sign forward in
front of me to stop me falling.

But it didn't hit the floor.

No, it hit the floor after slicing its way through
something long and green coming out of the door.

The whole place fell silent. Until a piercing noise
shattered it.

"MAAAEEEEVVVEEEE!"

CHAPTER
4

Good news: I hadn't killed one of Stormy's dogs. Absolutely terrible news: I had slashed Maeve's dress. Maeve Murphy.

Star of the film. Formerly in a body-hugging dress with a train. Now in two long bits of dangling skirt. One bit firmly skewered under my sign.

I froze. Maeve froze.

Sadly, the Maevenators very much un-froze, and surged towards me. The way they were waving their giant candy canes told me I had 0.06 seconds before I got bludgeoned to death with bits of gingerbread house.

There was only one thing for it … flee! I dropped the sign, shook off Stormy's dog, and with a yell of "sorrrrrry!" ran towards the door as if my life depended on it.

It probably did.

I sprinted into the cinema and slammed the door behind me. Where could I hide?! I raced down a short corridor, then another, desperate to put distance between me and what had happened.

What *had* happened?!

Had I really ruined Maeve's dress?

Please tell me I hadn't ruined the premiere too?! Yup, now my running was world record speed. Thank goodness my hoodie had been up. Please let no one have recognized me.

Checking no one was following me, I slumped against a wall and opened my phone. Phew. Nothing from Grace other than asking where I was. This was a good sign. If this had made the news, Grace would be the first one to know.

"Goody bag?" A man thrust a small paper bag into my hands, ignoring what a sweaty, shell-shocked panting mess I was. "Don't forget to rate and review the film! Five stars is what we want."

There was no time to reply – security guards were behind him. My blood ran cold. Were they coming for me? I turned my back and pretended to be on a very important – and sudden – phone call. "I SAID BICHON FRISES NOT CAVAPOOS!!! DO YOU NOT HAVE

EYES?!" a lady's voice screamed. "AND RED M&MS. NOT PURPLE. I'M NOT A MONSTER! AND YES I KNOW THEY DON'T MAKE PURPLE ONES, THAT'S WHY YOU HAVE TO ORDER AHEAD!!" A ball of bright pink feathers, a Stormy in the middle of them, whooshed into the corridor. "HOW AM I MEANT TO WORK UNDER THESE CONDITIONS?!"

But that distraction was just what I needed, and as Stormy started ranting about "the smell of ice giving her migraines", I slipped away to somewhere even safer. The loos. Hallelujah! They were empty. Time to try and process the last five minutes.

I leant over the sink and stared at my reflection in the mirror.

I was a total mess.

And on the other side of this door were the world's most glamorous celebrities – and my family on the loose.

And Maeve in a ripped dress.

How had I really thought I could get through this and stay invisible?

Eurgh. I splashed cold water on my face, checked the loo seat was down and collapsed on to it.

But my phone was vibrating.

Grace: *Just got inside. WHERE ARE YOU????*

And then again:

52

Mum: *You missed out on a lovely interview! Meet us by the pickle abs mix please XXX*

I think she meant pick 'n' mix.

Mum: *pickle abs mix*

Mum: *ARGH*

Mum: *Pickle abs*

She gave up.

Fun Sponge: *I will NEVER stop laughing at that.*

Oh great. Tess had sent a photo of me in full sprint mode.

Only Grace was getting a reply.

Me: *Staff loos. Tell no one. Can I meet you after the film?*

Grace: *You sure?? There's free Ben and Jerry's. AS MUCH AS YOU WANT.*

Grace: *And that includes fudge sauce.*

Tempting. But I had to remain firm. I typed back.

Me: *CRYING ALL OVER AGAIN.*

But I didn't want to see the film, think about the film, know about the film, or even eat the free ice cream for the film. Well, maybe that one, a bit.

Me: *Message when you're out.*

Me: *And sorry.*

Grace: *SORRY??? I have popcorn, am sitting so close to Maeve's seat I could sniff her hair, and there's an empty* seat which means v soon I might be witnessing Joseph D Chambers in the FLESH 😬😬😬

OK. Maybe I wasn't the worst friend in the world.

Grace: *Have I mentioned he's* 🔥👟

I *think* that was a good thing.

Grace: *btw my bag fits loads of popcorn so you shall feast after all* 😋😋😋

Grace was officially the best. I was dying to tell her what had happened – her face would make this all so much better, but it was a story that needed to be told in person.

Me: *You are a legend.*

Me: *Am going to tell Mum and Dad I've got food poisoning.*

Grace: 👍

So I did. But the screening was running late and I had to field a ten-minute call from Dad trying to track me down. In a stroke of genius, I flicked on video to show my sweaty face and said the only way I would feel better was if they supported the film and watched it while I drank some water and stayed in the bathroom. Which did the trick and he agreed that as long as I stayed in the cinema, we were OK to meet after the film. Result! Just enough time for me to make a full fake recovery in time for our booking at Pizza Express. Those dough balls weren't going to eat themselves.

But half an hour later, my messages to Grace stopped getting delivered. Her phone must be off for the film. And as safe and quiet as it was in this bathroom, I couldn't spend another two and a half hours in here. I tied my hoodie round my shoulders. Not great, but at least people might not recognize me from earlier. I poked my head out the door and looked round the hallway. PHEW. The people with clipboards had disappeared and it was just normal cinema staff sweeping up and packing away the displays.

I walked out carefully, trying to blend in with the background, looking for my next hiding place. And there it was! A huge storage room with the door open, nothing inside except props, a popcorn cart and, best of all, zero people. Perfect.

"You!" A guy Tess's age appeared out of nowhere. He had perfectly slicked-over blond hair, a headset like Clipboard Man and was wearing a super-smart suit. I froze. Was he talking to me? "I don't think you're getting paid to be doing…" I looked around, but it was only me here. "Nothing?"

"I, er, don't work here?" Not sure why I said it like a question. I held out my wristband. He physically recoiled.

"You're a … guest?!?" Avoiding making eye contact,

like I was contagious, he lifted up the wristband to inspect it. "A triple A, top VIP-level guest?"

"I *guess* so."

"And *that's* …" He looked me up and down … "what you decided to wear?" Did his eye actually twitch?

"I, er … also guess so?"

"So, whose list are you on…?"

I really didn't want to give him any details. But I also wasn't sure how to avoid them.

"My family. The, er, Bells?"

He scrolled on his phone. Down and down, until.

"Wait." He looked up at me. "Are you … Molly?"

Uh-oh. Where was this going?

"That is what people call me. Yes." Awkward silence. "Because that is my name."

The guy nodded slowly, like I'd solved the mystery of why pizzas are round but their boxes are square.

"Little. Elf. Girl." He swept his hand through the air as if visualizing it. "Almost ten years later." Instinctively I shrunk backwards at the E-word, as if my hoodie could somehow ingest me whole. HOODIE, PLEASE INGEST ME WHOLE. "Now THAT is a press story I would LOVE to put out – 'You Won't Believe What the Cutest Elf in the Whole Wide World Looks Like Now!'"

"No way!" I blurted out. But I could picture it all too

clearly, along with a terrible school photo of me. "Nope."
I shook my head. "Just no. That's not how it is…"

"So you're *not* Elf Girl?" He looked thoroughly
confused.

Gulp. "Erm, well, sort of. Maybe. But not really. Not
any more."

"Oh, come on. Your fans would love to see it!" I
snorted. *Fans?!* This guy was more delusional than
Stormy! "Everyone would love to see it."

. Not true. I was already seeing it, and it was making
me want to have a lie-down in a quiet room. For ten to
twenty years.

"They wouldn't. And no one is going to. EVER. *Ever.*"
Just in case he wasn't getting the message.

"So if I was to invite you to all the press events for
Sleigh Another Day you'd say…"

"NO!" I said it so forcefully a lady walking past turned
round. I smiled at her. "Thank you."

The man raised his eyebrows, his lips pursed. "I'll
take that as a *maybe*. Anyway, I'm Elijah." He thrust his
hand out for a shake. "On the press team. Well…" He
shrugged. "Soon to be. Right now, I'm on an internship
taking a break from uni. But we've all got to start
somewhere. And that PR assistant job has my name all
over it." He bit his lip, smiling at the thought. "Global

accounts, flights around the world, top hotels. I'm so ready for it."

"Well, good luck with that." I had no idea what to say. Other than thank you for the life story. *And please could I leave now?* "Sounds like a great job."

"On paper. In reality, the cast make it a niiight-mare." He rolled his eyes. "How hard would it be for two leads in a Christmas romcom to actually talk to the press about … oooooh, I don't know … love? Not naming any names, but Joseph" – that seemed like a name to me – "won't do any press. Complete diva in the making. And Maeve. How are you meant to get a handle on her?!"

I nodded, trying to look sympathetic, even though problems in my life were normally things like "who ate the last Hula Hoops?" Also, I really didn't want to talk about Maeve. Or the film. Or anything actually.

"ELI!" A gruff shout came from behind us. "Do you think you're getting paid to just stand there?" A man who looked a little like my dad, if I'd ever seen my dad properly shave, or wear a suit, or maybe even brush his hair, slapped Elijah on the back. He winked at me. "Joking, of course."

"Hello, Tim." Elijah hid his phone, flustered. "I was just saying how great the coverage has been."

Was he? Tim shook his head.

"Don't. I saw that fan thing. Did we really spend all this money just to whip up a million internet sleuths trying to track down an out-of-control Joseph-freak? No. If we want that Christmas number one spot, you need to pick it up. Coverage, coverage, coverage, Elijah."

"But—" Elijah tried to interrupt.

"No buts. Just front pages. Viral clips. Trending headlines. Shots of Maeve and Joseph. Preferably together. Very together. Stoke the flames. You know what it takes. Doesn't matter what they're talking about, as long as people are talking…"

I nodded, trying to look serious, and not like I was making one big massive mental note to tell Grace ASAP that Maeve and Joseph were together. She was going to explode.

"But…" Elijah lowered his headset.

"But do you want that job or not?" Tim slapped Elijah on the back, then switched his attention to me. "You're a young person." Was I? I felt like I'd aged thirty years in the last hour. "You like the internet. I bet you do all that dancing stuff." He tried and failed to … I dunno … dab? Twerk? Whatever it was, it was disturbing. "Maybe you can help Eli understand. If there isn't a story – it's our job to make one. Get people clicking. Now…" He looked round the corridor. "Someone said Stormy needed some ice that wasn't so cold … and didn't smell of *water*?" He peered at his phone. "So…"

He double clapped his hands.

And just like that, Elijah went running off after him. The world of film was even weirder behind the scenes than on screen! But … that gave me an idea. What if being behind the scenes meant finding raffle prizes for Grampy G's Grotto?

Checking no one was watching, I slunk into the empty storage room and pulled the door shut. Too shut. Because when I tugged on the handle it wouldn't budge. Oh well. After what had happened today, a lock-in with me, myself and a popcorn cart sounded most excellent. I filled up one of the red-and-gold glitter cardboard popcorn containers. Eurgh. The *Sleigh Another Day*'s logo. I turned it out of sight. I'd asked for donations not presents this Christmas, but if I could have one present, it would be never seeing or hearing the words "sleigh another day" again.

Totally exhausted by everything, I picked my way through a stack of red velvet cinema chairs, past a polystyrene giant snowman and squeezed by a cardboard cut-out Tom Holland (Grace REALLY would love it here). I stopped by a big black curtain hanging down from the ceiling. I bet behind here would be the perfect place to sit and hide.

The perfect place to figure out how to survive the next few weeks.

The perfect place to ... get the biggest shock of my life.

CHAPTER
5

ARGHHHHHHHHHHHHH!

I shrieked. Jumped back. Threw my popcorn straight up in the air.

I wasn't alone!

Someone was walking towards me!

Hundreds of kernels pinged off them in every direction. Over *him*.

A poor guy in a cinema uniform. Who was probably having a quiet break until I yelled at him and covered him in corn.

"Oh … my … sorry … goodness … I'm…" Nope. Words. Not Coming. Out. I waved my hand about. "Accident?"

Not sure why I said it like a question.

He emptied some popcorn out from behind his

cinema name badge. *C'mon, Molly.* Do something helpful. But what? I stepped forward and flicked a clump of kernels out of his hair. *Wait.* I froze. Was rooting around in a stranger's hair OK? Nope. But neither was attacking him with snacks. And he still hadn't spoken?

"SORRY. Is what I'm saying." I paused, in an awkward frozen lean-limbo. "And also, there's some in your ear. Like, *really* in your ear."

He tilted his head on one side and bashed it. A piece fell out, bounced off his shoe and landed on the concrete floor with a "plip". We both looked down at it. Then back at each other. Oh … OK.

He wasn't just a guy, my age, in a cinema uniform, covered in popcorn. He was a really hot guy, my age, in a suddenly weirdly cute cinema uniform, covered in popcorn.

"I mean…" he said in a super-smooth American accent, picking popcorn off his Ciniview sweatshirt. "I prefer salty myself. But," he grinned. "I'll take what I'm given."

"You're American?" I said, with the same level of shock as if I'd discovered he had a spare nose.

"I guess so," he said with a grin.

"Interesting," I said – absolutely no idea why. "I've never met an American before." What was I on about?!

63

"But obviously I've seen lots on TV and things." He was trying not to laugh. But I couldn't seem to stop talking. "Like…" and for some reason every single person I'd ever known disappeared out of my head. "Neil Armstrong."

WHY, IN TIMES OF STRESS, WAS MY BRAIN ONLY GIVING ME MY YEAR 7 PROJECT ON THE MOON LANDINGS?!

He raised his eyebrows and nodded. "Yeah. Me and Neil. The two Americans."

I tried not to react. "There *may* be more … anywhere up to seven is my guess."

But as he laughed more popcorn fell on to the floor. I picked it up. Why? What was I going to do with it? Eat it? I shoved it in my pocket. Great. Now it looked like I was saving hair-floor-popcorn for a snack.

"I'm not going to eat it later. If that's what you're thinking?"

"I wasn't." He shook his head side to side. "But – now I am." His accent made everything sound cool – he could probably say "I fell in a puddle" and still sound smooth.

"To be clear, I didn't mean to assault you." He was definitely keeping a safe distance. "Or should I say A-SALT." I cracked up. Ten per cent joke, eighty-nine per cent nerves (one per cent I had no clue about anything after the day I was having). "Like *salt*. Salted popcorn."

But he was giving me a funny look. "Because I threw it all over you?" I added feebly.

"Have we…" He squinted. "Have we met before?" Oh no. OH NO. Please tell me he didn't recognize me from my red-carpet disaster! He might tell his boss! Was tripping into a Hollywood star a criminal offence? Or even worse, did he recognize me because of that stupid theme song? He leant forward and ruffled his hair. Yet more popcorn fell out. Was it multiplying?! Where was it even coming from? Was his hair a black hole of popcornicity? "Were you at the team meeting earlier?"

"Nope." I wasn't elaborating. "Not me. We've never met." There was NO way I was admitting I was a Maeve-attacking, family-band-singing weirdo, who only thirty minutes ago had got a message from her best friend saying her youngest sister was neighing at the opening credits. Oh, and that I'd locked him in with me.

"So you don't work here?" He was still giving me that look.

I shook my head innocently.

"*Weird*. Your face feels familiar." My heart raced. I could *not* handle an Elf Girl conversation right now. Emergency subject change needed.

"Just one of those faces I guess? Anyway." I cleared my throat, like we had much more pressing matters to discuss. "Shouldn't you be at the screening?" His eyes narrowed suspiciously, like I was about to let the cinema know he was bunking off. It didn't help that I glanced down at his name badge. What did it say … Kyle? "Intel is the *Love Villa* crew have got *serious* ice-cream demands."

He looked relieved and sank back on to a black leatheresque armchair. His phone was already in the drink holder. "Nah. It's my break. Consider me fully off duty right now."

"Free snacks, free films and getting to hide back here? Sounds like a great job to me." Grace's idea of heaven.

"It is until someone catches me. I *technically*, maybe, should have been back ages ago. But." He looked around. "In here seemed way better than the chaos out there."

I nodded. "Hard agree."

"And I can really recommend these…" He looked at the big squishy armchair attached to the other side of the armrest drink holder. I sat down, his chair rocking back a bit as I did.

"Nice, huh?" Kyle asked, his eyes closed.

For a split second I relaxed. It really was nice. But then it all came flooding right back. Maeve. Elf Girl. If Grace was currently sniffing Joseph thingy's hair.

"Soooo." I stretched back. "Hold on to those vibes. Cos I *might* need to tell you I think I've locked us in."

Kyle opened his left eye. I turned my head to face him. It was the first time I'd properly looked at him. At those dark brown eyes. Tiny scar on the bridge of his nose. A splatter of dark freckles running up his face. His black hair just a tiny bit longer than being shaved. The thin gold chain around his neck.

"So it's not my fault my break is going to be even longer?" He grinned. "The good news keeps coming."

"Are you not enjoying the premiere then?" Surely to work in a cinema you'd be into that kind of thing?

"No way." He turned his head to face me too. "They're always bad, but this one is a complete mess! Everyone lost their heads after that fan attack on Maeve Murphy." Fan attack?! Did he mean me!? What was the world record fastest time for a face going bright red? Whatever it was, I'd just beaten it. Did they really think I'd attacked her?! Luckily he had his eyes closed again, so didn't know he was sitting next to a human beetroot. "And if I hear that 'Love Your Elf!' track one more time, I might do something I regret with a candy cane." OH MY JINGLE BALLS. "It's been on loop all day. All weekend…"

I laughed. Slightly hysterically. A mixture of fear, panic and trying to pretend this was all OK. Trying to pretend that stupid song had absolutely nothing to do with me! Nor the Maeve thing! I'm actually very, very normal! Here I am just laughing at how normal this all is! Hahahahahaha.

"Yup." Deep breath. "It's the worst."

"And that little kid!" He opened his eyes and shook his head. "'... the cutest little elf in the whole wide world!'" he started to say with the best impression of the elf's voice. Of my voice.

"STOP!" I said, holding my hand up. "Or I'll find more popcorn to throw."

He laughed. "Maybe that's why that fan went on the rampage with that sign." *It wasn't a rampage?! It was a badly timed fall!* "That song pushed them over the edge." He had no idea how right he was, but I wasn't even slightly tempted to tell him what had really happened. "Funny, though. Want to see the video?"

"Nothankyou," I said almost before he'd finished speaking. "I don't really like..." *What?* "... videos?"

"Right." He blinked. "So ... maybe a stupid question, but if you don't like *videos*." He paused. "And if you don't work here, then why are you here?"

Ah.

"I'm here." Gulp. "At this cinema." I was speaking on half speed. "Because..."

OK. Here it was. The choice. Fess up to who I was. Risk him figuring out where he did maybe recognize me from. That my family were The Brussel Shouts. That I was the fan who stopped the whole premiere...

Or...

"Because..." I scanned the room. But all I could see was props from the premiere. A fake sleigh. Giant branded baubles. A bag of reindeer feed ... ohhhhh. "My family brought the reindeers here." What was that prang in my stomach? Oh yes. IMMEDIATE REGRET. Why didn't I just say something normal like "my mum is a lawyer on the film". Whyyyy?

He cooed, impressed. What did Grace say about extending the truth? Details made it believable. Less likely to get caught out.

"Yup. My family are reindeer handlers. That is what they do. But other than that, they are very, very normal people." Kyle nodded, his eyes wide, taking it all in. You and me both, Kyle. "Did you know they have hairy noses? And feet? Very hairy feet." I paused. "Reindeers, that is. Not my parents."

"I ... did not." He took a sip from a Diet Coke can. "But that's *quite* the image."

What else did I know? I thought back to Billy's extensive chat about them.

"And it's the females who still have their antlers at Christmas."

"I did not know that." Kyle looked genuinely interested. Details had worked! "How did they get into that?"

Details had NOT worked!! "Erm, you know. Went to Lapland once. One thing led to another."

"I see," he said politely, as if we'd all been there.

"And now my parents travel the country with the" – what on earth was a group of reindeer called? I tried to think, but Neil Armstrong just came back – "er … flight?"

"Flight?"

It was herd, wasn't it? HERD.

"That's what we call the ones who pull the sleigh."

"Cool." Kyle nodded. "And what are they called?"

"Gabe and Ange?" Silence. "Oh, you mean the business!" That made more sense. "Reindeers R Us?" *Reindeers R Us?* Grace was never going to stop laughing when I told her. Kyle picked up his phone. "I wouldn't. We don't have a website. It's very much word of mouth."

I tried to look like that was totally obvious to anyone who worked in the industry. The reindeer-hiring industry.

"Oh, OK." He put his phone away, as if embarrassed by his lack of reindeer-acquiring knowledge. "I guess it explains why premieres aren't your jam… This must all be normal for you?"

A normal Saturday for me: Grace trying and failing to teach me a dance routine, and then seeing how many free samples we could get from the hot pretzel stand in town before they recognized us.

"Soooo normal." I looked at the floor in case he saw the fear in my eyes. "All those D-list celebs?" I sucked in some air through my teeth. I wanted to sound as disconnected from the film as I could. "And this film looks terrible. Apparently Maeve and Joseph thingy are a nightmare." Did that sound like something an unimpressed daughter of a reindeer handler would say? Who knew?! "What about you? Are you a fan?"

Kyle stretched back.

"Well, I'm dodging my usher duties and hiding out in a storage room, so draw your own conclusion." He looked a tiny bit guilty. "To be totally real, Christmas films don't do it for me."

I smiled. Finally. Someone who felt the same way about Christmas as me!

"Me neither! And my best mate said this one is as Christmas cheesy as it gets. Apparently every character has a Christmas-themed name and it's snowing in every scene. Oh, and the acting is so bad it's funny for all the wrong reasons." Not exactly Grace's words, but hopefully that made it sound like I really was avoiding it and not just on the run from the red-carpet police or elf fans.

Kyle softly whistled, but he was smiling.

"And I thought *I'd* been harsh about it…" He laughed and held his hand up in a high five. "Here's to romantic comedies being the worst." I slapped his hand. "And us all dying alone and miserable at Christmas."

"Now you're talking!" I slapped it even harder. But his phone was wobbling about in the drink holder, making the loudest rattle. We both looked down.

The screen was faced in my direction and there was a call coming through with a picture of a girl standing on a beach, her back to the camera. Super cute. Although what was that name?! "Better Half 👩❤️🧑".

I had to swallow to stop myself snorting. Seconds ago he'd been pretending not to be a cheesy romantic, but he was as bad as Grace!

"Sorry." He snatched the phone and cut the call. Which didn't seem that nice a way of dealing with your "better half". "I'll call her back in a bit."

"You sure…" I said as it rang again. But he just cut it.

"Yeah, it's nothing urgent." I couldn't help but notice he flicked "Do Not Disturb" on.

But I had enough drama right now, without getting caught up in someone else's.

"So…" he said, extra cheery. Had he noticed the weird silence too? "You haven't told me. Who is my mysterious popcorn attacker?"

But something about how he cut the call had taken me back to feeling even less like sharing than normal.

"You can call me Dasher," I said calmly. "And I already know you're Kyle…"

He looked confused with my mind-reading skills, but then followed my eyes down to his name badge.

"I prefer Rudolph actually." He grinned. If Grace was here she'd say it was a cute grin. But unlike Grace, my heart was password protected. Triple security locked. The safest way. "Ru to my friends." He held his hand out. "Nice to meet you, Dash."

"You too, Ru." I shook it back. I guess it was nice to meet him too – I hadn't thought about small elves or red-carpet not-rampages for at least two minutes, which felt like some kind of record. And once the weirdness of the call faded and we started chatting, we didn't stop. I think it was something to do with all the stress of today, this week, combined with the safety of him having no idea who I really was, and us never seeing each other again, that after my bombshell that in the UK we put pyjamas under our pillows, and him going in deep on how Brits were meant to wash their faces when our hot and cold taps were separate, I ended up telling him all about Grampy G's Grotto. We'd had loads of ideas for the party, and I was really looking forward to Grace finally getting to do her *Nutcracker* dance – she was pulling out all the stops as Simon had never seen her in action. Ru said it sounded awesome, and way better than his Christmas, which was working till Christmas Eve then heading back to America just after. He didn't seem bothered about leaving the UK, and I got the impression his parents moved loads for their jobs. He didn't go into detail, but apparently it was something to do with this cinema chain, which I guessed was how they'd swung him this job. And somehow that led me on to how annoying Jess (sharing real family names was too risky) was and how I was going to be stuck sharing a room with Tilly for ever, and how I was still waiting to hear back from Zaiynab about The POWR. Ru asked if he could see some of my lyrics, but I gripped my fingers round my notebook in my pocket and told him I didn't have any with me. But as I explained how much I'd love making music, I realized I'd told him more than I had to a single person back home since I'd moved. Well, except Grace, but she didn't count as she was basically me.

"That's so cool, Dash. Although, shame you haven't got any stuff with you. Not even on your phone…" Ru said, knowing full well I would do. But I didn't react. "I can't even write good text messages, let alone lyrics."

I shrugged awkwardly. "Well, the band haven't said yes so…" Maybe my lyrics were rubbish after all? And talking about it with anyone who wasn't Grace felt all niggly like when I wore my pants that had shrunk. Time to move on. "Did I tell you there's a house in my village that puts up over two hundred Christmas lights?" Ru didn't need to know it was mine.

"Intense. Are all the neighbours into it?"

"I'm definitely not," I said truthfully.

Ru stretched his legs out. "When I was little, my grandparents used to do this thing where they hung a pickle ornament on the tree—"

"Like a mini Branston?" His grandparents sounded like a match for my mum and dad! But he looked as confused as me.

"Are we talking the same language?" He turned his phone round and showed me a picture he'd just googled.

"Oh, a *gherkin*!"

"Well, yeah." Not sure why he was looking at me like I was the confusing one, when he was the one hanging small cucumbers on a tree. "And on Christmas Day, the first one to find it got an extra present from Santa." He smiled. "It used to be chaos…"

I could imagine. In my house there would be branches and baubles flying everywhere.

"Sounds fun." I smiled, thinking back to the first year we'd got a real Christmas tree, and Tess and I had slept in the lounge so it would be the first thing we saw when we woke up.

"It was," Ru said, with a soft smile. For two people who didn't like Christmas, it seemed like we both used to. A lot.

Eurgh. Stupid Elf Song. Stupid everything.

I shimmied my shoulders, trying to shake off the festive, and sat up. Now was NOT the time to start feeling nostalgic – it was the time to make sure I avoided everything Christmassy until this whole stupid film had gone away.

It was like Ru read my mind. He grinned, as if the memory was long gone. "Not as awesome as having fish and chips for breakfast though. Genuinely happened in Camden a few weeks ago."

And we got stuck into a (heated) debate about whether fat chips or thin ones were superior (OBVIOUSLY THIN ONES) right up until a buzzer rang and we realized the time. 7:55 p.m. The real world crashed back in.

Five minutes till the film finished.

Five minutes until my parents were on a mission to check I hadn't keeled over and died in a vat of popcorn.

Five minutes until Ru risked meeting them in full concerned flow for my fake food poisoning, when right now he thought they were busy trimming reindeer hooves (I'd had to get inventive).

"I better head." I stood up. "Although…" I sat down again. "I've locked us in, haven't I?"

But after we both tried pulling, pushing, leaning, even giving the handle a talk on positive mental attitude, the door still wasn't budging. And there were more footsteps outside. And Stormy yelling, "No one listens! Signing autographs is emotionally drraaaaining." Followed by, "And someone needs to get a pooper scooper."

In desperation, I asked Ru to give me space as I vented my stress on the handle, but when it didn't work I called him back over. He was faffing about with a popcorn container.

"Guess there's nothing for it." He rocked back on his heels. "Three…" Was he really going to attempt a run? He crouched down into a semi-sprint position. "Two…" Then he stood up. "Although, before I potentially break my shoulder, you do *definitely* need to leave, right?"

"Yeaaahhh." I looked at the heavy wooden door. "But it's not breaking-bones level of urgent." Maybe minor fracture, but not break. There was always plan B: staying here until Mum and Dad had gone to notify the police of my disappearance and they brought in a battering ram, or at least a key. Or plan C: slowly dying in this room, and my final resting place being on the bed of floor popcorn we'd tried to clear up. Which *actually*, now I'd considered it, sounded quite good and could be upgraded to plan A.

"Cool, in that case … ONE!" Ru thundered towards the door. Almost as fast as me down the red carpet, his left shoulder dipped forwards. "ARRRRR!" he yelled, bracing for impact.

I braced for impact! But the door swung open.

Wide open. And Ru fell right into the hallway, straight on to the feet of Elijah, who was holding the handle.

Elijah looked at me, then at the crumpled pile of human on the floor. Immediately his face turned from confused eye twitch to pure thunder.

"*You!*" Elijah pulled at Ru's T-shirt, yanking him back to his feet. He looked him up and down. "You, Kyle, are coming with me."

"But…" began Ru, but Elijah was already marching him off towards where some other ushers had just gone into a staffroom. I ran out into the corridor, watching as Ru tried – and failed – to apologize. We hadn't even said bye.

But Ru looked back. And mouthed just one thing. Not "bye", but "popcorn".

Right.

And just like that he disappeared through the door marked "STAFF". The last I'd ever see of him. And for a split second I was alone.

Until the doors into the screen sprang open, the low murmur of noise became a loud roar of chatter, and people spilled out in all directions.

The film had ended! And I hadn't found a single thing to use for a raffle prize! I was a terrible friend. I ran back into the room for one last look. As much as I'd love a vintage cinema chair it was going to be hard to fit one in a pocket, so I grabbed a couple of branded popcorn containers. Slinking back out, I pulled my hood up and shrank back against the wall, scouring the heads for Grace and practicing my "I've miraculously recovered from my sudden burst of food poisoning" face.

My phone pinged.

Tess: *Look what I just found. Enjoy* ☺

I opened the video. It was a loop of someone in a black hoodie looking like she was about to stab Maeve with a giant sign that said "Joseph D Chambers ♥♥♥ be my Christmas present!"

It was fair to say the fan looked deranged. And on a rampage.

And it was also fair to say, the fan was … me. I was the fan.

So *that's* what the sign said!

I hadn't even seen Joseph D Chambers, let alone wanted to wipe-out his love interest. Not that whoever posted it and wrote the caption cared.

"CRAZED JOSEPH D CHAMBERS FAN GOES ON RAMPAGE AGAINST RUMOURED LOVE INTEREST MAEVE."

The top comment was even worse.

"FIND HER #JUSTICEFORMAEVE #MAESEPH".

It had 1,231 likes.

I hated my sister.

And I also hated that because of the crowd, you couldn't make out Stormy's dogs knotting themselves round my legs. The only relief was that my hood was up and it was impossible to see my face. If anyone found out it was me, it could be even worse than my Elf Girl secret getting out! But now I felt like my hoodie was evidence and yanked it down. Phew. There was Grace's black hair piled up.

I felt better already.

Head down, I shuffled through the crowd. I could not WAIT to tell Grace what happened on the red carpet. Or about Ru. Or hear her film review. Knowing her, she'd probably managed to bag Joseph's number. Or become besties with Maeve.

But when I saw Grace's face, as she pushed towards me, my stomach dropped.

Everyone around her was smiling and laughing, but tears were streaming down her face.

"Mols. *What am I going to do?!*"

CHAPTER

6

I could kill Simon.

Lucky for him my parents' reindeer were imaginary, or I'd have already sent them to trample him.

NO ONE did this to my best friend and got away with it.

I crouched down and wrapped my arms round Grace's shoulders. There were only two toilet cubicles in this Pizza Express, and we'd been in this one for fifteen minutes. But bodily functions could wait.

Grace needed space. To rant, then cry, then rage, then despair, then stare at her phone. And I needed the space to not ring Simon and tell him exactly what I thought about him. (Grace didn't want any drama. And apparently stringing him up with my parents' pigs in blankets Christmas lights could be deemed "dramatic".)

Tess had got it immediately. When she whispered to ask why we were heading straight to the toilets and not the table I'd mouthed "Simon" and she nodded, not needing another word. Sometimes having a big sister could be OK. Sometimes.

"How could he do this?" Grace sniffed, holding her thumb down to pause the video. She'd played it so many times it probably had as many views as the one of "Maeve's attacker". I'd already told Grace what had really happened with Maeve to try and cheer her up, but it only got a half-smile, that's how bad things were. I hadn't mentioned Ru yet, the timing just didn't feel right. "HOW?!"

Even though I'd seen this story thirty times already, maybe this time I could see something that made sense? It was a post from this guy at our school of his mate getting his hand caught in a bowling ball and sliding down the alley after it. But in the background, hanging out in Shut Up And Bowl, was Simon. Who had told Grace he was home babysitting his brother. Not kissing another girl under some plastic mistletoe. A proper eyes closed, hands-all-over-her-back snog. He was even wearing the new suit he'd told Grace he'd got for their anniversary.

My stomach clenched like I had not-fake food

poisoning. Every time Grace clicked back and it played again, I hated Simon more. And even more when I looked at my best friend, her eyes swollen from crying, her gorgeous sparkly eyeshadow smeared all over her face. This was meant to be the ultimate day to cheer her up, my way of kick-starting salvaging her Christmas cheer, and this is what he'd done.

I clenched my fists, trying to direct my anger. I wanted to say something positive but I had … nothing. I leant back against the loo roll holder and passed Grace another tissue. Considering this was meant to be the most A-list day of my life, I'd spent a weirdly long time in toilets.

"Why couldn't he just have told me?" Grace sniffed.

"Because he's an idiot. A total idiot." I dabbed eyeshadow off her cheek. "A prize-winning, massive turnip of an idiot. But not in a Brussel Shouts turnip way. In an *actual* way. He does not deserve you AT ALL. All he deserves is a long and painful death. And a permanently cracked phone screen." I couldn't stop. "And kneeling on every single plug there is to kneel on."

When Grace had turned her phone on after the film, Simon had messaged another pouting selfie. But he'd been so busy trying to look smoking hot (which he hadn't managed) he'd missed the Shut Up And Bowl logo on the mirror. Grace had been confused, clicked on the location and all the videos came up from it. Including this one.

So not only was Simon an idiot. He was an idiot who couldn't use the internet.

I rested my head on Grace's knee, my brain spinning. How could I make this any better? Simon hadn't just broken her heart; with one single photo he'd broken her whole belief system. Grace loved love more than anything, and if anyone deserved a happy ending, it was her.

Gently, I pressed pause on the video.

"I know this is the worst thing in the world right now, but I promise, if this is what he's really like, you're so much better without him." Oh no. Fail. Her eyes were filling again. I scrabbled around for something better. "Honestly. This isn't love. This is just one stupid boy. And you … you are the best person I've ever, EVER met. And just today I must have met at least twenty new people. So if you think, over fifteen years, that's actually loads of people. And you really are the best one." She sniffed, and shrugged her shoulders. "Oi, don't give me that. *Everyone* thinks so. Why do you think my parents basically want to adopt you? They'd happily swap me for you, and don't even pretend that's not the case. Even Tess likes you, and she doesn't like *anyone*."

Grace wiped the sleeve of her dress across her nose.

"But it's our year anniversary." Her shoulders slumped even further. "I've already bought his present." Ouch. I felt another stab of rage as I pictured the super cute photobook of them over the last year that she'd spent weeks making. "I love him, Mol. I thought he felt the same way."

I growled. I was SO mad at him! "That's because he told you he did!" I'd heard it a zillion times when they said bye. Grace saying "I love you" and him replying "No, I love youuuuu", and it going round in so many circles I'd gone to get some crisps from the vending machine and they were still saying it when I got back. *C'mon, Molly.* Deep breath. "How were you meant to know he was a total liar? That's on him. Not you!!"

Grace sighed. If we were at home, I'd stick on a cheesy romcom to cheer her up, but I had a feeling we might be switching to slasher horrors for the foreseeable.

"Would pizza be a thing that could help? Just for tonight? Apparently Dad's ordered extra dough balls." He'd messaged me to ask if everything was OK. I'd told him we had girl stuff going on, with liberal use of the blood emoji to prevent further questions, and then said, "but dough balls could help."

Grace smiled. It was tiny, but I'd take it. "I ... I do like dough balls."

Yes, Grace! A stupid boy could take your happiness but he can never take your garlic bread balls of joy!

But there was a knock on the door. Well, another one.

"Not now…" I hissed. How unreasonable could someone be? We'd only been in here for twenty minutes. *Some people.*

But Grace stood up. "I can't sit here for ever." She rubbed her hands over her face. "I just need to not think about… Not think that…" Uh-oh. Her voice cracked. "I had one billion plans with…" She gulped. "… *him* – and they were all going to be perfect and … *sniff* … now all I've got is…" Another gulp. "Dough … *sniff* … balls."

I cuddled her tight.

"Not true. Dough balls. And me. And we are NOT going to let evil Sly-mon" – I was quite pleased with that, but now was not the time to dwell – "ruin today. Or *any* day. Especially not Christmas. Sure, it's not an ideal situation, but" – I looked her dead in the eye – "we're going to get through this together, OK?"

"OK." Grace nodded gently. "You and me. No boys. And a good Christmas." She rubbed under her eyes, getting the worst of the mascara dribble off. "It's what you always say, 'Life isn't like the movies'." She sniffed. "Just took me a while to realize." She picked up her phone. "Block annnnd DELETE." She clicked her screen with determination. And then looked sad. Very, very sad. I squeezed her tight.

"Strong start. And don't even think about your year anniversary. Year, *schmear*. How about we celebrate our … *five*-year anniversary." I already had an idea to make a photobook of all of our best bits to try to make her smile. "Honestly, Gracington, after a truly epic Grampy G's Grotto and hitting that fundraising target, this time next month you'll be all like 'Simon who?'"

Yup. All we had to do was get through the next few weeks together. Then Christmas would be out the way, this stupid film would have been forgotten about, Grace could have started to see Simon for what he really was, and I could get my life back to normal too.

"Guess it's time to face the world then." Grace pushed open the cubicle door. The queue of women clapped (especially the one at the front with her legs crossed) and we headed out. But as we hurried down the spiral stairs, I banged into a guy running up in the opposite direction.

"Ouch!" I said, before realizing it wasn't a stranger after all. "And also, sorry."

Elijah looked more shocked than me. I peered behind him. He was on his own. Not that I was looking for Ru. And not that I was already brushing off breadstick crumbs (they'd been my toilet snack) in case he appeared.

"I'm not eating here," Elijah said, in what I think was most definitely a flap. "I'm just on my way somewhere more ... high end."

If that was true, I wasn't sure why he had a napkin tucked in his shirt, but who was I to point it out? But I didn't want to chat either, as I didn't want Grace finding out about Ru before I'd had chance to tell her what had happened, and even more importantly, I didn't want to risk her dough balls going cold.

"Grace, Elijah, Elijah, Grace," I said quickly, before turning to Grace. "OK to catch you up in a sec?" She said it was fine and carried on downstairs. But there was one thing I wanted to check with Elijah. "I hope that Kyle wasn't in trouble," I said, ducking out of the way of a waitress carrying platefuls of pasta. Elijah looked at me like I was talking about hanging up pickles. "He didn't mean to be gone so long but I accidentally got us locked in."

"Ahhhh." Elijah nodded, finally catching up. "He didn't mention that. Typical Kyle."

"So he's not in trouble?"

"Sadly, not as much as I would like." Elijah suddenly smiled unnervingly sweetly. "But I am glad I ran into you actually. I had no idea the cutest little elf had been so very busy..." He said the E-word! In a panic, I scanned around, checking no one heard.

"Can you keep your voice down, please?" I hissed. Even one more person knowing was one person too many. And what did he mean about being busy?

"Sure. If you tell me if you've reconsidered my invite to the *Sleigh Another Day* events?" I shook my head firmly. I'd made it through the premiere without being recognized, and now I was even more determined to avoid all things film-related and keep it that way. "The Liverpool Docks lights switch on this weekend?" I shook my head. "Edinburgh then? We're building a whole winter wonderland at the castle. You can meet the cast…" I was still shaking my head. "All ending with a bonanza on a boat on the Thames."

Not even as tempting as a single crumb of dough ball.

"Sorry, Elijah, but it's not my thing."

He put his hands on his hips, like Billy does when someone calls a horse a "pony".

"But Elf Girl all grown up and onstage with Maeve and Joseph. Imagine…" OK, I imagined it … and hated everything about it. "*Such* a better press story than what happened today. A dangerous fan on the loose and all that."

"Elija—"

"It would all be so romantic. So Chrismagical." That wasn't even a word. "You could bring your boyfriend, girlfriend, whoever, for some special Christmas memories…"

I rolled my eyes. "Not my scene, sorry. And my bestie is the only other half I need." So he could stop trying that route.

"OK, well, in that case. There is *one* thing I haven't mentioned. Since we last met things have changed a little."

Why was he fishing his phone out?

"I *may* have seen the CCTV footage of the fan going on a rampage with poor Maeve." My blood ran cold. *And would everyone stop saying rampage?! It was an accidental trip!!* "So, unless you want the world to find out you were the one that thought it was a good idea to attack the nation's sweetheart with a very painful-looking sign, I *respectfully* suggest you say yes to coming to whatever event I invite you to."

Had all the potpourri fumes in the loo made me lose my mind or … was Elijah blackmailing me?!

"But … it-it was an accident?" I realized I was gripping on to the handrail, the stairs suddenly feeling all wobbly. "An accidental dog-based trip!? It wasn't even my sign?!" No one could even know I was at the premiere! Let alone the fan on the rampage! OH NO, NOW I WAS EVEN THINKING IT TOO! There was no way I'd be able to explain any of it. I'd be totally outed as Elf Girl!

"Sure, I saw the whole thing. But if just the last five seconds got leaked online... From the other angle, with Little Elf Girl's face looking so very shocked..." He winced. "I'm really not sure the world would see it that way. Imagine what all those Maevenators would say...?" Elijah shook his head, as if trying to dislodge a terrible thought. "Doesn't bear thinking about. So, how about we keep this our little secret?" He winked. "You come to Liverpool, show the world who Elf Girl is now, give the press something nice to talk about, and I will keep this footage away from any naughty, prying eyes who would love to go viral with it." I watched in horror as the video looped again. "Deal?"

CHAPTER 7

TO DO:

- *Ideas for lyrics (not about Simon treading barefoot on every single pine needle in the world)*
- *Survive the last days of schoooooool*
- *Raid Mum and Dad's fancy-dress box*
- *More ideas for lyrics (not about attacking Simon with mechanical snowman)*
- *Not think about Saturday*
- *Start geography assignment*

"Late night Christmas shopping is fun," they said! "The shops look magical," they said!

No one mentioned it would be minus one million

degrees and I'd either be freezing outside or sweating under my scarf and coat and hat inside, as everyone grabbed candles like it was *The Hunger Games*.

"Having fun?" Grace asked, clutching the calendar she'd just picked up for her dad, full of photos of the two of them. I shuffled my body to block out the couple behind me, who were all over each other.

"So much!" I said, trying to smile.

"ALottaWaffle, here we come!" she said, looping her arm through mine. I grinned. Grace wanted to take me to try out their festive menu for the first time ever, and if novelty waffles made her happy, I was MORE than in. Tonight was the night she was meant to be celebrating her anniversary with Slymon, so instead we were having a shopping, snacks and sleepover evening, and in the interim I was on a mission to hide how much I hated being out and about doing Christmas stuff. Grace didn't need to know that ever since the premiere all I'd wanted to do was hide inside, especially now the film was in cinemas, because this wasn't about me.

All week Grace had been bursting into tears whenever she heard certain songs. Or certain shows came on. Or even when it rained. Apparently that reminded her of Slymon too. As did grass. Hot drinks. And tables. Recovery was going to take a while. With everyone else

Grace had been putting on a brave face. Partly to make Simon think she wasn't totally devastated, and partly so her dad didn't suspect they'd broken up and get even more worried about everything. Last night Grace had also admitted to me she didn't think it was OK to look miserable when you were surrounded by tinsel.

And I'd been trying to be the friend she needed – the Christmassy friend she needed. I swear my Spotify thought it had been hacked due to my sudden interest in *Now That's What I Call Christmas 1,000!* And I hadn't got round to telling Grace about Ru, even if he did keep popping up in my head. But that was just because he was the first proper American person I'd ever chatted to. Yes. That was a very normal reason to keep thinking about a boy.

"The PERFECT spot for some Grotto plotting, amIright?" Grace said as the cute cafe came into sight. Its windows were steamed up and they'd wrapped a huge light-up ribbon from top to bottom and left to right, like the building was one giant present. Arm in arm we walked in, the warm air hitting us as quickly as "Jingle Bell Rock" on the speakers. My Christmas playlist must be getting to me as I found myself singing along. The cafe had NOT held back. There were lights hung from the ceiling, red-and-white candy cane ribbons wrapped around the chairs and even mini Christmas trees on the counter.

"Sure is," I said, as we grabbed the massive sofa. I saw Grace check to make sure it was a SFZ (Simon-Free Zone). "Clear." I nodded, confirming we were safe. "So…" I flopped down. "Are you ready to put the fun in fundraiser? Eat so much pudding we feel sick, sort of dizzy and sweaty – but in a good way?"

Grace grinned. "Yu-huh."

Good. This evening was working. But as I turned to tug my coat off, I jumped. Argh! On the next table were Zaiynab and Matt. Who, almost two weeks after seeing them at the switch on, still hadn't got back to me about the band.

I waved feebly and wished I wasn't wearing the penguin jumper Grace had lent me.

"OMG! Look!" Grace pointed out the window. "In fact, don't. DO NOT." All I could see was condensation. "Unless you want to see a poster for *Sleigh Another Day*. On the side of a bus? Which come to think of it … did I even see at all?"

Eurgh. I dropped my head on to the table with a bang, before remembering Zaiynab and Matt might see, so tried to style it into a very vigorous rummage in my school bag instead. I was so OVER that film! Half our school had seen it this week, and the corridors had been full of people humming "Love Your Elf!". It was torture. Luckily, no one had figured out we'd been at the premiere, and no one suspected that my mum and dad were The Brussel Shouts. Just how I needed it to stay, which was going to get trickier as Elijah had been in touch with my parents to sort me going to the event in Liverpool this weekend. I was dreading it. Grace had been checking social to make sure no one had figured out who #dreadcarpetgirl was and I'd dodged that too. Plus, full-time super sleuthing had been a good distraction for her and it meant I hadn't had to see anything about the film, so a double win.

I finished fake rummaging in my bag and pulled out the unopened envelope I'd stuffed in there this morning. It was finally time to open it. I knew what was inside, but seeing made it even more real. More terrifying.

ADMIT TWO: LIVERPOOL LIGHTS UP!
GET FERRY AND BRIGHT AT THE SLEIGH
ANOTHER DAY WINTER WONDERLAND
LIGHTS SWITCH ON!
RIDE THE FESTIVE FERRIS WHEEL AND
FEAST ON SANTA'S SNACKS AT THE
ALBERT DOCKS AS THE CITY GETS LIT!

The thick gold invitation reflected my face back at

me – and it didn't look happy. How was this tomorrow? I wasn't mentally prepared. But when I'd messaged Elijah to say I wasn't sure I could do it, he'd sent a screengrab of my face from the red carpet and suddenly I'd decided maybe I could after all. But with one condition – he had to let Grace come with me. The perfect thing to keep her mind off Simon.

"Remember The Plan," Grace said calmly, plucking the invitation out of my hand. I'd told her that Elijah had invited me to show the world what Elf Girl looked like now. I may have kept the whole blackmail thing out of it, as I didn't want her to worry or not come, so I said agreeing to it had been my idea to make it up to my parents after the premiere. "You just have to turn up. Do everything as we planned. And I'll be on the ground checking social. Elijah can't say you didn't show the world Elf Girl. But your identity stays hidden! Job done." I smiled weakly. Grace made it sound easy, but if anything went wrong I was at serious risk of being unveiled as Elf Girl. I had to hope Elijah wouldn't freak out either, but he *had* said I could access "a glam squad" – and I'm just taking up his offer. "Mol, I promise, if I managed to look unbothered when I was made to sit by Simon in chemistry earlier, *anything* is possible."

"How you didn't shove that conical flask up his nose, I do not know."

Grace smiled. An evil, happy smile. "It would have felt soooo good."

"Moving on." I got my notebook out. "Next thing on the agenda. Grampy G's Grotto." We had three weeks to pull it off, and it was fair to say plans had kind of stalled this week with everything going on.

"Honestly, if we didn't have that to look forward to there would be zero Christmas cheer round mine."

"Well, prepare to unleash FULL ON Christmas cheer. All the Christmassyness you'd normally have crammed into one single evening. And I will deal with *everything* so you don't need to speak to you-know-who."

We both really wished we hadn't arranged to have Grampy G's Grotto at Simon's parents' restaurant, but there was no way we were cancelling.

"Perfect." Grace smiled. "So I'll stick to … entertainment, right? And guest list, of course. I've got emails for most of my family. They can't wait!" Last count we had about thirty people coming. "My dance friends have said they'll help with the *Nutcracker* thing. And did I tell you I reckon I can wangle a karaoke machine from my teacher?" Grace waggled her eyebrows as I scribbled it all down.

"Great, although can we keep my parents away

from it at all costs?" She nodded solemnly. "And I'm on decorations annnnd…" I looked at the list: "raffle prizes".

"Ah," Grace said, like she'd remembered something I didn't want to hear. "About that. I'm not quite sure how it happened. But…"

"Buuut…?"

"I *might* have chatted to Holly Hospice about it last night." Well, that sounded OK. "And I *might* have invited a few of Grampy G's friends." That was OK too. "And some of the staff." OK, so the party was getting bigger. "And when I told them we were hoping to finally hit five hundred pounds for their Christmas party fund, they were so happy and started talking about how they would have to raise some more to decorate the social room so it was nicer, and basically, I think I accidentally might have maybe said that actually we were going to raise a thousand pounds and pay for that too."

Right. Grace grimaced. "I'm sorryyyyyy. It's been a bad week, OK?"

I didn't want her to worry, even though the fundraiser had been stuck on £326 for months now.

"It's OK. We've got this."

I wasn't really sure we had, but I'd just have to find a way to figure it out. I was sure they'd understand if we didn't quite hit it.

"If it helps." Grace rested her head on my shoulder. "The lady on the phone cried. In a happy way." No, that didn't exactly help. "And I really meant to say it was just a target, but then said we'd definitely, *definitely* do it."

OK. Now I was panicking.

"You ready to order?" The waitress interrupted us. Grace gave me a guilty, yet strangely excited, smile and asked what the specials were. I went for a peppermint and pretzel marshmallow slice, but after she wrote it down she didn't leave.

"Not being weird, but do I know you from somewhere?" she said, looking at me.

"I don't think so," I replied, smiling so she knew I didn't mind her asking. "I did come here for my sister's birthday though. You made her a horse made out of chocolate mousse. Highlight of her life."

"Nah." She shook her head. "I only started this week." Uh-oh. "Do we follow each other on social or something?"

Considering I'd never posted a single photo, I was pretty confident the answer was no.

"Not me. Sorry."

But at that exact moment "All I Want for Christmas" finished playing and "Love Your Elf!" started blaring through the speakers. Was Spotify trolling me?! I felt my face go bright red.

The waitress clicked her fingers. "Of course! *Little Elf Girl! The cutest little elf!!*" My heart actually stopped. No one had said that to me for five years! "It's you, isn't it?" The waitress looked super pleased with herself. "My mum did say she thought The Brussel Shouts were local."

Oh, jingliest of balls. People knew about my family's stupid band?! I tried to breathe. In… Out… In. But the whole place was spinning! Had Zaiynab and Matt heard?! Were my secret-Elf days over?!

"No no no nooooo," Grace said, shaking her head very hard. "That's definitely not Mo—" She stopped midway through my name.

"I've never" – deep breath – "even heard of that song?" Could everyone tell my voice had gone tight and high? "If it is a song. *Is it a song?*"

Dad's voice crooned "You're our tiny festive friend!" through the awkward silence. And *this* was exactly why I stayed indoors for the festive period.

Grace spluttered. "In fact, I'd heard the family who wrote it actually live in Scotland. Or Australia."

"Okaaaay." The waitress looked at Grace, then me, then Grace again. "Shame. I love that video. Was watching it last night. My favourite ever Christmas number one."

"Number thirteen." It popped out before I could stop myself. I shrugged. "At a guess…"

But after a very suspicious look, she finally left. I exhaled so hard, I basically deflated.

"Grace," I whispered, clutching her arm, as I checked Zaiynab and Matt were none the wiser. "Tell me this isn't happening. HOW did she know?"

"I dunno," Grace whispered back. "But we have to keep calm. She's only one person. And I think we threw her off the scent." I was going to have to check YouTube later, wasn't I? That stupid music video from years ago, with my stupid green face. If people had started to watch it again, I was in *serious* trouble. And the stupid song was still playing. How long did it go on for? Two hours?! It felt like five days already.

"Honestly, Grace. If anyone find outs my life will be over. You know what happened to Cliff? I mean, Daisy." The name was stuck for life. "And to Noah when he knocked over that candle?" Grace nodded slowly. Poor Noah got his hand covered in wax and two years later he was still getting tagged in Madame Tussauds pictures. "You-know-who" – I jerked my head towards Zaiynab and Matt – "will never speak to me again." I picked up a tiny, tiny marshmallow, but dropped it back in my drink, too sad to eat it. Double tragedy.

And now Dad was ringing. "One sec…" I gestured outside, relieved to have an excuse to avoid hearing child-me singing the last line. Maybe cold air might help calm me down. But Dad just wanted to know if I wanted to join them to do an interview in London. Which didn't make me calm at all. It made me want to move to Lapland and live in an igloo far, far away from anyone. I put the phone down and bent over double.

Someone was yelling, "Whhhhyyyyyyyy!"

And that someone was me.

"You OK there?" Please no. Please don't let that voice belong to who I thought it did. I stood up slowly.

"Just, you know…" I tried to look as normal as someone who had just been yelling to themselves in the freezing-cold night could. "…vocal warm-up stuff."

"Cool." Zaiynab nodded – she looked so cool in a black fake leather jacket. Did cool people not feel the cold? And I was wearing a penguin jumper. I WAS WEARING A PENGUIN JUMPER! I folded my arms tight in front of me. "Kind of neat we ran into you. We wanted to let you know that sadly for you we've narrowed it down to a final two." Ouch. My stomach sank. Had I even come close? "Just a final stage left. Getting one more set of lyrics in."

I tried to nod and look neutral, and not like I was having the worst three minutes of my life.

"We've already got the track." Matt sighed. "But we're struggling for lyrics that feel right."

"Well, I hope you find someone good." It was hard to look that enthusiastic when my dreams had just been crushed, and I didn't have a coat and had lost feeling in three out of four of my limbs.

Zaiynab's eyebrows lowered. "What? Are you out then?"

"Out?"

"Yup. You're one of the final two." My mouth fell open! I was still in the running! They liked my stuff! "I only said sadly cos it meant more work for you…"

"Whoa. I mean … what?!" I might be in The POWR?! "I mean, I'm in. SO IN!"

"Great, we'll DM you the track…"

But before I could say thanks, the waitress burst out of ALottaWaffle holding up her phone.

"IT *IS* YOU!" Oh no. Oh no oh no oh no! On her phone was the video of The Brussel Shouts… "Elf girl?"

Zaiynab and Matt looked at me, confused. I looked at the waitress, hoping she might somehow fall down a drain. But she wasn't only one inch wide, and there was no drain, and the video was still playing … AND WHAT COULD I DO?!

I could… Nope, literally no idea. But Grace could

help. Grace always helped! I bunched my fist, and keeping it behind my back, banged on the misted-up window by where we were sitting.

"It really isn't." I banged some more. *Please come out, Grace!* "Honestly," I looked at Zaiynab and Matt. "There's been some kind of mix-up."

"Everything OK?" Grace appeared like some kind of Christmas angel. She looked round at what was happening. "Mol, I thought you might need this." She held out my coat, right in front of the phone. Genius.

"Thanks, Grace. It is very cold brrrrrr." I was talking extra loud to mask the tinny sound coming out of the phone. I had to get everyone to leave. And quick! "So very cold that we can't just stand here chatting. Vest weather, as my aunt says. And hypothermia is no joke." Please let me stop talking. "Toes can fall off and everything. So, I'll bid you *adieu*." I actually bowed at Zaiynab and Matt. Why was I like this?! "But thanks SO MUCH, you guys." I side-shuffled towards the door, Grace sidestepping next to me, both of us ignoring that a very confused waitress was still looking down at the video and then back at me. "And top tip time! You should probably save your battery. The cold makes it really drain."

Safety was in touching distance! But that's when a couple holding hands walked round the corner, the guy giving the girl a quick kiss on the cheek, their arms swinging as they laughed.

They looked really in love.

And they looked really like Simon and a new girl. Because they were.

"Shall we go in?" I swivelled round and tried to bundle Grace inside. But she'd already seen.

"Si...?" she said quietly, almost to herself. But the waitress was waving at the girl. And she was steering Simon over. And he realized too late who else was standing here.

At least the video finally stopped. But then again, so had my heart. Simon didn't even drop the girl's hand, not until she hugged the waitress as Zaiynab and Matt headed off.

"What are you doing here?" the waitress asked, not realizing the atmosphere had turned frostier than a snowman with two snow-girlfriends.

The girl grinned. "Just saw *Sleigh Another Day*."

The exact film Simon said he wouldn't see with Grace. *And* he'd gone on their year anniversary.

"And what a night to see it," I said, my eyes locked on Simon. I wanted to say more but knew Grace would hate it. What kind of a guy would do this?

But Simon just shrugged. "Yeah, it was great. Although,

some bad news." What's worse than "I'm cheating on your best friend"? "That party thing? Turns out we're double booked. You're going to need a new venue."

"Are you kidding me?" Had he really just cancelled the one thing we'd had booked for Grampy G's Grotto? I looked at Grace. She was just standing, staring, not even blinking.

"Sadly not. But I'm sure you guys can be resourceful." He didn't care one bit! "Anyway, we've got a booking we need to get to."

"Have you heard of Pomodoro & Pasta? It's meant to be lush!" the girl said excitedly as Slymon steered her away, no idea that was exactly where Grace had booked for their anniversary. I called after her to say it was meant to be great – this wasn't her fault after all – and with my arm around Grace trudged back into the cafe. Grampy G's party had been the one thing to make her smile. And if Slymon thought he was ruining that too, he had another thing coming.

"Well, that went well," Grace said, drying her eyes after a therapeutic five-minute mix of crying and creatively insulting Slymon. Thank goodness we had seriously amazing waffles to cheer us up. And by the time we'd finished them, Grace had graduated from sad to furious.

"Who needs boys when we have waffles?" she said,

leaning back. I was so full I had to undo the top button of my jeans.

"Agreed." I stuffed a final forkful into my mouth. I'd already promised Grace she didn't need to worry about the Grotto venue, and I'd sort it.

"This Christmas. No more Slymon. No more boys. Just you, me and as much Christmas as we can muster."

"Hear, hear," I said, burying the thought of just how many sparkly gold drinks and bad jumpers I was going to have to deal with.

"You were right, Mol. Forget all those silly films. All those fake happy endings. All those stupid fluffy snowmen with light-up carrot noses that wave their arms and say 'I love you *snow* much'." That seemed like quite a specific reference, but now wasn't the time to question it. "I've decided this year I'm going to be … a one hundred per cent single Jingle Lady." She dropped her head on my shoulder. "You want to join me?"

"Sure," I said, although I hardly needed to confirm considering I'd never had a boyfriend and the only guy I'd met recently seemed like he was just as bad a boyfriend as Simon. I picked up my glass and held it out. "Here's to the Jingle Ladies."

Grace tapped hers against it. "Jingle Ladies indeed!" She grinned. "And may Christmas be fully epic."

"Fully! Starting with" – I pulled out the popcorn containers from my bag – "it's not much, but could these be the first raffle prize?" I put them on the table, along with an AAA gold wristband I'd found. "I can try and get more stuff from Liverpool."

Grace held them up like they were baby Jesuses.

"Mols! In a hundred years' time, when *Sleigh Another Day* becomes a cult classic, these could be worth more than a house!" She noticed the look I was giving her. "Not that it *will* become a Christmas classic. In fact, thinking about it, I'm sure no one is probably going to watch it after all. Too, y'know…" Yes – too funny, too festive, too many five-star ratings. I'd seen the reviews. Everyone loved it. "Festive Film of the Decade" had been the headline after the premiere. Grace popped one of the popcorn containers out into 3D and sniffed it. She jerked her head back, like it smelt bad. "Why is there writing in it?" Was there? I hadn't spotted anything. "It's a…" She tilted it towards the light. "…number, I think?"

She was right! There it was. In pencil. A scrawled mobile number.

She slammed it on the table. "If this is Joseph's number, can we forget about the whole Jingle Ladies thing?" But she saw my eyebrow rise. "Joking. Jingle Ladies is for life, not just for Christmas."

"Hear, hear..." I laughed. But was that a drawing underneath the number? The outline of ... a dragon. With a ... nose ring? "C'mon then, super sleuth. What's that? Your crime podcasts have trained you for this moment..."

"You're right. There must be a simple explanation why there's a phone number and a reindeer—"

"THAT'S A *REINDEER*!" I shouted so loud, even the waitress who was now avoiding us looked over. Of *course* it was! A really bad drawing of a reindeer. Antler horn things, long face, a round nose over the top (which made a lot more sense than a dragon with a nose ring). My heart thumped.

Was this Ru's work?

Had he left his number for me?

But why?!

He had a girlfriend. Although this could just be as friends.

"Mollllls." Grace was giving me the most suspicious of all looks. "Why are you getting so weird about this?"

"I'm not," I snapped, a bit too quickly.

"So you *don't* know whose number it is?"

If I was going to mention what happened with Ru, now was the time. It wasn't like anything *had* happened. But after just seeing Slymon, the timing felt way too bad.

I shook my head, not quite able to say "no" out loud. I never didn't tell Grace the truth.

"Phew." Grace grinned. "For a second there, I thought you were going to say you'd met someone..." She laughed. This felt weird. Why did it feel so weird?

"Bail on the Jingle Ladies already? Never," I said firmly, trying to make up for not fessing up about Ru. "Call me Molly Natasha Jingle Bell." I stopped, realizing I'd basically been named for this exact moment.

"Jingle Bell, I love it!" Grace picked up my pencil and passed it over, the rubber facing towards me. "And just as well. You had me worried for a second."

What mattered more? Rubbing this out to make sure we had prizes for the auction and show I was a committed Jingle Lady? Or keeping any chance I had of ever speaking to Ru again?

Before I could doubt myself, I rubbed the number out. All traces removed. Decision made.

This Jingle Lady was ready to sort Grampy's Grotto and survive Christmas.

CHAPTER

8

TO DO:

- *Pack the green paint!*
- *Village hall form*
- *Check red/white socks have dried*
- *Order Jingle Lady Christmas card*
- *Remember to tell Bil the cracker joke: Why does a pony make a terrible carol singer? Because it's a little horse.*
- *Start geography assignment*

Outside the Portakabin window, a crowd screamed. Huge searchlights swivelled over their heads as a heap of fake snow emptied down on them. Any other time of the year having a load of freezing sludge-water poured on you would be a criminal offence, but in winter … they were actually chanting 'More!', waving homemade posters, chanting Joseph and Maeve's names and filming every last second.

I leant forward in my spinny chair and looked in the mirror.

Was I really doing this?

"Don't forget to smile." Tess was loving every second. She flicked out my pointy collar. "And work that look. It suits you."

The only thing this look would suit was a plant. Or a pea.

I looked down at my head-to-toe elf costume complete with body paint. I'd always thought being backstage in "hair and make-up" would be glam. I definitely never thought it would be so … green.

"The only thing I'm going to work," I hissed, not just because I was fuming with Tess but because the green face paint had set my face semi-solid, "is how fast I can get this over and done with."

Tess's uni friends were waiting outside with Grace, as they weren't allowed in the "crew" bit and Elijah had escorted me and my sister to this trailer. I was SO happy Grace was here though – last night she'd bawled her eyes out to *Nativity* and despite promising they were happy tears, I wasn't so sure, so hopefully this trip could cheer her up. If it wasn't for her being here, I would have run straight back to the car where Dad was waiting already.

Although now I was pea colour I didn't want to run anywhere, except into a bath. Or maybe into some mashed potato to make Grace laugh.

I looked in the mirror and took a deep breath.

Don't panic. This is what you wanted, remember?

My cunning plan. If Elijah was making me be here, making me pose with the cast on the big stage, showing the world Elf Girl, then that's exactly what I was going to do – my way. Which is why I'd changed into a replica costume from the original video and a make-up artist was currently turning me green with the body paint I'd bought. My hope was that no one would be able to recognize me underneath it all, yet I'd still stuck to my end of the bargain.

As I stared at the horrified green face looking back at me, Tess snapped yet another picture.

"If you put this on social, I will officially kill you."

Tess rolled her eyes. "Elf gone wild. We love to see it!" She laughed. I didn't. "Relax. It's going nowhere. Unless, of course, I find out you've been borrowing my black jacket again." Oh, I see – she was securing blackmail material. She and Elijah should be besties.

"You should see if Elijah is looking for more people for his team," I said, enjoying that she didn't know I was insulting her.

"Talking of Elijah, Pankaj messaged me…" He was one of her uni friends who was working here, handing out flyers. "He's *sure* Elijah was on his course but got kicked out…" The make-up artist coughed. Or maybe spluttered. Either way, Tess wiggled her eyebrows. "You didn't hear it from me, though…"

My phone buzzed.

Grace: *Transformation complete?*

Then a gif of Ru Paul with the words "When you become the image of your own imagination, it's the most powerful thing you could ever do".

I'm not sure Ru Paul meant wearing a ginormous pointy red-and-white stripy hat with a bell on, but I took a selfie anyway.

Grace: *Your elfie game is* 🔥. *Also don't forget to get GOSSIP.*

I laughed and sent back another of me working my angles – which are hard to find when you're bright green and have your hair pulled up in pigtails. But messages were coming through on the family chat where Tess had just shared her half-blinking picture of me.

Mum: *Going green is good for your elf!*

Dad: *Costume is 10/10. Maybe we should all wear them for Grampy G's Grotto!*

Mum: *Proud of you, Molly Moo xxxx*

Then a video of Billy from Mum. Bil always had something nice to say, so I pressed play.

"You look like broccoli!!!!" she yelled, waving with both hands.

Or not.

And there was no way Mum and Dad could wear fancy dress for the Grotto. Grace and I hadn't told anyone about the venue change yet, as we were waiting till I'd lined up a new one. But that shouldn't be too long. I'd already emailed our village hall and it was free, so once I'd filled in the form it would be confirmed, and we could send out the updated invite. I'd wanted to do it already, but everything had been so busy and my brain was already at risk of shutting down with too many open tabs – not exactly helped by the message I'd got late last night. That I still hadn't replied to.

Unknown Number: *What do you call a reindeer who messages someone out the blue hoping for a reply but knowing they probably won't get one?*

Unknown Number: *Rude-olph.*

Unknown Number: *And also, a reindeer with surprisingly good typing skills.*

The messages then stopped until an hour later.

Unknown Number: *Already regretting that. Deeply. Down to my hooves. Can we pretend that never happened?*

Not going to lie, they'd made me smile. Well, smile then frown, as I wondered how Ru had got my number. But mainly smile.

But would a Jingle Lady reply to it? I wasn't sure. And there was no rush, as I wasn't going to London anytime soon.

"Ready for the finishing touches, lil' elf queen?" Jack the make-up artist twirled my chair so I was square on to the mirror.

"You mean there's *more*?" He zhuzhed the ends of my pigtails.

"Honey. There's ALWAYS more."

I gulped and reached out for one of the hundreds of packs of make-up wipes.

"In that case, can I take these for later? No offence, but I don't think this is going to be my evening look."

Jack smiled and started to draw a bright pink circle on my cheek. "No problem." He was the only one at this stupid event who'd made me feel relaxed and not like this was the most stressful day of my life (second only to the premiere). His Liverpool accent was chef's kiss too. "A good ol' scrub and this face paint should come off."

I didn't like how he said "should".

"Mols, stop moaning." Tess tutted, even though I hadn't said a word. "So many people would *love* to be getting this A-list make-up treatment."

Tess was almost, *almost* right. It was kind of cool being in a trailer having my make-up done by a pro who had more boxes and toolkits and belts of make-up than an entire Sephora. But… I looked at my reflection. My green reflection. And … just, no.

"So, you didn't have to do any elves like this in the film?"

Jack shrugged. "Not that I can remember… Also, side note, love that you are the only person in the country not to have seen it yet."

"And it's going to stay that way." I wouldn't even look at a poster, let alone watch the movie.

"Merry Christmas to you too." Jack winked. "Anyway, I was mainly on special effects. That Santa beard and aging make-up took for *ever*. Com-plete nightmare. Joseph had to sit for three hours every single day to get it on. Never complained once." He started the other pink circle. "Unlike someone else I know…"

I ignored him. I knew from his big grin he was winding me up. "I heard he was a bit of a diva."

Me getting gossip = happy Grace.

"I think he's just a little ... complicated." Sounded like code for diva to me. "At least he had Maeve." Ding! Gossip jackpot. "Anyway." Jack booped me on the nose with a blusher brush like he'd realized he'd said too much. "For what it's worth, I think you make this look gorge."

If by gorge, Jack meant "like a really angry gnome" then totally. But there was a knock at the door and without waiting for an answer, Elijah strode in.

Then saw me. And came to such an abrupt stop he almost tripped over.

"What" – his mouth was wide open in horror at my reflection – "is ... THAT."

Silence.

"Er, do you mean me?" I asked innocently.

Elijah ripped off his headset. "What else do you think I'd mean? How many other people are in here looking like a green goblin?"

"Trying not be offended at my elf work..." Jack muttered.

"You look RIDICULOUS." Elijah was almost shouting. "No one can see you like that!"

"I think it's kind of cute." Tess flicked my hat bell.

"Cute? No way!" Elijah growled. "You look unrecognizable!" Just the word I was hoping for! Luckily my face paint stopped my grin muscles working. "As if we'll get any press about *this* as a reveal… And we've got thirty minutes before the event starts." He closed his eyes and started deep breathing. "I bet they don't have to put up with this on *All I Want for Christmas Is Drew!*" He took another deep breath. "Keep calm. Not a problem. Yet again, Elijah will sort everything…" He pulled his headset back on and started barking, "Change of plan!"

"Chill, Eli." The suit man from the premiere walked in, looking very calm and un-Elijah. "How many times do I have to tell you? Even when it's falling apart behind the scenes, it's our job to make sure everyone thinks it's a total success." He put his hands on Elijah's shoulders. "Christmas number one. This is all a distraction. Keep focused. Keep up conversation. We need that BIG idea."

Elijah shot daggers at me, muttered "sorry" to his boss and stormed out. I didn't see him again and half an hour later I was shuffling (how on earth elves got any work done in these shoes, I did not know) down to the huge Ferris wheel towering over Albert Dock. It was ready to be lit up, each pod sparkling red, white or green, and along the docks were the huge pieces of set I recognized from Leicester Square. The main attraction was a giant sleigh that you could have your photo taken in, but there were also igloos, wooden chalets, even an ice rink with the *Sleigh Another Day* logo in the middle, where professional skaters were performing, all dressed up in Christmas tree outfits. And towering in front of the crowd was the stage where the cast were coming out. Where I was meant to be coming out. My stomach fizzed with nerves. There were so many people!

"DON'T JUST STAND THERE, ELF!!" Elijah bounded over with a megaphone. Guess I answered to "elf" now.

"It's Moll—" I started to say.

"Three minutes till switch on!" he yelled. I wasn't sure he needed a megaphone when he was four centimetres away, but from the way he was sweating and waving his clipboard, he didn't look in the mood for feedback. "And change of plan. Forget the stage. The reveal's off. We need you in a pod seventeen." He shooed me with his free hand and lowered the megaphone. "Quick! The normals are watching!" Was that what he called non-famous people? "So run run goblin."

I weaved through the crowd. Pod seventeen? Pod seventeen... Where were you?

"Sixty! Fifty-nine!" The crowd started counting down with a giant timer that had taken over the screens. I looked back at them. So many people staring right in my direction. So many phones up recording. So many people who hopefully wouldn't recognize me in this outfit.

"Thirty … twenty-nine…"

Pod seventeen finally trundled down! With the biggest leap, I threw myself into the pitch-black glass bubble. But with these stupid pointy red shoes on, instead of landing gracefully, I skidded, whizzed across the floor and splatted down on to the hard wooden planks.

And on to something else.

Human feet?

I mean shoes. Argh! Being an elf was getting to me.

"You OK there…" a low, slightly cockney voice said. A hand reached down.

"EIGHT! SEVEN!"

"Cos no pressure, but in six seconds I think you're going to be immortalized as 'Elf Sprawled on Ferris Wheel."

OK. That was enough to move me.

"TWO…"

I scrambled to my feet.

"ONE!"

The whole place flickered into a glowing web of red, gold and green lights. Huge Christmas shapes lit up in the water. A giant snowflake. A huge neon-green Christmas tree. Even the outline of The Beatles in Christmas hats, which I wasn't really sure fitted in with the film, but it was festive, so who cared? The entire dock had exploded with twinkly Christmas lights. Even I had to admit it looked magical.

Human guy whistled, impressed. He was about my age but dressed in human clothes, with messy brown hair falling over his face. Had I just had a quick lie-down on the feet of a cross between Harry Styles and Tom Holland? He walked to the edge of the pod and waved out to no one in particular, before turning back to me. "You OK? Cos even for an elf, you look kind of shocked."

"Sorry, yeah, I'm fine." I patted myself down, as the crowd erupted at the silhouetted shapes of Maeve and Joseph walking out. I could have sworn they were holding hands, but it was hard to see from up here. And was that Stormy barging them both out the way, dragging a tiny white fluffy dog along? The sound of Elijah yelling "Clap! Clap! Clap!" drifted up. I spotted him at the edge of the crowd, flapping his arms, his megaphone pointed directly into the head of a bored-looking dad.

"Think he wants people to clap," I said, with a laugh. "And sorry about squashing your feet. Elf life is a wobbly one."

"No problem." The guy smiled; a smile so gleaming it should come with a "ping". I could feel Grace swooning just at the description of him … if she wasn't a Jingle Lady and off all guys for the foreseeable, of course.

I leant against the glass, feeling brave behind the make-up, costume and fake bits of face.

"Kinda cool, huh?" I said, looking at Liverpool stretching out below us. I'd love a photo, but the invite small print had said NO PHONES, NO PHOTOS in capital letters, double underlined. I still had mine hidden in my green tights, though, just in case. "Elijah's smashed it, to be fair…" I stopped. "Sorry … do you even know who I'm talking about?"

Human-guy nodded. "Who doesn't?"

"Are you something to do with the film, then?" I paused. "Although if it's a 'no', then this is a really weird place to have ended up."

He laughed. "Long story. But short answer is yes. Elijah roped me into this last minute. Well, more gave me zero option…" He trailed off. "And what about you? Or is this is your usual Molly-on-a-weekend look?"

I nodded. "One hundred per cent. Every Saturday. Why wear—" But I stopped. "Sorry, how do you know my name?"

Was Elf Girl recognizable, even under all this?

"Elijah mentioned you, that's all…" He shrugged. Did he look awkward or was it me projecting? "I'm Harry, by the way. And you didn't finish. What's your film connection? Or are you just a mega-fan?"

I didn't want to go into any detail. "Also a long story. But not exactly a mega-fan, no. I haven't even seen it yet. Been busy wrapping presents at the North Pole, all that stuff."

Harry nodded solemnly. "Understand. It's a hectic time of the year." Truth was, a tiny bit of me had started to want to see the film. Just so I knew what everyone was talking about. But after that waitress had recognized me and Grace had confirmed views of the old music video were creeping up, a much bigger elf-shaped bit of me wanted to obliterate it from existence. "Although…" He sat down on the small wooden bench. "I thought everyone was dying to see Joseph D Chambers in action." He pretended to swoon.

"Speak for yourself."

"At least it means you've been spared sitting through that terrible, terrible title song." I froze. "What kind of ridiculous family music ensemble could write such cheese?" A noise came out of me, slightly like a balloon deflating. But Harry laughed. "Joking, Molly. I know exactly who are you. Elijah filled me in. In fact" – he bounced his shoulders – "it's kind of a tuuuune. Although that might just be because I've been brainwashed by hearing it a zillion times a day on TikTok."

He'd been what?!

And why was he doing some kind of elfy-dance?

This couldn't be happening!

I dropped my head so fast the bell swung round and whacked me in the eye.

"Tell NO ONE it's me!" I knew Elijah was on a mission to reveal my identity, but even telling just one person felt too much already. "And for the record, I personally think the director must be out of his mind choosing that stupid song."

Harry failed to hide a grin. "Out of *her* mind." Cringe. "I'll tell my mum you said that."

Oh, jingle bells. His mum was the director?!

"Oh, man, I'm SO sorry. I didn't mean it." I mean, I *did*, but…

"No stress." He held up his hand. "Team out-of-control parents, am I right?" OK, he got it. I laughed and slapped his hand. "Is that why you're here on your own?"

"Nah. Elijah said there was only room for one. My best mate is somewhere down there." I waved to where I was getting Grace vibes from. And, like we were psychically linked, my phone vibrated. I fished it out.

Grace: *Don't panic. But … no, in fact* do *panic.*

Grace: *In fact. JUST RING ME.*

"PHOOOOOONES AWAY!!!!" Elijah bellowed as we trundled past the bottom of the circle. I shoved it down my elf sock. "I can still see the GLOW!!!!" he yelled again, shining a torchlight right in my eyes. "OFFFFFF."

Fine! I switched it off. But I needed to ring Grace. If this was Simon-related, I was going to kill him. I could see the headline now:

ELF GOES ON RAMPAGE.

OK. Why was that making me feel happy? Maybe I was about the rampage life after all?

"You OK?" Harry looked concerned.

"Hypothetical question: if I murdered someone looking like this, do you think I'd get away with it?"

He thought for a second. "I think the mugshots would be very interesting."

I laughed, and chatting away, the hour passed way quicker than I thought it would, and it took me by surprise when the brass band marched onstage playing Christmas carols for the grand finale. And as they worked their way through "Silent Night" and "Once in Royal David's City" – the lights twinkling and crowd swaying – Harry and I stopped speaking and just listened, looking out over the water. Harry and I stayed silent until the very last note of the very last song. And for a second, way up in the sky, I pressed pause on all the thoughts that were stressing me out. Grace's message. Elf Girl. The Grotto. The lyrics I hadn't written for The POWR. And it was weird. In the hole they left, a new thought crept in.

Should I message Ru back?

But Harry was nudging me. "Photo?" We were at the very top of the wheel. "It's the last circle, and Elijah can't kill us when we're three hundred feet up."

I flinched.

"Don't look like that. It's just for us. And look." Harry held his battered handset up. It was the same ancient model as my dad's but had a *Sleigh Another Day* sticker on it. "This thing's so old we'll just be two blurs."

"Fine." I stood next him. "But one take only."

He took it as I was still speaking.

How had Harry managed to get the perfect light on his face? His chin back, textbook smile. There was even fake snow behind him. But me? I was a blinking green person, who looked like they were mid-chew on a particularly challenging Christmas toffee. Oh well. I typed in my number so he could send it over and then it was time to say bye. I immediately rang Grace.

"Where are you? And are you OK?"

She sighed. A really long sigh. A really long happy sigh? "OK?! I just saw Joseph D Chambers, so, erm … slightly more than OK actually!"

Phew. She didn't sound upset.

"So what's up… No one posted any pictures of me, did they?"

"No! Not one. You're in the clear."

I did a celebratory dance-shuffle, much to the amusement of Harry, who had just walked back past. "So … what is it?"

"What it is … is…" Grace took a deep breath. "How do you think the village hall will cope with bringing the outdoors *indoors*?" She paused. "Mol, I MANAGED TO GET A SNOW MACHINE FOR THE PARTY." Her voice wobbled as she jumped about. "Grampy G's Grotto is going to go OFFF!!!!!"

I was so happy it was good news, not her being upset. But I couldn't head off to celebrate with her until Elijah had given me the all-clear, so we agreed I'd ring once I was done and she would go with Dad and Tess to Wagamama, then come back to pick me up. First stop was the posh portaloos (that had full-length mirrors on the doors!), where I scrubbed at my green paint so hard I triggered a workout alert on my watch. When I finally looked more normal (although, I'd swapped bright green for bright pink), I headed to the production office and found Elijah leaning against a golf buggy.

"Hi," I said. He didn't even look up from his phone.

"Sooooo… You can say thank you now." He was

scrolling like his thumb was in a race. "Best view of the city, am I right?"

"Yeah, it was pretty cool actually." I leant over to try and see the photos he was looking at. "How did all the press go?"

"Would have been better if I could have revealed who Little Elf Girl was." He finally looked up. "Oh, and you decide to look like a normal human girl *now*, do you? Thanks so much."

"Anytime." I smiled.

"Glad you said that. Because after today's effort, I'm going to need you to come to Edinburgh next week." He what?!

"But—"

"But wouldn't that red-carpet clip get so many views online?" He gave a quick smile. "Don't worry, you can bring Grace. I'll chat to your parents, get it all sorted. We've invited some pretty major influencers down to the pop-up winter village. Should be fun."

Fun?! Fun for me was sitting in a dark room until January.

"Fine." I crossed my arms. "I'll do Edinburgh." I lowered my voice. "And then that clip is MINE."

"We have ourselves a deal. Although, one question. A top secret big idea one. What do you think the Bells would say about a little remake of the 'Love Your Elf!' video? A brand new look that feels a lot more NOW. Get some cameos, give it the star treatment." Elijah smiled smugly. Could he not see how horrified I was?! "Joseph wouldn't do it, no way. He won't do a single thing to do with this film. But Maeve *maybe*. Especially if we gave some of the streaming proceeds to charity." He got lost in his awful idea. "And we're pretty tight with Ed Sheeran."

Ed Sheeran? ED SHEERAN? How would I manage to keep my identity secret if I was forced to be in a video with Ed "Zillions of Fans" Sheeran? I might as well run into school dressed as an elf screaming, "I'm the cutest little elf in the world and Zaiynab, Matt, my nice normal life, BYE, it was nice knowing you."

"As delightful as it sounds, it's a no from me," I said firmly.

Elijah rolled his eyes. "Yet again, Molly, thank you for your assistance in helping me get press and get that job. So very much appreciated."

But I was here, wasn't I? And none of that was my responsibility.

"So am I good to go then?"

"Sure. Although…" He checked his watch. "Can you do one little thing? Head to the 'Christmas in London'

photobooth set-up and get one solitary photo on the bench."
My eyebrow rose. What would he do with it? "Don't give
me that. I won't use it anywhere. I just want to know if it's
working as the photos are coming through all distorted. Oh,
and can I borrow that hat? I want to show it to wardrobe as
an idea for some crowd props in Edinburgh."

Fine. I handed it over and headed off. Grace and
Dad wouldn't be back for an hour, so this meant now the
crowds had gone, I could also have a nosey around for
any spare film bits for the raffle. Oh! And I could email
the village hall with the confirmation form and to check
about the snow machine.

I grabbed a gingerbread steamed milk from catering
and a handful of Lebkuchen biscuits (my fave) and
headed in.

WOW!

A huge snowy London street opened up, street lights
flickering on the cobbled streets, snow falling, the sound
of the brass band playing carols floating in the distance.
Red, snowy post boxes, old-fashioned shop windows lit
up with boxes of chocolates and gorgeous gifts, even a
nest of robins hopping about on branches. In the middle
was the photobooth bench where they'd been getting
everyone to pose – the gifs were scrolling by on a fake
bus stop video screen opposite.

Apparently it was a recreation of the street and bench where Joseph and Maeve's characters kissed, and, according to a man I'd walked past earlier, was "swoontastic". But he *was* wearing a jumper with an up arrow that said "This Guy Is Christmas Crackers", so not sure how much his opinion could be trusted.

I did what Elijah wanted and sat down on the bench, smiling for a selfie. It really did look like a picture-perfect Christmas scene. I watched the gifs scroll through on the screen. Couples doing stupid poses. Pretending to throw snowballs. Pulling on the ends of a giant bow on an even more giant present. Kissing under the mistletoe. I looked up at the bunch dangling above me. It was probably good Grace was eating katsu curry, not seeing all these loved-up couples, having their perfect Christmas moment – just like the ones she'd wanted to have with Simon.

Even though it was all so fake. So set up.

More flicked by ... a guy not realizing the camera was going and getting caught in the middle of pulling his jumper off, his girlfriend cracking up. Two guys kissing as they held up a "Happy Holidays" sign. Two young kids holding hands. Erm ... why was I smiling?

Was my icy heart thawing?!

Molly. Get a grip.

I tutted at myself and pulled out my phone. Time to stop getting sucked in by all this fake Christmas romance. It was as artificial as those mechanical robins. And I had a booking form to fill in. But as I waited for a signal, I found myself looking back up.

Two old women smooshing their faces together, making a heart with their hands, a dribbly boxer dog staring up at them. Cute.

Molly, NO!

Life isn't like the movies.

Life is a guy telling you they love you and then seeing him snogging someone else on Stories. And taking a girl on a date on your year anniversary.

Life is meeting someone who makes you laugh, who sends funny messages, but they have a girlfriend and so there's no point even thinking about it.

Because what life really is … is being a Jingle Lady with your best friend, Grace.

Yes. That was more like it.

Molly Bell wasn't a melting heart-shaped snowball – I was a piece of Christmas coal.

Phew.

But that's when I heard a crunch of footsteps.

"Room for one more?"

CHAPTER

9

If there was one person I didn't want to see right now, it was him. Well, Simon, and then him. And maybe Mr Phillips, my geography teacher, as I still hadn't finished my end of term assignment and he was starting not to believe me that there was a nationwide printer ink shortage.

"What are *you* doing here?" I spluttered so hard, some chewed-up Lebkuchen dislodged out of my tooth. I wasn't expecting to see Ru ever again. Let alone on a fake London street in Liverpool. And I hadn't replied to his messages?! Whyyyyy?! Being guilty over phone was fine, but irl I felt baaaad.

Mustn't panic. Maybe we could both pretend the messages had never happened? Maybe we could both pretend I still wasn't glowing bright pink. Still, better than green.

"I *could* ask you the same thing." He raised an eyebrow, and shuffled his feet in the fake snow. "Not that you'd reply…"

Great. We were going there.

What did I have? Broken phone? Nope, it was literally not-broken and in my hand.

"Ah … about that." I paused. "My phone's been, er, playing up."

I tapped it, giving it a "what a naughty little thing" look.

"Sure…" But Ru grinned. I instantly felt a bit better. He was letting me get away with being rubbish. "Guess I'll just take it as a win that I'm not head to toe in snacks this time."

I waved my bag of Lebkuchen menacingly. "Don't speak too soon." He laughed and sat down next to me, plonking a pile of books down. "How did you get my number anyway?"

He pressed his lips together. "A reindeer never tells… But *Elijah*. Elijah gave it to me." Interesting. Elijah never said a word to me. "Although he referred to you as *Elf Girl*?"

"Elijah, huh?" Laugh laugh laugh. "What is he like?" AN ELF-OUTING DEMON, THAT'S WHAT. But at least it meant Ru hadn't put two and two together. "But you didn't answer. Aren't you meant to be in London?"

"London…" Ru's nose wrinkled. "That was the plan. But then … everyone started to freak out about this film maybe not getting Christmas number one and now they're throwing *everything* at these events."

"Meaning?"

"Meaning…" Ru paused. "They want anyone they can get – all hands on deck. I swear half of the college students here have all been roped in." That made sense, the whole crew here had seemed strung out. But he sighed. Sighed?! I snorted. Hard life was it, being paid to travel round the country and meet celebs?

"I'm sorry. Can we talk again about how you hate your job?" The best I could get near me was working in a garden centre.

"It has its moments." Ru smiled. "Running into you might be one of them."

Erm.

What?

Was he being creepy? Or friendly?

I could be flattered, if my red-flag radar wasn't sent to "high" and flashing, and I wasn't imagining what his "better half" would say if they could hear and what was that ringing in my ears? Oh yes, my Jingle Lady alarm.

Time to make things clear.

"Yeah, it's nice to see *friends*." I picked at some icing

on the biscuit, not able to look him in the eye as I said it. But after what Grace had been through I wasn't just going to sit there quietly. "In fact, it's a shame you missed my bestie, Grace."

"I would have liked that." Ru didn't seem fazed. Good. "Is Simon here too then?"

"*Eurgh*, him!" I took an angry bite of Lebkuchen. "No. They split up. We caught him cheating on her. THE ABSOLUTE IDIOT."

Ru looked genuinely shocked.

"But I thought they were super tight?"

"So did *everyone*." I paused. "Well, except Simon." But I didn't want Ru feeling sorry for Grace – Grace was too good for that. "But she's doing great. Way better without him. In fact, now we're officially Jingle Ladies." I shimmied my shoulders. "Staying single together." Yes, it was cheesy but I wanted him to know Grace didn't need a someone – a Simon – to enjoy Christmas. And nor did I.

"Just checking." Ru looked over his shoulder. "Can you legally say that on the set of a romcom?"

"Well I did. And I am. Cos when your best mate asks, you say yes, right?"

"For sure. Especially if her ex was such a fool."

I liked that Ru was #TeamGrace, but this all seemed

a bit much coming from him. Even as friends, I couldn't help but wonder if his girlfriend would mind him giving his number out to me like he did? Messaging me? Maybe it was all the sugar, or being a Jingle Lady, but I decided to find out.

"So, hypothetically, if you had a girlfriend, would you think it was OK to give your number out to other girls?"

He shook his head. "Hypothetically, and actually, no. Never." He paused. "Although I've been single for so long, I can hardly remember."

Single?!

"Single as in…?!" Mouth! You did not have the authority to say that!

"Single as in … like a Jingle Lady, I guess? Just with less" – he shook his shoulders like I had – "hashtag sleigh!"

But what about the "Better Half" thing?!

I pictured my phone and how Tess was saved in it as "Fun Sponge".

Had I got things very wrong? Ru was single? And had given me his number? And I'd rubbed it out?

But if he was single then…

Nope. My brain spun in circles. And when I looked at him, it got worse. Especially as all there was at the end was a flashing big stop sign saying "Jingle Lady".

Ru looked down, fiddling with his hands, suddenly as awkward as me.

I had to get this conversation back into some non-awkward territory.

"Great. Right. Good to know, just as, you know, a good fact for a friend to know." Turns out non-awkward wasn't one of my skills. "So, erm … cool." I nodded.

"Cool." He nodded.

Silence. Awkward silence.

"So, erm…" When in doubt … biscuit! "You want a Lebkuchen?"

As we chewed, I had a serious word with myself.

Molly! Jingle Ladies do not get flustered by single boys!

Not even very cute boys who write funny text messages.

It was just this film set making me be weird.

The fake snow probably had odd chemicals in it.

Ru sniffed the steam coming off my drink. "First these cookies. Now, whatever that drink is…" He sniffed again.

"Gingerbread latte. No coffee. Just oat milk. The Best."

He raised an eyebrow.

"Has something … happened, Dash? Are you all

advent calendars and festive sweaters since we met?" He pretended to gasp. "Wait! Is that why you couldn't reply? Too busy moving those mini reindeer?"

He'd remembered my story about "our Christmas-obsessed neighbours" (that he had no idea were actually my family), but I rolled my eyes. "Says Mr Pickle tree. Nah. I was just thirsty. And this is tasty. Not festive, really."

"I stand – well, sit – corrected." Ru shuffled back on the bench. He looked so different to when I'd first met him. Big black puffy coat, smart trousers, scruffy Converse, but then this perfectly groomed face. Grace would have said a perfectly groomed very handsome face, but that's not something a Jingle Lady would pick up on. "So you survived the rest of the premiere then?"

"In a way." I wiped some foam off my nose. "How was the rest of your shift?"

"Well, Elijah threatened to move me on to bathroom cleaning, if that answers your question? Anyway, how's all the Grotto prep going? Not long now, right?"

I rolled my eyes. "It would be way better if Simon hadn't cancelled the venue. Honestly, what a wetwipe. And did I say he went to see *Sleigh Another Day* with another girl on his and Grace's anniversary?" As I waved my arms about, crumbs flew everywhere. "He's an emotional robot! Sorry, I think I have undealt-with rage. A lot of undealt-with rage."

"Let it out, I say." Ru discreetly brushed the crumbs off his cheek. "And tell Grace I'm sorry."

"Will do." Although I'd have to tell her you exist first. "So, are you going to Edinburgh next weekend?" Maybe, just maybe, the two of them could meet?

"Yup. Only Edinburgh then London to go. Then it's Lapland, which I'm actually psyched about. Then my work is done and I'm free."

"You're going to Lapland?" He'd said it in the casual way I'd say "the big Asda".

"Didn't you know? They added it on."

"Perks, much?!?!" I said, making a mental note to google London cinema jobs for me and Grace.

"Not gonna lie, I think it helps when your parents are friends with the bosses." Did he not understand that the main perk I got from my mum was her letting me off a forty-eight-day library fine? "They're doing a big open-air screening at the" – he did air quotes – "'home of Father Christmas'. Which, of course, definitely exists."

"Sorry." I hit my gloved hand down on the bench so hard that fake snow flew up. "One more time … you're going to LAPLAND?" I sighed. "I really need to sort out what I'm doing with my life. Can I get your job when you head back to the States?"

"Travelling round the country with a flight of reindeer doesn't exactly sound like a tough life." What was he… OH, THAT'S WHAT HE WAS TALKING ABOUT?! "I mean, it actually sounds like Santa's life…"

Thank goodness he made a joke so I had time to get my face reactions back in order.

"Well y'know…" I said, though I didn't know. "There's a lot of…" I tried to think back to any of Billy's videos. "Reindeer poo. And, er, feet clipping?" No, that wasn't right. "Hooves! Hairy hooves."

"OK, what's worse – Elijah and a megaphone or reindeer poo?"

I weighed it up. "Tough, but I'm going 'Elijah'. You know, I heard him pitching a story on 'inside the mind of Stormy's dogs'." The journalist looked as confused as me.

"What would that even be…" Ru rubbed at his eyebrow, trying to figure it out. "Feed me? That butt smells nice?"

But this was a perfect opportunity! Grace wanted gossip, and gossip is what I could get. "So, come on then. If you're backstage all the time, you must have some serious stories…?"

"Stories?" Ru looked up at me. The huge indoor lights made his brown eyes sparkle. Not that I noticed. *Jingle*

Lady, Jingle Lady. I looked away. "I'm normally too busy removing popcorn from places it really shouldn't be…"

"Oh, come on! Elijah's always telling me what a nightmare everyone is. You must have seen *something.*" More silence. I could get the hint or … I could totally ignore it. "At least tell me if Maeseph are together?" Ru blinked, like I'd broken some kind of unwritten rule for people who worked here. "I won't tell anyone if that's what you're worried about." But I stopped. "Although, full disclosure, I would definitely a hundred per cent tell Grace, but she's basically me."

Ru looked at me. Really looked at me, like he was trying to figure me out.

"Honest answer? I haven't seen anything. And even if I had, it's not really my business." Ouch. But he clocked that I looked like Sosig when he gets bopped on the nose. "Sorry, I've just seen it so much at work … the cinema. One rumour and suddenly the world thinks it fact. Like Taylor Swift's twin."

"Taylor has a twin?" That *would* make sense. She did achieve a LOT.

Ru chuckled. "Well, no, but … you get my point." Fine. I'd just have to ask someone else. I did have Harry's number now. "And talking of prolific genre-changing songwriters. Any news from your audition?"

I got it. We were changing the subject.

"I'm in the final two." I did a little celebration dance. "So, the plan is to write some lyrics tonight and send them tomorrow. Then it's wait and see time."

"Awesome." Ru looked impressed, which felt weirdly nice. No one other than Grace knew I wrote stuff. "You sound pretty chill about it?"

I cackled. "Sure, if 'chill' means checking WhatsApp every two and a half seconds."

But before he could reply, his phone rang.

DAD.

Ru saw me looking, so he cut the call. His phone was as battered as Harry's. And it was ringing again. He flicked mute on and pretended it wasn't for at least two seconds that felt like one minute. This was like déjà vu.

"You should get that." Why was he so weird about speaking to people? I mean, no one likes phone calls, but at least I could answer my dad.

"Nah. It's nothing..." He didn't look very happy for "nothing".

But it was ringing again. He stood up, turning his back to me before he answered.

"Uh-huh."

"Yup."

"Sure."

"OK … OK. It's fine. I'll see you at breakfast."

It sounded more like a work call Mum took, rather than a family one. And when he sat back down he looked miles away.

"Everything OK?"

"Just work stuff. My parents never stop." He sighed. "So, what were we saying…" There he was. Smiling. Back in the room. Well, fake London street.

"I *think* you were saying I was going to be more famous than Taylor Swift …'s twin." I laughed.

"That was it! Seriously, though, maybe Elijah or Tim might have some good contacts? Now that the theme tune is trending. It's top ten, right?" My stomach fell. Instead of disappearing into obscurity, that stupid song was just getting bigger and bigger?! After setting my face to neutral and having a silent scream, I tuned back in. "… He's obsessed with getting all the cast in a new music video for it." What? I thought that plan was top secret?! How many people had Elijah told? If Dad got even a whiff of it, it would be SO hard to get him to say no! Ru laughed. "Your face is telling me this isn't a good idea."

"Something like that." But my mind was racing. This couldn't happen. My family in a video with Joseph, Maeve and Stormy would make my life even worse than it had been before we moved. And that was before Elf

Sheeran popped up to co-banjo with Mum! "...don't suppose you know what they said?"

I tried to sound casual, and not like my life depended on it.

"A flat no, I think."

PHEW?! I sighed so hard with relief that my fringe went vertical. "Thank GOODNESS." Ru looked slightly puzzled by just how relieved I was. "What the world does not need is another terrible Christmas music video, right?"

"Can I make an observation? Forget what I said earlier, I'm not sure idyllic Christmas streets and festive hot drinks are doing much for your season's cheer, oh Jingly Lady."

He was right. I needed to get off this bench. But that's when I noticed what books he'd put down.

Maths text books. A French vocab test book. Wow. This guy knew how to have fun on a Saturday night.

"You brought your school stuff with you?" I flicked the French book open. "*La chauve-souris?*" I paused. "Means bald mouse, apparently." I couldn't be bothered to elaborate that it's what they called bats. "Have you got exams or something?"

"Something like that." Argh. Excuse me while I face plant the fake hedge. He could be worse than me at straight answers. "Oh!" He reached into his pocket. "I forgot. THIS is why I came here." He was holding my elf hat. "Elijah asked me to give you this. Figured it was a private joke or something to do with the fundraiser?"

"Something like that." If he could dodge questions, so could I.

"He also asked me to take a photo with you in the photobooth." Ru nodded towards the screen with the big "Say Cheese" button blinking away.

"Nah." I shook my head. Ru didn't need to know that I was already doing way more than enough for Elijah. "Although it did give me the idea for a DIY photobooth for Grampy G's Grotto!" People could donate to use it? Then we'd only have another … £650 or so left to raise.

"Your first prop could be this…" Ru passed me a mechanical robin that had fallen on the floor.

"Deffo. And if you see anything else, we're still on the hunt for raffle prizes." Yes, it was a bit cringe to ask, but I imagined Grace's face if I got some proper signed merch and it made it all OK. "Like anything signed by the cast or a props that are going spare?"

"I'll see what I can do…" Ru said, in a way that sounded almost promising. Although, if he knew about the music video, maybe he was better connected than he was letting on? Maybe his parents could pull some more strings? I stood up, but my notebook dropped off my knee and flopped open on the Christmassy lyrics I'd been working on for The POWR.

"Wait…" Ru picked it up. "Did you draw this?" Around my ideas I'd sketched Grace's smiley face under a big "Jingle Ladies". And on the other page my family sitting round a Christmas tree, a horse wrapped up underneath it. "You never said you were pro?!"

"Thanks," I said, snatching it back up. For all my being careful about not letting Ru know about the stupid song and why I was really here, somehow looking at this felt like he was getting a shortcut to the real me. I stuffed it back in my bag.

"Was that Grace?" Ru asked. "She looks just how you'd described her."

But he'd already seen too much, so I mumbled "yes" and started to walk, narrowly dodging the mistletoe. But once we were on the move, we began to leave all the weirdness behind, and I started telling him all about how Tilly had just won a pony-grooming competition with a Shetland called Spud. I put my foot in it by starting to say Billy, but styled it out with a coughing fit and blaming a rogue crumb. Ru didn't pick up on it, and instead just asked more questions about Grampy G's Grotto and I told him about the snow machine. And how I'd gone full YouTube tutorial to make 3D paper snowflakes. And that I was going to borrow the lights from the 'OTT house on our road' (aka mine). And despite not knowing Grampy G or Grace, he didn't look bored once, and told me it was going to be awesome, and offered a hand if I needed help googling back-up venues. And his enthusiasm made me slowly forget all the stress about being Elf Girl and instead start feeling like Grace and I really could pull off something special for her granddad.

"No waaaaay." Ru stopped dead at the end of the fake street, a big grin on his face. "Is that what I think it is?!"

I looked round the corner to where he was pointing.

Oh no. *Pleeeeease no!*

A pen of five of the cutest, fluffiest reindeer were chomping on some hay.

THE MONSTERS.

And Ru was walking towards them. "Are these yours?" And now he was stroking the one with massive horns that was giving me serious side-eye.

But what could I say? How many reindeer-hire firms did one film need?

"Erm … yes?" I didn't make a single step forward though.

"So cool!" He stroked the one next to it. "You should

have said the Reindeers 'R' Us crew were still here! I can't believe I'm getting to meet them."

Nor could I, Ru. Nor could I.

I shuffled slightly closer to the pen. The big one sidled towards me. Were reindeer attacks a thing? Like how hippos were surprisingly dangerous?

"*Nice reindeer...*" I whispered, holding my hand out.

"Look at you, pretending to be scared to make me feel better." Ru laughed. I couldn't smile back; I was focused on not getting a festive antler up my nose. "So what are their names?"

I swear all the reindeer simultaneously looked up at me like five big furry lie detectors. *Enough shade, guys?!* I had to look away. The guilt was too much.

"Erm." *C'mon, Molly,* think of something. "Rodney. Derek. Malcolm."

Why had I just named all of Mum's library colleagues?!

"I thought you said it was the female ones who still had antlers at Christmas?"

Why was Ru a leading reindeer expert right now?!

"Yes. They are. And those are their names."

He quietly repeated, "Rodney. Derek. Malcolm" while stroking the middle one's neck. Derek, the big one, looked like he wanted to impale me. Not very festive,

Derek! Thank goodness my phone rang, and unlike Ru I couldn't answer quick enough.

Dad was outside, so we headed towards the entrance and stopped under the flickering light of a fake old-fashioned street light to say bye.

"Guess it's bye then," Ru said gently. But was he … leaning towards me?!

Why was he looking at me like that?!

Why was he tilting his head?!

"Dasher…" He stopped, his face incredibly close to mine. "Can I ask you something?" Gulp. I could feel his breath on my neck. I nodded, not saying a word. "Would it be OK if…" What was happening?! "If I asked…" It felt like my world had shrunk to just this one metre square. "Why your neck is … green?"

Ah! I almost collapsed back. What on earth had I thought was happening?!

"Long story…" Well, it might be short. I didn't know. I hadn't made it up yet. BUT I wasn't ready to tell him, to tell anyone, about my elfy past! Especially when we'd been getting on so well. And he'd also realize that under pressure I named reindeers "Rodney". "But it involves a very green, er, very avocado face mask.'"

His eyes narrowed. "And your … arms?"

"It was actually a full body mask." His eyes lifted up

to my head. "And hair."

And with the quickest bye possible, I trudged to meet Dad, the whole weird day scrolling on repeat through my brain. But as I headed towards town, not one single person did a doubletake or asked about Elf Girl. Even though the song was getting bigger, so far it *was* just the eagle-eyed waitress back home who'd connected the dots. Maybe I could survive this?

And maybe this Christmas was salvageable? Grace had enjoyed today. The party was taking shape. And I'd had a really nice time with Ru. Which wasn't a problem because we were just friends, and I was still one hundred per cent very much a Jingle Lady.

And as I stood in the pick-up area looking for Dad's headlights, my phone pinged. A voice note from Ru.

"Sorry, but reindeers are bad with phones. Just ask Derek." Even though it had only been ten minutes, it was nice hearing his voice. "All hooves and…" He stopped, lost in where the joke might go. "Hooves?" He stopped, laughed, then composed himself. "Probably should start again, but seeing as you probably won't reply to this I might as well carry on. I wanted to say I had a good time today." He paused. "Learning about naked mice was a highlight of course." Another pause. "And seeing you was also OK I suppose … maybe." I could picture the grin he was doing. And realized I was smiling too. But that was OK. Jingle Ladies could smile at messages and it didn't have to mean anything. "So, if you want to do it again in Edinburgh, let me know? I'll be there all weekend. Or don't reply and I'll get the hint."

But Dad's car lights swept in and Grace jumped out the millisecond it stopped.

"Don't panic," she said, breathless.

"You said that earlier."

"But this time I mean it." Uh-oh. "Two words." She gulped and the beginnings of Christmas cheer instantly melted. "There's a photo of what I can only describe as an elf and some kind of supermodel on the internet. And the elf is you."

CHAPTER

10

TO DO:

- Pack jumpers (make sure Mum doesn't sneak in long johns – AGAIN)
- Present idea – buy Billy a hoof pick?
- ~~Finish~~ start geography assignment
- ~~Raffle prizes – time to ask Elijah???~~
- ~~Check Tess OK to donate a photoshoot~~
- ~~Look up normal names for reindeer. Neigh-ames. Hahahahaha.~~
- Booking form for hall!!
- Make 200 snowflakes
- Try to get over Dad throwing away the first 200 snowflakes

"Slice?" Dad offered me some Chocolate Orange the second he stopped for the lights. Some people might not think Christmas chocolate was OK before 7 a.m. but those people were not my dad. For last night's dinner he'd just had mince pies.

But chocolate always helped. I chewed and stared out of Cara the Camper Van's frosty window as we drove past Holly Hospice, their little Christmas tree hardly staying upright in the breeze and broken lights dangling off their roof. I could see why Grace wanted to raise as much money as possible to help Grampy G's friends have fun.

Not that anyone else was awake yet. We'd had to set off SO early to get to Edinburgh for the *Sleigh Another Day* event. But I didn't mind. Just one more day and this whole film nightmare would be over. Elijah had asked me to do a Little Elf Girl takeover of the film's social account with "lots of elfies". I think his vision was for me to be in the posts, but Grace and I had come up with a much safer idea. I'd brought my elf hat and we were going to put the bell at the very bottom of each photo, like there was a tiny elf posing just out of shot. Then all I had to do was upload them, and wait for Elijah to hand over the footage.

Finally something going right. This week had been awful. I snuck a last look at the picture of me that had been posted. Before we picked up Grace and her dad, I needed to get my "it's fine, I'm dealing with this" face back on.

Eurgh. Every time I looked at it, I felt the same sick thud, like the world had tilted off balance. Harry smouldering and my stupid blinking elf face.

Why on earth had SleighAllTheDaysFans, the stupid film fan account, shared this photo with the world? And how had they got it in the first place?! I wanted to kill Harry.

689 likes.

45 comments.

1 caption that might ruin my whole life.

Ten years later and THIS is what the "Love Your Elf!" girl looks like! Can we call it an exclusive?! 😲 *Shout out to @MollytheLolly for turning up to the Liverpool light switch-on and taking such a great elfie* 😂 *! So jelz she got to hang with Maeve and Joseph! Mol, if you're reading can you give us the inside gossip on #Maeseph?! #hohoho #peacetoallelves #seeingthefilmsisgoodforyourelf #sleighanotherday*

Harry never said he ran a fan account, but when I'd immediately messaged him to take it down, he'd pretended to be clueless.

Harry: *Sorry Molly (also that rhymes). No idea what*

you're talking about. The only one I sent that photo to was you 😕

And the only person I'd sent it to was Grace. And there was no way it was her.

All week I'd been petrified someone I knew might start following SleighAllTheDaysFans, so I'd checked I was on private, changed my profile picture to a picture of a slice of toast and asked Grace to stop following me, so there were no clues the account they'd tagged could be me.

But who would do this? I couldn't bring myself to look at any of it, but Grace had done a full deep dive. Apparently it was a gossip account just for the film's mega-fans. Photos of the cast. Interview clips. Rumours about who was dating who. Behind the scenes photos and pap pics. Grace had tried to report the post. She'd chosen "inappropriate" as the reason it breached guidelines – no lie, though, sharing a picture of me as a blinking elf was deeply, *deeply* inappropriate. But it was still there.

I scrolled down the comments. At least there were less new ones every day.

"*Lol.*"

"*Why is he standing next to that mutant?*"

"Check out my TikTok. Link in Bio. I originated the ElfYoSelf challenge!!!"

I felt sick all over again. I stared out of the windscreen – all the streets and places that felt like home feeling at risk of changing for ever.

My school. Where up until now I'd just been Molly. Nothing out of the ordinary Molly. Not embarrassing-Elf-Girl Molly.

The newsagent. Where I'd been Molly. Sure, slightly obsessed with Freddos Molly, but not in-a-ridiculous-singing-family Molly.

The bus stop where Grace had pressed send on that first email to Zaiynab. And now The POWR were a few clicks away from realizing I was a national musical laughing stock.

But wait... I froze.

What was that new comment?!

"Is Elf Girl at St Augustine's??? I SWEAR she did a coding camp with me 😊 😊 Also. Campaign for better elf emoji starts here."

I groaned so loudly Dad heard it over his exceptionally powerful rendition of "Stay Another Day".

"Harmony time?" He turned the volume up even more, his eyebrows wiggling in excitement, making his

Santa beard wobble. Why he was wearing a fake Santa beard to drive Cara was beyond me. But I'd realized from a young age that asking my family questions was dangerous.

"DAD!" I had to yell. "THAT WASN'T A HARMONY! IT WAS ME GROANING."

"Well, that doesn't sound *lit*." He was still deep in his using-words-he-didn't-understand phase. I didn't have the energy to explain. "What's up, Mol?"

The fact he said things like that, for one. The fact that I'd begged him to dress normal and he was wearing a Christmas jumper that said Feliz Navi-Dad with a picture of his own face on was another. "Nothing," I lied. Our argument last night had confirmed that trying to explain was pointless.

"The Brussel Shouts have been asked to go on" – he'd begun cheerfully. I'd hoped he was going to finish the sentence with "a permanent hiatus" – "*The One Show* to talk about Love Your Elf!"

I'd begged them not to go, said I'd never ask for a single Christmas present ever again, but all Mum and Dad had said was "potentially", which is British for "it's the answer you don't want to hear".

Eurgh. Everything was getting so out of control. And even though I'd sent off the new lyrics they'd asked for,

Zaiynab and Matt hadn't said a word about the band. Was it because they didn't like my lyrics? Or had they figured out my connection to the worst band in history? Because at school I couldn't shake a feeling. Had people started whispering when I walked past?

If this was the most wonderful time of the year, the other eleven months must be pretty terrible.

"Well, whatever 'nothing' is, this should help…" Dad turned up his favourite Christmas song. "Let It Snow" by Dragos Cicu. "And did I tell you it's SNOWING in Edinburgh!" He sighed, a big grin on his face. "It's going to be *magical*."

We pulled up outside Grace's house. Their cottage was the only one on the road that didn't have a single decoration up. Dad beeped. I wasn't sure how Mr W was going to feel about his neighbours getting woken up by a bright orange camper van, with flashing Christmas lights, blaring a tinny "Wish You a Merry Christmas" at 7 a.m., but I also wasn't sure he had a choice. Mr W and Grace walked out of their house doing polite sorry waves to the next-door neighbours, who were flinging their bedroom curtains open, looking less than impressed.

I jumped in the back and watched as Mr W climbed in, taking in the tinsel on Cara's gear stick, brand new

Christmas ham air freshener and drink holders that had been turned into pots of Lindt balls.

He sat down silently, potentially in shock, as Grace and I hugged hello.

"Can I just say." Grace inspected the van. "Cara is looking particularly divine."

"Glad someone appreciates it." Dad shot me a look in the rear-view mirror. "Which reminds me, I've been chatting to Sam," Dad said cheerfully, as if there wasn't a mute man blinking next to him. "And he agrees. How about we get the ol' band back together for Grampy G's party? The Brussel Shouts taking to the stage for one last time?"

Dad had a glint in his eye, lost in his vision. His terrifying vision. He moved his hand in the air.

"Molly ... on backing vocals." Never going to happen. "Maybe bass guitar too?"

"You know I don't play in public," I hissed. But he ignored me completely and carried on.

"Me ... vocal lead." He hit his chest. "Mum, rocking that banjo." Was that a thing?! "Tess on drums." She hadn't played in a zillion years. "Billy on ... tambourine and general dancing, and Grace, Sam, you can have whatever parts you want." Mr W steadied himself on the dashboard. "First live performance together in almost ten years!" Dad turned to the back seat, where I was aggressively shaking my head. "C'mon, Grolly! Tell me that wouldn't bring a tear to the eye."

It really would bring a tear to my eye.

"Well, I for one would love to see it," Mr W said politely. "And I know my dad would have too. The infamous Brussel Shouts I've heard so much about? At the even more infamous Bromster Village Hall?" Oops. I still needed to send over the official booking form to the village hall, especially now we had forty people confirmed. I could do it on the train. Mr W leant through the gap between the front seats. "Grampy G would be so very proud of you two…" He paused, his voice choking up. Dad put his hand on Mr W's knee. We all knew how tough the last year and a half had been. Mr W shook his head and smiled again. "Did I tell you, I had a call from the hospice yesterday? They're getting a volunteer photographer to come down and film it too. The residents want to live stream it all for their own Christmas party." Uh-oh. His voice was really going. "Dad couldn't have asked for anything he would have loved more."

Grace reached round the front seat, pressing her face against the head rest, to give her dad a big cuddle from behind. "It's going to be awesome. I promise. And just imagine all the fun they can have with a thousand pounds?!"

That meant making over six hundred pounds on the night, but Grace was sure we'd do it. And I was sure I'd never seen Grace put her mind to something and not make it happen. Which reminded me, I hadn't heard back from Ru about any prizes to raffle off. Maybe I should ask again? We'd been sending messages all week, although I'd avoided saying yes or no to meeting up this weekend. I wasn't sure what the Jingle-protocol was, so wanted to wait until I'd chatted to Grace. But that hadn't happened. Yet. I was sure it would be fine, though. A Jingle Lady was still allowed to make friends. Good-looking, nice friends who had spent the week checking on how Grace was doing, asking after Derek, and sending all the celebration gifs when I told him I'd sent off the lyrics to Zaiynab.

I started to type.

Heyyyy. Just left for Edinburgh.

Nope. Sounded like a message Mum would send. Maybe more casual…

Wassup Ru

Immediate delete.

Why don't ponies like carols? Because they're a little horse.

Nope nope NOPE.

"You OK there?" Grace leant over.

"Yup yup, just…" I waved my phone like I was constantly messaging my huge network of friends. Not just Grace or my family.

"Zaiynab?" Grace asked. I nodded sheepishly. And felt dreadful. And quickly sent any old message.

Hey Ru. Early morning question. Any news on raffle prizes #nopressure #althoughactuallymaybethereis

And hid my phone out of sight. I had six hours on the train up to tell Grace. And once we were on board and the train started rumbling north, the snow getting heavier and heavier, the fields racing by getting whiter and frostier, and every second further away from home, from Simon, felt like a better time to bring it up.

"Now, you will be careful when we get there?" Mr W was reading an article about *Sleigh Another Day*'s battle for Christmas number one. I could just see a photo of Maeve peeping out of the corner. "I hadn't realized how enormous this whole film thing was. And Edinburgh is a big city, you know…" He said it like we had never left our little village, like we'd never even seen a car. "Full of…"

"Beautiful castles?" Grace said innocently. "Trams? Cute Christmas markets?" She nodded seriously. "Yes. It's a scary world out there."

Mr W raised an eyebrow. "That's not what I meant, Gracey. You're both very capable young women. I meant" –

he tapped at his paper – "all these Hollywood types you might be mingling with."

"I'd love to do *more* than mingle with Joseph D Chambers," Grace snorted. Her dad clutched his tea. "Jokes, Dad!" A joke that looked like he would take five years to recover from. He tried to compose himself.

"Well, if you come back with a…" He took another look at the article. "… diamond ear-jazzle." He squinted at the table and muttered, "I don't even know what that is – like Stormoo…"

"That's a dog, Dad," Grace said calmly. "Stormy's dog. And anyway, no I won't."

"Fine." He looked flustered. "Or your head filled with nonsense. Says here Cate and Bry Chambers paid two BILLION to send their dogs' ashes into space." Wow! Cate and Bry were going to be there? They were husband and wife Hollywood royalty! Grace grabbed the paper out of her dad's hands.

"Honestly, Dad, you have nothing to worry about." But Grace looked at me, jiggling with excitement in her seat. "Cate and Bry! Stormy and Stormoo. Maeve and Joseph?! Mols, iss this actually life!!!!"

And instead of looking cross, Mr W laughed. Maybe it wasn't just me that loved seeing Grace get her sparkle back.

But sitting doing nothing was hungry work, and when we whizzed through Penrith, I went for another drinks run. I finally checked my phone.

Ru had replied.

Ru: *I'm on the hunt. And greetings from Ed-in-borooo.*

Ru: *Want to meet? By the Christmas Tree Maze? 7pm?*

So he still wanted to meet? What should I say? What would a *Jingle Lady* say? "No" probably – but then I might run into him anyway. But if I said "yes", then I needed to speak to Grace ASAP.

But maybe that was it! Meet him *with* Grace. Then there would be no Jingle Lady awkwardness. Just three friends hanging out. *Jingle People!*

Me: *Sure! You can meet Grace.*

He started to type. And stopped. And started.

Ru: *Awesome. I'll see if I can find some Leebrecooken.*

Ru: *That's not how you spell it. I realize this now.*

I couldn't work him out. He'd only ever been really nice to me. Funny, helpful with the fundraiser, potentially dislocating his shoulder to get me out the locked room. But I couldn't help but feel like there was something he was hiding – and I couldn't put my finger on what.

And I couldn't put my finger on why I felt a weird knot of butterflies when I thought about him.

Or why was it impossible to walk down a train aisle without semi-sitting on at least five strangers' laps?

"If we don't have the most festive weekend of our lives," I said, sliding into my seat next to Grace, my hands dripping with hot chocolate from where I'd splashed it everywhere, "then we're doing this trip wrong." Grace had spent the week showing me super cute pictures of Edinburgh at Christmas time. "Eljiah's team have done a Christmas tree maze. And there's a snow globe that's so big there's a cafe in it!" It was a huge see-through dome lit up with icy blue lights, with snow whirring in it.

"You're the best you know, Mol." Grace fiddled with the sleeve around her paper cup, her glittery gold nails sparkling. The tiny reindeers I'd drawn on them looked awesome. "And just, thank you. For everything. The fundraiser. Being my Jingle Lady wingwoman through the whole 'situation'." She meant Simon. Guess she still hadn't told her dad then. "This…" She nodded at her dad, who had just put on the Christmas jumper Dad had bought for him and was taking a smiley selfie.

Maybe now was the time to tell her about Ru. I sipped my drink. Here went nothing…

"Gr—"

"Don't forget these!" Grace and I leapt back as Dad slammed down a Celebrations tin. He was wearing reindeer antlers, making him seven feet tall and needing to crouch to stand up. "Thought our fellow pass-en-gerrrrs" – why could he never say words normally? – "might appreciate some."

Was he really going to wander the carriage semi-squatting, wearing reindeer antlers handing chocolates out to total strangers? Yes. Yes he was. But … people didn't give him a horrified look. Something about a grown man in a bad jumper and antlers offering free chocolate at Christmas made people … smile. And chat. And soon everyone was wishing complete strangers a merry Christmas. No one even complained when he sweet-talked the conductor into letting him get out his pocket speaker to play Christmas tunes for the last hour and a half of the journey – and by the time we rolled into Edinburgh, the carriage was in a full singalong to "Winter Wonderland". It was Grampy G and Mr W's favourite song and they used to lead a singalong every year at their party. I soaked the moment in – even though I hadn't had much choice, maybe these film events hadn't been so bad after all?

Maybe despite all the stress, I was keeping my promise to Grampy G?

Maybe I really could help Grace have an awesome Christmas after all.

CHAPTER

11

I stepped off the train into the freezing-cold Scottish air, feeling the most full of Christmas cheer I had since I'd found out about the film.

THE FILM.

My Christmas cheer disappeared like the Malteser Celebrations.

"Come on, guys!" Dad yelled, like it was hard to lose six-foot-seven man in antlers. "It's just a short walk to the hotel!"

But fifteen minutes later we were panting and sweaty after a low-level mountaineering trek, complete with yanking heavy suitcases over cobbles. Not made any easier by me refusing to take off a very large bobble hat, or loosen my scarf, because I didn't want to be spotted with Dad just in case anyone recognized us together.

But Grace was right. Edinburgh was SO pretty. Even better than I imagined. A huge castle towered over the city, and along the high street was a Christmas market, little wooden stalls dotted about with the most delicious smells wafting out. There was even a tram! At the end of the market was the giant snow globe, already packed full of happy tourists. Which reminded me, I needed to keep an eye out for Harry. Grace wanted to interrogate him face to face about the social post – see if we could make him crack.

"Well, here we are…" Dad climbed some huge wide steps up to a massive green wooden door, a wreath as big as Billy on it. "The Winterfield."

This was our hotel? It was the poshest place I'd seen in my life! A man in a top hat opened the door for us, and inside it just got grander. As our dads filled in paperwork, Camilla, the super-friendly receptionist, showed me and Grace the huge Christmas tree at the bottom of the Hogwarts-esque staircase. No way! Under the tree were tiny, wrapped Christmas presents with our names on! Maybe Elijah wasn't that bad after all?!

"This way, ladies," Camilla said, leading us up the winding staircase and into our room. She didn't even let us carry our bags! Or mind that my snow-soaked Converse were leaving a trail of melted snow juice. "We saved the best rooms for cast..." She pushed one of huge wooden bedroom doors open. Did she think we were cast? I'm not sure cast would be holding hands and squeaking with excitement. We had our own room! With a balcony! And the best view of the castle! And was that a hot chocolate machine? And did the fireplace have two stockings hanging on it with our initials on? Be still my beating heart!

The bed was so big we could lie sideways and not stick out! I know cos me and Grace yanked off our shoes and jumped right on it.

It was very bouncy. We may have bounced on it. A lot. And then realized Camilla was still standing there, smiling to herself.

"I'll think I'll leave you to it... And if you need anything..." She gave a small nod. "Like emergency chocolates or – can I recommend the Christmas shortbread if you lassies are peckish – just ring reception."

We waved bye and Grace flopped down on the bed, arms and legs spread out like she was making a snow angel.

"It's official. We've hit peak Christmas." She swished her arms and legs up and down. "We're haven't even been in Edinburgh an hour and already it's the best ... day ... EVER!!!! All thanks to you."

"Thanks to YOU! Imagine if I was stuck here on my own being dragged around novelty tie shops." Dad had already bought one and I was worried how the next thirty-six hours could go. Grace took one of the freshly baked shortbreads.

"Your dad is an unstoppable force, Mol, so you might as well stop fighting it." Easy for her to say, her genetic relative wasn't the one unpacking Father Christmas pyjamas. She bit into a shortbread, crumbs flying everywhere. "Who needs boyfriends when you have free biscuits!" She had a point. And a lot of crumbs on her face. She held up another and clinked it into mine. "Jingle Ladies for ever!"

"For ever!" I replied. Then remembered I still hadn't mentioned meeting Ru. Maybe that would be better to do once we were outside?

We arranged to meet our dads later, left the hotel and set off to explore.

It was snowing, and Grace stuck out her arms and twirled up the street. The scene looked like a Christmas card. It always made me glow when she unleashed dancing Grace. Look at my best friend with her superhero skill hidden away. A couple stopped to watch her pirouette and broke into applause. Grace of a week ago might tell them that December was actually the month most couples broke up; this week she'd walked around saying, "I wonder how many more people will be dumped this month". But today … today Grace was bowing and saying, "Merry Christmas, one and all!" just like her granddad used to. We picked up some non-alcoholic hot toddies with big chunks of apple and orange in, and strolled up through the market then along the cobbled Royal Mile up to the castle. The snow was settling on the courtyard, so we found a quiet alley to build a snowman – which Grace named Simon – and then completely destroyed with the umbrella she'd bought. Grace grinned as she took a selfie with it (framing out a crying child in the background). Maybe she finally had turned a Simon corner?

I sent a photo of the obliterated snowman head to Ru.

Me: *Think Grace is feeling better. Meet Simon…*

But it went unread. Oh well, we'd be seeing each other in two hours… Two hours. I should really tell Grace.

"We're here!" Grace pointed at the huge sign stretching over an archway made of baubles which said: "Light Up Your Holiday Season With *SLEIGH ANOTHER DAY!*"

Behind it the castle walls and gardens were lit up with moving art that made it look like a fairy tale castle with little elves at the windows and reindeer outside, and scattered around were the bits of set that I recognized from Leicester Square and Liverpool.

We headed under the arch, checked in and, arm-in-arm, walked into the event.

In every direction was something Christmassy. I scanned around. No sign of Harry. Or Ru ... not that I was looking. In fact, Ru had mentioned he'd met someone called Harry at one of the crew parties, so running into them both would be a nightmare, as Harry could spill my elf secret, and out my imaginary reindeers.

Actual shudder.

"Mols." Grace grabbed my arm, taking a temporary break from eating the shortbread she'd stocked up on. "Tell me I'm not dreaming. Or I am. Or whatever is the one that means this is really good."

But I didn't have time to answer.

"THERE YOU ARE!" Elijah appeared from behind a large snowman. He was wearing the same long black coat, plain black scarf and black shoes as in Liverpool. He plonked a box down at my feet. "I've been lugging this round for *hours*."

It was a brown cardboard box, black gaffer tape all round. Scribbled on the top was one word, "sezud". But no, he spun it round and turned it the right way up – "Prizes".

No way! Had Elijah really come through for the

fundraiser?

"Are these for us?" It was heavy too!

"Would be a weird thing to give you if not. You might want to leave it in a safe place." He nodded behind him to some Portakabins. "Valuables in there."

OMG was it valuable? This got better and better.

"Thanks, Elijah." I went to hug him. He backed away. I returned my arms to my sides as if it never happened.

"No raffling them online. Or auctioning, or whatever." Ooh, I hadn't thought of that – maybe we could do that with the other things to help raise more money? "Raffle them in the room, on the night only. Seeing as they technically shouldn't be leaving set…"

"No probs. Honestly, this is SO cool!" I turned to Grace. "Grace, no big deal, but you are looking at some actual, proper exclusive Hollywood movie things to raffle for the fundraiser!"

It took a second for the penny to drop, but when it did, Grace lunged and hugged Elijah. She was lightning fast, too quick for him to dodge. "THANK YOU!" I enjoyed his grimace. "We're going to raise SO much money!!" She gave him another hard squeeze, her pom-pom dinging him in the eye. "That's for the hotel too. Though I feel a bit vommy after all the shortbread. And three hot drinks. But it's Christmas, right?!"

"Not all thoughts need to be out loud," Elijah said, brushing shortbread crumbs off his scarf. "Although…" He eyed us up and down, taking in our matching bright red light-up Christmas scrunchies we'd just bought at the market. "Molly, you've made an effort for a change. Nice to see you not green. Is this your influence, Grace?" Charming. "Because I approve. Unless of course there's another reason." Erm, like what? "Meeting anyone?"

"NO!" I spluttered. "It's all Grace!" I didn't want him mentioning Ru before I'd talked to her, but Elijah almost looked disappointed.

"Well, you both look very … festive."

"Thank you." I took it as a compliment, even though it definitely wasn't. "You look … warm?"

He flicked his scarf. "The word you're looking for is stylish. I don't do cheap fabrics. My skin's too sensitive. And this" – he waved his hand up and down my outfit – "is a walking fire hazard. Although it would look great on camera. In a music video." Not this again? I'd already messaged him twenty times saying "no". He turned to Grace. "Grace, I'm relying on you to talk your friend round. You can have a starring role. I'm sure there's room for a dancer." *Eurgh!* He was a blackmail genius! I wasn't telling him anything *ever* again. "It would be *such* a good last-minute video drop for the film, just before Christmas… Just before they pick who is getting the job on the press team…" He looked into the distance, a tiny smile starting. "Christmas number one is *so* close." But then it was like he just realized he was still talking. And I was still shaking my head.

"Fine!" He cleared his throat. "Whaddya think then…" He pointed towards the maze. "Going to look good on the gram? Is that what you young people say?" He was only about four years older than us. "Obviously, the snow is all down to me, and I had to ship these in …" He pointed to the three huge Christmas trees that were dripping in lights. "… from Norway. No biggie." He blew on his nails.

"Well, *I* did." Tim, the suit man from Liverpool, interrupted. "Someone had to do something, seeing as I've just scanned the papers and there's a big fat ZERO pieces in there about the film." Elijah's shoulders dropped. "Time's running out, Eli. This was meant to do the trick, so let's hope today we get some pick up. We need whatever it takes. Exclusives. Arguments. Who's kissing who. Photos, photos, photos. Unless of course you don't want that job…" Elijah went to reply, but Tim talked right over him. "Although that music video idea had legs…"

He walked off without even a "goodbye". As much as

179

Elijah annoyed me, I could kind of see why he was so pushy. His boss wouldn't take no for an answer.

"Sorry about him." It was the first time Elijah had sounded human. "He's got a lot of pressure from up top, I guess. If we don't hit that top spot for Christmas, we're ALL in serious trouble." He sighed. "And I'm definitely waving goodbye to that job." A crackle came over his headset, flicking him back into normal mode. "So please do a decent job today … first thing you need to do is pick up a production iPhone from the cabin. It should be set up and logged in…" He rattled off everything we needed to do – mainly feature Little Elf Girl "as much as possible" (I didn't say what was possible was "not at all") and give a look at the event through the eyes of someone "pumped about the film". I tried not to snort, but luckily Grace leapt in, going into detail about the bit in the film where they have a high-speed sleigh chase in Lapland, and Joseph's hair is all snowy, and … well, a lot of Joseph-based content … until Elijah had gone glassy-eyed and said something about needing to go and check the snow wasn't melting.

We collected the phone and spent the next half an hour wandering around. But with only an hour till we met Ru, and me getting stressed we'd run into him any moment, the time had come.

"Graaace." I slowed as we came to a light-up penguin

on a sledge (which made no sense. It's like all logic was off with Christmas decorations. Reindeer being ridden by a Christmas hedgehog? Sure, why not?).

"That voice means you either have something to confess to. Or … nope, just that first one." But she was smiling. Chewing shortbread, but smiling.

"So, at seven. Once we're done. If you're OK with it. We *might* need to meet somebody."

"Somebody?" Grace's eyebrows shot up so fast her hat bobble wobbled. "Some. *Body?*"

OK. I had to get this right. Make sure she knew the Jingle Ladies were all good.

"Just someone I met at the premiere. When I wasn't being fake-sick. Or attacking you-know-who."

"Someone you've waited" – she counted back – "two weeks to mention to me?" I had nothing to say to that. "Mols, you rang me when you saw that guy you liked in Tesco and you swore he'd 'given you a look in the bread aisle'." She had a point.

"Erm. But this isn't like *that*. I'm a fully signed-up Jingle Lady. He's just a guy. Not a *guy* guy."

Grace folded her arms and leant against a fake lamp post. It wobbled, but she knew it looked dramatic and film-y so didn't move.

"Right, Mollington. I've known you long enough

to know that that 'erm' and 'that' mean that it's not 'some*body*'. It's a '*hot boy*-ody', isn't it?" She exhaled, her breath turning to steam. My stomach knotted. Was she cross at me? For not telling her? Or was she angry because a Jingle Lady shouldn't be in this situation? "Oh my god, this is bread aisle boy but MORE. Isn't it?!"

"No. Not at all..." Well, maybe a bit. Well, maybe a lot. Maybe actually, dude from *Bridgerton* season one level good-looking. But it wasn't like that.

But how *could* I describe what was going on? Ru was a guy who I could chat to about anything – but I hardly knew anything about him. He was someone who kept checking in on me, and my best mate, and the fundraiser – but who seemed to ignore other people in his life. A boy who was just a friend, yet made me smile when I thought about him, like now.

Eurgh.

The shortbread must be making my brain do weird things.

"And his name is?" Grace was still studying me. Was she mad? My smile vanished. Please don't let her be mad.

"Rudolph?" I said, shrugging, my brain scrambled. "Well, Kyle, actually. And he's American."

"American?" Grace whispered, impressed, like I'd

said "unicorn". "What else?"

"He used to look for a pickle on his grandparents' Christmas tree?"

Grace leant forward, squinting . "That's really all you know?"

"No, I also know he has NO idea about "Love Your Elf!". Thinks I live on a reindeer farm. Have sisters called Jess and Tilly and…" I trailed off. "So, if we meet up, don't talk about any of that. Or the film. Or that stupid song." Grace was giving me the same blinking, confused look she did when we practised French verbs. "But he's just a friend. So if it's OK with you, we could meet up at seven. He's been really helpful with Grampy G's Grotto. And is dying to meet you. Oh, and he hates Simon." Phew. Think that covered everything. But Grace didn't say a word. She was just smiling at me. "And I am totally and utterly not interested in him." But Grace was still smiling. "So pleeease stop giving me that look."

"Only if you stop smiling like that."

"I'm not." But her saying that made me smile even more. Which was annoying.

"WHEN YOU SAID IT WAS A MAZE, I DIDN'T THINK YOU MEANT IT." We both jumped as a screaming giant furry snowball burst out of the maze. Oh no, it was just Stormy in a fluffy white coat and matching hat. "AT ONE POINT I THOUGHT I'D NEVER SEE MY FAMILY AGAIN!"

She clutched her dog, which camouflaged so well with her fluff it looked like her coat was barking. She flounced past, a trail of people scurrying after her (one hissing, "she was only in there for five minutes".)

But I was happy for the interruption and with no more chat about Ru, Grace and I set off around the lights trail. Grace wanted to make the content for the *Sleigh Another Day* social takeover, which was good with me. Seeing her so hyped about it, taking photos of all the Christmas details, waving at dogs in festive fancy dress, felt like the old Grace was really coming back. The one who loved Christmas, and believed in love, and happy-ever-afters, and that life could be just like the movies. And as a couple went past in a tiny sleigh for two, and Grace made a swooning sound, I started to wonder. Something I'd never thought before. Maybe, *maybe* next Christmas, if all this elf stuff blew over, and the Jingle Ladies disbanded, maybe it *would* actually be nice to know what it's like. To hold hands in the snow, and buy stupid gifts, and swap scarves and laugh like it was the funniest thing ever.

But Grace was on a mission to spot famous people, so I left her to hunt down some celebs and took a break on a bench. Dream scenario was that Joseph was milling about, not with Maeve after all, and fell immediately in love with my best mate. Triple whammy – a story for Elijah, a happy Grace and a perfect way to annoy Simon. I pulled off my gloves with my teeth and opened a WhatsApp from a number I didn't recognize. I had two missed calls too.

Zaiynab: *Hey, Molly. Sorry for the delay. Hectic week. But … if you're up for it… How d'ya fancy being part of The POWR crew? Your lyrics were* 🔥🔥🔥

"Grrrraaaaaaccceeee!" I yelled. Thank goodness I was sitting down! Had this really happened? "GRAAACCCE!!!!"

Had I really done it?!

I read it again. I'd really done it!

I'd got into The POWR.

That's why Zaiynab must have rung! To do a Simon Cowell-esque reveal.

Just as well she hadn't! I couldn't speak!

I really had written Christmas off too early. I did a celebratory dance on the bench, not caring who saw.

I was in The POWR!

No one at school had found out about Elf Girl.

This was my last film event.

Grace was getting over Simon.

She knew about Ru.

I could *probably* find a way of talking Mum and Dad into not being on *The One Show*. Maybe my peace offering could be that they play Grampy G's Grotto, after all? It was only Mr W's friends and family coming anyway.

Yes, yes and YESSSSSSS.

I pressed play on my voicemail just as I spotted Grace running over.

"I got in to The P—" I started to say. Well, more shout.

But I stopped as the voice on the other end of my phone played. I hadn't been listening properly.

Did she say she was called Sue? Not Zaiynab?

From where?!

Panicking, I put my finger in my other ear and went back to the start.

"Ringing back about the snow machine query…"

Uh-oh. This didn't feel good.

"What? What?!" Grace mouthed, excited to know what the news was. "Put it on speaker!"

CHAPTER
12

We'd been waiting here so long I could no longer bend my fingers, and my ears were nearing cryogenic freezing. It was time to face it. Ru wasn't coming.

Just when I thought he might be different Ru was turning out to be just another low-level Simon. I'd even messaged to ask if he was bailing, and he hadn't even bothered turning his phone on to get any of my messages. Not cool.

But it was the reminder I needed. *This* is why I was a Jingle Lady. This was *exactly* why I never let myself get close to anyone but Grace.

I trudged over to the cabins to find Grace. She'd gone inside to defrost and watch the interviews with the cast that they were streaming live from one of the chalets. One of the influencers had grabbed them and I could hear Maeve chatting away about having to kiss Joseph, and Grace making an "ooooooh" as she did.

I hadn't told Grace about the village hall call yet. She was having such a good day – I was just going to have to find another venue and get it sorted before she knew there had been a problem, I didn't want her to worry about a thing.

I'd listened to the message again when she'd gone to take photos of the reindeer (Derek sneezed aggressively at me and I fled). An annoyed Sue said they'd sent me a booking form but had never got it back. She was right. A flashback to the half-filled-in form on my laptop came back to me. And now they'd hired it out to the "Santa Paws Fur-stive Finale!" – a pet charity's annual fancy dress competition. I'd rung Sue and begged to even just share the venue, but she said that last year they'd had trouble with one of the hamsters so needed to keep it "invite only" for health and safety reasons.

I was *such* an idiot. But I was going to fix it and had already emailed every venue on my original list. But all I'd got back so far were three "no"s. And one asking if a £2,000 hire fee "sounded good". No! It sounded terrible. Is this how Mary and Joseph felt with the innkeeper? Although, was I comparing my bad party admin to giving birth to the son of God? Glad I was keeping it in perspective.

I dropped my head back against the outside of the Portakabin. There was no way I was going to not find a venue, even if I had to build one, brick by brick. I wasn't going to let Grace down and we *were* going to raise that thousand pounds for Holly Hospice. So I couldn't just stand here worrying about it – or the fact that Dad was currently wandering round Edinburgh joining in with buskers and handing out sweets like an oversized elf (I know, cos he'd sent a video) or that I was turning into a human ice cube. Grace and I needed to finish filming. Then I needed to get the all-clear from Elijah that our deal was done, so I could put this stupid film behind me and focus on Grampy's Grotto.

I knocked on the open door of the cabin.

"Is now an OK time to drag you away?" I peered in. Grace and Jack, my make-up saviour, were sipping hot drinks, gathered round an iPad.

"I will *never* be ready to be dragged away from Joseph." Grace sighed as she stood up.

"If I see him, I'll be sure to tell him … to hang on to his personal items and call security." Jack laughed as he pulled Grace in for a hug. "… I mean, say hello to this gorgeous dancer from Bromster." Grace beamed. Guess she loved Jack as much as I did. "Now, Miss Molly. You said your best mate had the *Nutcracker* dance down, but come *on!*" He snapped his fingers three times. "More talent in her little toe than some of these people have in their whole bodies. And that's when she's frozen! Imagine a defrosted Grace, not in long johns." Mum had snuck some into my case. "*Incredible!*"

But we had work to do, so said bye, and headed to the maze, diving straight into a therapeutic session slagging off Ru for being a total let-down. Grace also filled me in on the make-up kit Jack donated to the raffle and I changed my mind at least twenty times about whether to tell Grace about the venue. But we were so busy chatting we forgot the rule of keeping left in mazes and ended up totally lost. Each tree had been decorated with something different. My favourite was the one covered entirely in dog decorations – but now we'd walked past it four times the novelty was wearing off. We stopped to take a picture of us looking lost by it, which was when we heard a crunch of footsteps on wood chippings.

Was there some dark hair sticking out over the top of one of the smaller trees?

Some hair belonging to Harry of "I swear I didn't post that" fame?

"Oi!" I shouted. Into a branch. One of the dancers from *Strictly* popped up. "Argh!" I gasped in their face. "Not you." She disappeared back into the hedge. Today really was very weird. "Harry…" I shouted. "Harrrry!!!!"

"Aren't we mad at him?" Grace whispered, confused.

"*Half* mad." He did keep saying it wasn't him. "But you can interrogate him, and if anyone can get us out of a maze, it's him."

She looked impressed. "Is he super clever?"

"Who knows. But he is very, very tall."

But there was no reply. Maybe it wasn't him? Grace explored the left turn and I waited by the tree decorated with tiny Lego figures.

"Molly," said a familiar cockney voice from behind. I spun round – it *was* Harry. He grinned. "I thought I heard you, but it was hard to get to you when we're in, y'know, a maze."

"Yes." I half-smiled at him, so I could keep the half-mad bit on standby in case I needed it. "I've heard they can be a little tricky to navigate."

The dancer from *Strictly* appeared again, stared at us and scurried off.

"I swear she's been in here for three hours." He shook his head. "Doesn't she realize you can just push through the trees?" He tilted one of the trees and suddenly I could see the next path. Harry tried not to laugh. "Please don't tell me you hadn't figured that out either."

"Of course we had," I said defensively.

"OK, it could be this way?" Grace reappeared, but she was looking back down the path she'd just come from. "But it also might not be. So if we don't want to be stuck in here and leave my dad at the mercy of your dad forcing him to attempt the bagpipes in public, then we better get going…" But as she spotted the tall, smiling Harry next to me, her words ground to a halt. And so did she.

I waited for the smart remark from Harry. About us being stuck. Or bagpipes. But the only noise was snow softly hitting the ground and some carols in the distance.

Harry was grinning at Grace. Grace was grinning at Harry. And … OK … this maze suddenly didn't feel big enough for the three of us.

Erm… Guess I was going to have to say something unless I wanted my last hours on Earth to be slowly freezing to death as Grace and Harry grinned at each other.

"So, Grace, this is Harry … of uploading the photo of me as an elf fame." Harry's face dropped.

"Even though it catsolutley abigorically…" He shook his head, flustered. "I meant absolutely categorically wasn't me." He said it so firmly it was hard to imagine it was a lie.

"And this" – I pointed towards my best friend – "is Grace. All round excellent human, lover of all things festive and officially has a toe that is more talented than anyone here."

She wiggled her foot.

"And soon to be turning to cannibalism if we don't make it out of here. I cannot eat another bit of shortbread or Lebkuchen. But Christmas cannibalism is OK, right?"

Harry laughed. "If pigs in blankets are OK, I'm sure human in coat is also fine." He smiled. And blushed. And looked back at her and... HELLO, GUYS! I'M STILL HERE!

How had I not thought about this sooner? Harry was 100% Grace's type. But maybe she'd been too sad about Simon for me to realize? Or did I just have Jingle Lady blindness?

"Let's go then." He rubbed at his scruffy hair. "...I've got a good idea how to get out... And by *good idea*, I mean pushing through the trees or ... this map." He flicked it out. "Which I'm willing to use if Molly agrees it wasn't me who put that photo up."

"Molly isn't willing to do that ... yet." I looked at Grace, who nodded in support. "But for the sake of Grace's h-anger ... I'll agree to a hiatus."

"You can buy the next round of hot chocolates to say sorry," Grace said to Harry, not missing a beat. "Churros too. Not that you did it, of course."

Harry rolled his eyes, but he was laughing. And he

carried on laughing as he and Grace led the way out, both deep in conversation.

But hanging behind was fine. I needed to check my messages. But there was nothing. No venue news. All I had was a message from Ru.

Ru: *I am so sorry! I got dragged into a work thing and didn't have signal.*

Ru: *If you're free, and want to see the world's worst skater in action, I'm heading down to the staff only session on the castle ice rink if you fancy it?*

I did not.

Ru had messed me around, and now I was having a way better time with Grace and Harry. And any spare second I had was now about finding a venue. But I'd tell him in a bit, let him sweat after he'd made me wait all that time.

I put my phone away and looked up. Result! We were at the exit of the maze.

But I stopped dead.

There was something terrible. *Someone.*

Standing next to Jack, checking her phone and looking cold and bored, was Maeve. Maeve actual Murphy.

Argh! I leapt behind a tree and crouched down. What if she recognized me?! As the red-carpet attacker? After all my hard work to let it die down, to stop Elijah sharing the clip, and now I was metres away from a lawsuit!

Please let Grace and Harry walk straight past. *Please, please, please.*

But when Maeve saw Harry, she smiled.

"Oh, hiya, Haz…" Maeve waved as if this was totally normal. As if we'd run into each other in the school loos. And Harry waved back. I peeked through a branch. Grace was just opening her mouth and shutting it. Fair enough. Maeve looked even cooler in her normal clothes than she did in the movies. She was in Doc Martens, straight faded jeans and a bomber jacker. Her long ginger hair was piled up into a messy bun and her fingers were covered in rings, her black nail varnish all chipped.

"What's up, Maevster?" Harry gave her a quick hug. Yup, Harry was officially more flustered by my best mate than by actual Hollywood royalty. Just the way I liked it.

"Have you guys met?" Harry turned to Grace. I crossed my fingers. *Please don't let them notice I'd gone.*

"This is Grace." Harry grinned.

My heart thundered in my chest as Grace walked over to Maeve. Yes, she was moving her limbs like a robot, but I bet she was going to think of something cool to say.

"Is it creepy to say I literally love you?" Nope. She

wasn't. "No, that's creepy, isn't it. But I've said it now. I'm Grace … and I love you." Maeve laughed. "Also, do you want some shortbread?" She held the battered packet out. "Maybe too much pocket fluff to be delicious, or even not-a-food-poisoning threat…" She trailed off. "But if you're hungry…"

Maeve took one. "Life saver. A tofurkey baguette is not my definition of lunch. Girl's gotta eat!" She took a massive bite, Grace watching with such love, like each chew was sealing their friendship. "Mmmm. And these are good!!" She swallowed. "But we were thinking of grabbing some food if you guys fancy joining?"

Nope. There was no way I could be in a well-lit room with Maeve. I was just going to have to stay in this hedge. For ever.

"Maybe, but one of our friends has gone AWOL." Harry looked back at the maze. "Weird, Molly was right here."

Oh no, Harry. Ohhhh nooooo. There was no way I was moving. Never. Not for anyone.

But Jack stepped forward in my direction, his hand on his hip.

"Molly. Get out from behind the tree and stop being weird." I stopped breathing in case it somehow could make me translucent. "And yes, I can see you."

Jack literally reached in and pulled me out.

I fell forward, right towards Maeve, some twig impaled into my hat. In hindsight, this probably wasn't the best entrance to convince her I wasn't completely unhinged.

"Course. There you were. In a … tree?" Harry said, trying to keep a straight face. "Maeve, this is Molly. She's actually more normal than she seems."

Hmm. I'd dispute that. Maeve smiled – she looked like a goddess. And I looked a hedge monster.

"Niiii," I said. Which was a mixture of "no" and "hi". "Sorry, I meant ho."

Nope. This wasn't getting any better.

"I'm Maeve," she said as if the whole world didn't know. "Do I…" She tilted her head, giving me an intense look. I buried my face down as much as I could into my scarf. "Do I know you from somewhere?"

I had to play this cool. Not raise suspicions. "Nope. No. No. Noooooooooo." I laughed. "Nicht. Nein. Just one of those faces."

"*Such* a familiar face…" But Maeve didn't look freaked out – she just gave me a really warm smile. "Well, if you guys don't have plans, shall we head? I'm SO hungry." Grace turned and gave me a look. The look of someone who was one second watching a film, and was now IN IT. Maeve didn't even finish her sentence before Grace had said yes and started walking. But I had to drop the phone off with Elijah and grab the box so I said I'd catch them up.

"Well, you look like the elf that's got the candy cane," Elijah said as I ran back into the room, where all the production phones were back on charge. Please don't let him tell me off for not being in any of the content. "Something happen?"

"Nah." I tossed him the phone. "Just grabbing food with friends, that's all."

He raised an eyebrow. "No other plans?" I shook my head. He was so nosy. I could see why his job was trying to make stories.

"Sorry, Elijah. No gossip for you."

He pretended to be offended. "As if… Just want you to have a good time. What are you up to tomorrow?"

I shrugged. "Don't know. But Dad's making us get up early to do a walk, so I might check out that bakery by our hotel for breakfast."

Elijah nodded. "Oh Crumbs!"

"Is that a bad choice?"

Elijah actually tutted in despair. "No, that's what it's called. Oh Crumbs." *Right.* "Anyway, I wanted to say, nice job today. You guys did good." I wasn't expecting that! "That livestream with Stormy's dog got major traffic."

"All Grace's idea." I smiled. It was nice to get something right for a change.

"Why do you think I said yes to bringing her along?"

"Because I said I wouldn't come unless you did?"

Elijah rolled his eyes. "Details, details. Although … I do still need one thing…"

"If you mean the music video, still no." I'd done my part.

"And there's *nothing* that could make you say yes?"

I shook my head. Nope, there really was nothing worth giving up the normal life I'd worked so hard to protect. "Sorry…" I walked over to the big box of stuff he'd given us earlier. "So, does this mean we are done? You delete the clip and no more *Sleigh Another Day* for me?" I tried to pick up the box. It was so heavy!

"And I thought elves were meant to be good with parcels…" He grinned. "Don't stress, I'll get it biked to your hotel. Leave it there."

"Thanks, but … is that a yes? About the clip? In fact, can you send it to me and then delete?" Having the evidence might come in useful if Maeve did recognize me. I could prove it was an accident.

There was a pause, which felt like an hour.

But then Elijah took out his phone.

"Sure." It was his personal one and brand new, unlike the production ones we'd all been using. "Got it safe and sound?"

I turned my phone so we could both see it and opened up my messages. *Oof.* I needed to reply to Ru. His message was still just sitting there, asking about skating. But that wasn't important right now. Above it was the thumbnail of the clip which had just arrived from Elijah.

"The eagle has landed," I said solemnly, and with a nod, Elijah showed me his screen and deleted the original. "Happy now?" I watched as it disappeared, a weight disappearing off me too. "Although, if you change your mind about the music video. "You know where to find me."

But I did feel better, which is why once I'd met back up with the others, despite googling venues for Grampy G's Grotto whenever I had a spare second, I ended up having a ridiculously fun evening. First stop was a coffee shop in a tiny alleyway off the Royal Mile then Maeve got us a people carrier with blacked-out windows to take us to a path that ran along a small river. The huge buildings along it looked like they should be in a Harry Potter film, and when we headed up some stone steps, suddenly we were slap bang in the cutest little row of shops, the doors decked with wreaths, the windows full of snow and beautiful Christmas decorations everywhere. Forget *Sleigh Another Day*, *this* was like a film set. And they'd closed the whole top floor for us in this posh restaurant called Scran and Scotty! Grace and I froze when we saw the prices, but the manager came over and said the whole meal was free. Maeve's life was ridiculous!

And maybe it was the sugar high, or maybe it was having the film events over, or maybe it was that Elijah had deleted the clip, or maybe it was seeing how Grace looked at Harry, or maybe it was that Maeve didn't recognize me, or maybe it was the fact I messaged Ru to say we couldn't meet, like a good Jingle Lady should, but I didn't even cringe when Mr W and Dad turned up. In matching kilts. And things got even better when we got back to the hotel and went through the raffle prizes from Elijah. Grace sprinted down the hotel corridor in her gown and slippers to drag her dad out of bed to come and have a look.

I'd never seen someone go teary eyed over a prop fake hot chocolate before. But Mr W did. Everything was all signed by the cast – prop after prop, even a script from Maeve. We really *were* going to raise so much money for the hospice. We really were going to do Grampy G proud.

As long as I managed to not ruin it all, and get us a venue.

And I had almost no time to sort it out.

CHAPTER

13

TO DO:

- *Find a venue! **URGENT PRIORITY*****
- *Get shortbread for Mum and Bil*
- *Stop Dad buying more novelty ties/kilt/ mini bagpipes*
- *Make 195 snowflakes*
- ~~*Start geography assignment??*~~ *Shortbread for Tess in return for geography assignment help?!*

Mmm, pillows, soo soft.

Mmmmm, air smells of cookies.

Mmm. In not much more than a week we'll be counting up how much we've raised from Grampy G's Grotto.

My eyes pinged open. I shot up in bed.

It was pitch black but I was instantly wide awake, like snow had been dunked on my head.

Grampy G's Grotto was almost here! I HAD to sort the venue TODAY. Sundays were notorious for lots of things happening, right?

I just needed to wake up!

Embrace the day!

Get in a positive mindset!

I checked my phone.

One message on my netball team group and one from the girl I sat next to in music.

Both saying the same thing.

They'd seen *Sleigh Another Day* last night. And then done a deep dive, and seen a photo on the fan account, SleighAllTheDaysFans. And was Little Elf Girl me?!

I replied with the only thing I could.

ME: *lol*

This was a disaster – "lol" couldn't protect me for ever.

People in my real life were starting to suspect my big secret.

I crashed back on to my bed and rolled face first into the big pillow.

Whyyyyy did there have to be three more days left

of term? If one person at school suspected, that meant soon everyone could.

Which would be RIP life as I knew it.

Au revoir to being in The POWR.

Hello to having "ring your jingle bell!" or "believe in your-elf!" shouted at me across the street, and being the butt of every joke about gnomes, elves, and anything small and green. People weren't fussy when it came to laughing at me.

Surely it shouldn't be OK to get this much bad news before … 7 a.m.

Grace was fast asleep, her "Sleep Mode" eye mask pulled down. Well, fast asleep except for murmuring something that sounded like … Carry? Larry?…

OMG. *Harry!!*

Was Grace dreaming about Harry?

She was definitely dream-smiling. And now she was dream-laughing. So loud she woke herself up.

And now she was not-dream blinking at me.

"Tell me it's not time to get up?" She rubbed her eyes, her mask pushed up.

"It isn't." I climbed out of bed. "But I am. Going to get us brekkie." I wanted to make full use of Oh Crumbs! doing free breakfast for hotel guests. "Requests?"

But Grace was already back asleep. I peeked out the

window – it was dark and everywhere was covered in fresh snow. I pulled on some faded jeans, my warmest socks and felt around for the biggest jumper on the chair where I'd thrown everything – which turned out to be the one Dad bought me yesterday. It was black with fluffy snowballs on together with a big fluffy snowwoman. Not exactly catwalk style, but the snow was getting heavier and maybe a smiley snow person might help me shift this mood. I pulled it on, scraped my hair up into a messy bun and messaged Dad to let him know where I was off to.

I headed out on to the empty street and after walking round the square, spotted Oh Crumbs! immediately. It was the only place with lights on, and looked super cute, its big windows steamed up, a smell of cinnamon buns wafting out.

The only customer in the bakery was an old lady concentrating on a crossword. She gave me a big warm smile when I walked in. At the counter there were so many pastries to choose from – gingerbread and Biscoff croissants, Christmas-spiced babka, bauble-shaped pain aux raisins. A nice man in a snowman-shaped apron talked me through each and every one, my mouth watering more every second.

He packed the eight I chose into a red-and-white

stripy box tied with a red ribbon. But when I went to take it, he pulled it back with a grin.

"You can't just leave with those," he pretended to be offended. "Our hot chocolate is legendary. Especially with a wee one of these." He picked up a gingerbread highland cow and popped it on to a plate. "So how about I keep these warm" – he slid the box under the counter – "and you can warm up over there" – he nodded to a sofa at the back of the cafe by a big radiator – "with a hot chocolate and one of these?"

I didn't need to say yes. He could tell by my goofy smile, I was fully IN. And by the time I'd taken off my hat and scarf, he'd already put a tray down.

Just what I needed. Snacks and time to properly work out how I could find a venue.

And to think about how to stop this whole Elf Girl picture getting out of control.

Christmas was two weeks away. If I could just get to Boxing Day, I *should* be able to survive for another year.

But it wasn't good news. My inbox confirmed I still had no venue, and after a load of "no"s my only hope rested on a yurt hire company who said they might be able to stay up an extra day after a wedding. They warned it could be below freezing inside and there was no electricity, but I'd cross that bridge when I came to it. Maybe the party could be *Frozen* themed?

I chewed the hairy face of the cow, a horrible thought growing. I needed to tell Grace … didn't I? Yes, she'd be upset, and I had to hope she'd forgive me, but she'd rather know. Right.

Right?

… but maybe I'd do it on the train back, so she could enjoy Edinburgh first.

"A gingerbread latte, please. But no coffee." I dropped the horns I was eating. Was that…? "Just hot milk and syrup. Oat milk, please."

The guy behind the counter smiled. "You mean the kids' one?"

"Well, you say potato, I say *potato*…" Nothing. "Yeah. The kids' one."

The guy ordering was in a long dark grey coat, beanie pulled down. Was it just coincidence he sounded American? But when he turned round and saw me in the corner, he smiled. A big Rudolph smile.

I felt a happy jolt. Then a damp one as a chunk of cow bum fell into my drink, and my hand got splooshed.

"Can I join?" Ru nodded to the entirely empty bench next to me. "Or is it a breakfast for one situation?" He paused. "Or … am I going to keep on talking until I get the hint you're not talking to me any more." Another pause. "And then apologize again for what happened yesterday…" I still hadn't said a word. "And then maybe see if I can reverse that by offering you these…" It was a bag of beautifully iced Lebkuchen, the ones I said were my favourite back in Liverpool. "Thought I'd beat the crowd and get here early as apparently, it's the best bakery in town." He bit his lip, embarrassed. "And maybe, *maybe*, Elijah said that *maybe* you were staying around here and maybe, *maybe* I kind of hoped I might bump into you. And give you the aforementioned Lebkuchen." He shook his head and looked down, looking all kinds of awkward. "And maybe I should stop saying Lebkuchen. Or just stop talking altogether." He stepped back and rubbed his forehead. "I should go, shouldn't I?"

And I wasn't sure if it was the hot chocolate or the thought of him trekking all the way here before 8 a.m., but I did feel less cross.

"I *am* talking to you." As of this exact second only. "But mainly to say I accept all baked gifts." I slid my coat out of the way, making room for him. Even a certified Jingle Lady could have a friend-based hot drink with someone.

Ru pulled his coat off, taking his phone out of the pocket and sliding it into his black jeans pocket. "Excellent not-at-all Christmassy sweater by the way."

I tried to look annoyed. "Snow people are for life, not just for Christmas."

"Course." Ru grinned and stirred his drink. "Seriously, though, I'm really glad I ran into you. Everything was so chaotic yesterday and I really thought I would be there, but then something came up and then my signal went and it was just … a mess."

Now was my chance. If he really wanted to apologize, he could be honest with me for a change. "So, what came up?"

Was it bad that I wondered if being vague meant it could be "better half" related after all?

He shrugged. "Oh, boring stuff. Elijah stuff."

Aaaaaaand.

Don't speak, Molly. Make him sweat. Make him spill some actual details.

I sipped my drink to stop my mouth opening.

Be intimidating! Be firm!

"It's a long story."

I continued sipping my drink. "Well, I have a lot of time."

Ru sighed. "It's just, I should never have said yes to this job, I guess. But my parents kind of said I had to. And with them knowing the bosses … *everything* I do gets back to them. Like going AWOL at the premiere.

And since then, just when I think I've got a moment for myself – like yesterday at seven p.m. – somebody finds something for me to do."

Well, that made sense, I guess.

"But you do get to go to all these places."

He nodded, embarrassed. "I know, I'm sorry. I need to stop whining! Privilege, much? I've done some awesome things and met some great people." He looked up. At me. Did he mean me? But before he could say any more, his phone alarm went off. Fumbling in his coat, mumbling "sorry", he pulled out a battered old phone and switched it off

"Um, do you have two phones?" I asked.

He shrugged. "Not through choice. Elijah makes all crew have them. Soooo, how was it yesterday. I didn't really get to see it. Everything go OK with the animals?"

Oh yes! Why else would I be here? "Yup. All went very smoothly. A very well-behaved flightherd." I nodded, trying to look wise.

"Any pictures?" He pulled at his beanie like he was starting to overheat. "Missing Derek was a real let-down. I think we had some major chemistry."

Great, now I was overheating too. I scrolled through my camera roll.

"I don't actually have any on my phone." I shrugged.

"Don't like to mix work and pleasure." What was I talking about?!

"Are they on Instagram?" Ru said, genuinely interested.

"No account," I snapped. "My parents are weird about privacy." Could not be further from the truth. "Reindeer privacy."

"Well, I'm with them. I don't have any accounts either." But did this mean he was safe from seeing the post about me being Elf Girl? Finally, some good news!

"But you *can* see this fearsome creature." I showed him a photo I'd taken a few days ago of Sosig.

Ru zoomed in. "Pomsky, right?" Wow, no one usually knew what Sosig was. And bigger wow – I'd dodged the imaginary-reindeer bullet. "I used to have one really similar. Ziggy. Before my parents went all 'no pets' and 'no ties' and we never stayed anywhere long enough to even get a cactus." He fiddled with his saucer. "And they're not the kind of people I can bribe to change their mind … not even with cute cookies."

"Well, their loss." He'd never told me properly what they did, but they sounded intense. "Are they here with you in Scotland?"

He cricked his neck. "Kind of. But last night they had some kind of crisis meeting… And they jumped straight back into it this morning. When Mom started on her third coffee, I figured it would be a good time to head out."

"Sounds stressful." Last night for me had been trying to stop my dad making Maeve show him every single filter ever invented.

"*Everything* with my mom and dad is stressful. And I don't even have a Jess or a Tilly to share it with." Cringe. Ru was never going to meet my sisters, but I still felt awkward that I'd made up their names.

"You can borrow J—" No, I couldn't say it again. "My sisters anytime. Anyway, what did you get up to last night?" He'd already told me he was really looking forward to looking round the city. "Was ice skating good?"

"Didn't do it in the end. Pizza for one in the hotel sounded more tempting." I felt a tiny twinge of guilt. Should I have at least invited him out?

"Did Elijah get you a good hotel? Ours has a Christmas tree that goes right up the stairs." He raised an eyebrow. I quickly corrected myself. "Not that I like Christmas trees."

"No." He tried not to grin. "Who does? Especially somewhere as picture-perfect holiday-season as Edinburgh." I loved how he said it. *Ed-in-broooo*. He took his first sip of his drink. "Oh, hold up…" He took another. "You weren't kidding when you said you were on to something with this?!"

"You can take it back "home" and pretend it was all your idea." Not that I even knew where "home" was, other than somewhere in America. "Wherever that is…"

"San Diego. Did I not say?" Nope, I was starting to realize the closest I'd got to a fact was the pickle hunt. "Well, it was Toronto for a bit, but now I'm back in Cali. If you're into beaches, I would recommend. But if you want some of this…" He nodded to the big window.

"Bin lorries?"

"No," he snorted. "Snow. These trad Christmas vibes. Then I'd give it a miss."

Was he honestly implying California was dull? He clearly had never been to Bromster.

"Well, I'm sure it beats where I live…" I tried to picture him wandering around my village high street – its one newsagent, one post office and one blue plaque that looks impressive but on close inspection is a joke one that says "Martin Jenkins, number one husband and Inventor of the Egg Toaster, lives here". Ru, with his American accent, and stories about travelling the world, and… Nope. I genuinely felt those two worlds might explode if they tried to co-exist. "On TripAdvisor, it says best thing to do in my village is visit a duck pond. We don't even have any ducks. Oh, and visit a bit of old wall that used to be a castle but now isn't, it's just twelve bricks."

"Sounds quaint."

"Come and visit and then say that again!"

But he just smiled. "I'd love to."

Erm. Was this weird? Why did I feel weird?

I gulped some hot chocolate.

"Well, if on the way to San Diego or Lapland or wherever you happen to go through Bromster, let me know."

Ru grinned. How was it possible to look so cute in a woolly hat? And how much sugar was in this hot chocolate?! I suddenly felt very hot and weird.

"Oh, I meant to say… Guess who Grace met last night? And when I say 'met', think *fireworks*. And long awkward looks…" Like the one we just had? *No, brain!* That was not an OK thought to have?!

"Erm…" Ru sipped his drink. "Maeve?"

"Yes, but no… Guess again."

"Stormoo?"

"No. And I'm still not over that name."

"I blame Elijah. He told her it was 'inspired'." Ru laughed, but I was starting to see a different side to Elijah.

"He's not all bad, y'know." Mostly, but not all. "He came through with some pretty epic raffle prizes."

Ru's eyebrows rose. "Is that so?"

"I know, I was surprised too. Oh, and it was Harry, by the way."

"Ohhh." Ru's eyes lit up. "That IS good gossip." He checked himself. "Not that I do gossip. How much did she freak when she found out about his mom?"

Oh man. How had I forgotten to mention that Harry's mum was the director! How had Ru thought of this before me?! Immediate two best mate points deduction.

The cafe was filling up and a couple, about our age, were walking past us to the toilet. I swear the girl was giving us a weird look. Oh, not today, Satan! I did NOT want this to be the moment Ru discovered my true elfy identity. I dived down and rummaged in my bag.

"You OK?" He peered down.

"Yup. Totally. Just think I dropped my ... er." I didn't wear contact lenses, so what could I say? "Edinburgh Castle pin badge?"

I was glad he couldn't see me mouth "what" to myself. Was that really the best I had?! But he immediately got down on all fours to help look. We found a pound coin, one wrapped chocolate coin, a biro lid and zero imaginary badges, and by the time I'd bravely said I'd have to write it off, the couple had gone, our drinks were drunk, I'd been out for an hour and I was beginning to worry about the not showering situ. It was time to get back.

So … why did I not make an excuse to leave? And why did I stay chatting in this perfect little cafe for another thirty minutes, right up until there wasn't a single spare seat in sight? And Grace had woken up and sent me a bed hair selfie?

Was it because I knew that this was the last time *Sleigh Another Day* was going to be in my life?

Which meant the last time I would ever see Ru.

But I had to go.

"I really better get back. Grace without breakfast is not something I want Edinburgh to have to deal with."

"At least let me walk you. If you want me to, that is." Ru stood up. "I could get another round of hot chocolates for you and Grace as my sorry for holding you up…"

"And for bailing on last night?" Tess had taught me well – guilt really could be dragged out. In fact… "Maybe you could seal the deal with some raffle prizes?"

"Gotta respect the hustle." He laughed.

And even though my hotel was two minutes away, somehow we made the walk last ten. And as Ru chatted away, snow still falling, it hit me that we looked just like all the couples Grace and I saw. The ones in the films she loved. Especially when the festive lights above our heads pinged on as we walked under them, like we were doing actual Christmas magic.

But my hotel door came into sight and it was time to say goodbye, for one final time. Why did this feel so huge? I'd only met him a few times.

"So guess this is it then…" Ru stopped. I looked up at him. At his big, deep brown eyes.

"MOLLY!" A voice boomed down the street.

Oh no.

"MOLLLLYYYYY-MOOOO!"

Oh no. Oh nooooo!

I slowly turned my head, almost scared to look. But yup … worst case scenario CONFIRMED.

My dad. Back from his morning run, with sweat patches in places I didn't even know you could sweat from, jogging over – Mr W trotting next to him.

Guess Ru knew my name then. One unwanted step nearer to FED: Full Elf Disclosure. My chest tightened.

"Thought that looked like my middling daughter! Can't see a blinking thing without my glasses." Dad lunged so hard, the elastic in his leggings went white. PLEASE LET IT HOLD. This was *exactly* why no one from school was allowed to meet him! But Dad smiled as he clocked Ru next to me, holding a tray of steaming hot chocolates. "Normally can't get this one up before ten.

Unless of course there's food involved." Dad pretended to just spot the drinks. "BINGO!" Laughing, he held out his hand to shake Ru's, even though Ru clearly had zero hands free. Ru bent his body down to try and finger-shake it back. "Gabe. Or Molly's Dad. Or Mr B. Or taxi service, as I'm mainly known. Even Spider-Man only had two names, y'know!" Wow, dads really did have unstoppable bad-joke energy. "And this is Sam. Or Mr W. Or Usain Bolt Snr. He just ran rings around me!"

Grace's dad saw Ru's struggle and deployed for a polite wave.

Dad lifted up his arm. "Wow. I really whiff, don't I?!"

And that's when Grace banged on the window above, wrapped up in the hotel dressing gown and double-handed waving. She really was living her best life! I waved back and mouthed "one sec" and then "we have HOT CHOCOLATE!". She started dancing around, arms in the air.

"Pleased to meet you, Mr B," Ru said politely. Dad actually repeated it with the same American accent.

"An American, hey! Well, that's kinda cool, y'all…" Dad's American accent was the worst. I wanted to say something, put an end to this torture, but all I had in my brain was, WHY DID DAD HAVE TWO PERFECT CIRCLES OF NIPPLE SWEAT?

"Not as cool as Reindeers 'R' Us," Ru said to Dad. Who looked totally blank. "Don't suppose you have any photos of Rodney and Derek? I miss those guys!" OK. Dad looked peak confused. The only option now was running.

"Well, thanks for these." I grabbed the drinks out of Ru's hands, trying to flee the scene. "I should get them upstairs – get showered. Not that I'm going to shower them. A drink would be a weird thing to shower. Shower myself."

It was fair to say Ru looked more than a little bewildered. "Oh, OK. Will I see you in London then?"

I felt a weird happy tingle? Why? Ru wanting to see me again? Or not being totally alarmed by my dad. "Maybe?"

I white-lied. It was a "no" really. Elijah hadn't asked and even if he did, I wasn't doing anything to do with this stupid film ever again, but I couldn't handle a final goodbye in front of my dad.

"I'll take that," Ru grinned. "And say hi to Grace! And Jess and Tilly!"

I literally sprinted inside before I could see Dad's face.

Before I could process that I was never going to see Ru again.

Grace was waiting in the corridor outside our door, with all the questions.

"My best friend doth lie-eth!" she wailed dramatically. "You said you were going for pastries. Not to pick up some cute Scottish guy? I thought you were meant to be a Jingle Lady?! Right? Ms Molly Natasha Jingle Bell!" Grace was on the balcony peering after Ru. "I mean, all I could really see was a beanie. And a coat. And what looked like a really awks handshake with your dad. But I could just tell." She made a low "mmmmm". "I bet he had nice teeth, didn't he?"

Should I just tell her?

"I wasn't picking up *anyone*, Grace." She mouthed, "right". "I am still one hundred per cent Jingling all the way with you. He's just that guy I was telling you about. Ru. Rudolph. Whatever." So why was I reeling from just saying bye to him for the last ever time. "That we were meant to meet yesterday."

"Hmmm." Grace craned her neck even further. "You didn't mention that he was hot. Well, from above anyway."

"It all goes wrong when you're eye level." I laughed. Truth was, Ru was drop-dead gorgeous from every angle. From above (I may have noticed when he was looking for my imaginary badge), from the side (sitting on the bench) and most probably feet first too. But this factual appraisal wouldn't help Grace believe me that there was nothing going on. "Anyway, he says 'hi'. And got us these as a sorry for yesterday." I plonked the drinks down. But Grace was still peering out the window. "I forgot I could have got them for free, but he said they give all the staff twenty quid a day just for food and drinks, so this can be a thank you from the film too."

"Sounds like a keeper to me." She sat back on the bed. "Not that you're interested."

"And not that you're interested in Harry..."

But Grace's smile vanished.

"I'm not." She said it slowly, seriously. "Don't get me wrong, he's great. But so was Simon at the start, and look what happened there. Anyway." She gave me a knowing look. "I'm a Jingle Lady, remember?"

"Fine." I opened the box of pastries. "Have a mini croissant. And, in totally unrelated news, if you *do* ever want Harry's number, he's saved under 'Liverpool Harry'."

Grace threw a pillow at me, and after an impromptu pillow fight we were soon back outside, building a snow dog that looked like Sosig, getting bribery shortbread for Tess and trekking up to the castle – where we ran into Harry. I made an excuse to go and buy an 'urgent novelty tie' for Dad so I could leave them alone. As I headed down the street, my bags banging into my leg and thinking about what Grace was going to report back, I realized I was smiling.

"Dare I ask what that smile is for?" A voice called out from a little table outside a cafe. I spied Elijah having a coffee under a heater and walked over.

"You don't want to know." He raised an eyebrow. "Grace stuff." He looked less interested. Rude! "Although, thanks again for those prizes. They're awesome. Slightly hard to carry back on the train, but awesome."

"No biggie. I was hoping to run into you actually." He finished the last dregs of his coffee and stood up. "I know our little *deal* is over but…"

"Please don't let this be about that video." I'd got Dad to promise last night he wouldn't do it, in return for him trying Scottish dancing with Maeve and Jack.

"Nope. It's how would you like to come to our final event in London?"

"Not at all." The finish line for getting through Christmas was in sight and I needed to shut down the Elf Girl suspicions at school, not run the risk of making them worse.

"And there's *nothing* I could do to sweeten the deal? Get a yes? I thought maybe you'd be ready to finally show the world the real Elf Girl."

I shook my head. "You thought wrong." Although… I pictured Ru asking to see me there. And how I'd never see him again. And… NO! STAY STRONG, JINGLE LADY! "Maybe you should have asked when you still had that footage."

He raised an eyebrow. "Maybe things change, Little Elf."

"Oi!" I hissed, checking no one heard. But I had to get back to pack my stuff, so I left him to it and walked down the Royal Mile, soaking up gorgeous Edinburgh. Soaking up the atmosphere as everyone got into the festive spirit.

And maybe some festive spirit soaked into me too. Because on the train back I *might* have helped Dad hand out his new supply of chocolates.

And as we were driving home in Cara, I *might* have introduced Grace and her dad to my family's rendition of "Let It Snow". And not said no to the antlers Dad had bought us all.

And Mr W *might* have told us his big news.

Grace's uncle and his kids had booked flights down from Newcastle for Grampy G's Grotto. Literally a flying visit to make it here and back before Christmas.

Which meant sixty people were now coming to Grampy G's Grotto.

And Grace whooped with excitement.

And I said "cool" rather than "HELP HELP HELP," which is what I was thinking.

And I didn't quite manage to tell Grace about the venue situation after all.

As I climbed into bed, I knew however awful it was, I had to.

It was already getting too much hiding my Elf Girl secret – I didn't want to have to hide a secret from Grace too.

CHAPTER

14

TO DO:

- *Venue venue venue!*
- *TELL GRACE about the venue venue venue.*
- *New lyrics for The POWR meet*
- ~~*Bribe Tess*~~ *Start/finish geography assignment*
- *Survive last day at school*
- *Make 177 snowflakes*
- *Figure out how to wrap a hoof pick?!*

Can you send a video of your line? My parents won't believe it's you!!!!

How much for Joseph's number???

I heard you were going on Gogglebox?!

Can you get Stormoo to guest on my dog's channel?!??

Were just some of the questions I'd been asked/yelled at across the hall/messaged from unknown numbers yesterday. Or in my physics teacher's case, written on my homework. But no. She was *not* getting a video from The Brussel Shouts to play on Christmas Day.

I got a D for that homework.

It was the last day of term and Elf Girl was officially out of control.

Circled screengrabs of Grace and me in the background of the *Strictly* dancer's stories in the maze were doing the rounds.

The picture of me in fancy dress in Liverpool felt like it had been shared in every single chat.

The video for "Love Your Elf!" was playing on every single phone, computer and even on the head teacher's iPad.

And wherever I walked, the looks happened. The whispers and laughs.

My whole class knew I was Elf Girl.

And unless I did something drastic, soon the whole school, the whole world would too.

My life was over.

Which wasn't even the worst thing. The worst thing was that it was nearly time for Grampy G's Grotto and I still hadn't found a venue. Or told Grace.

I spooned up a blob of cranberry sauce and let it splat down on my plate. The canteen was chaos, everyone excited to break up in a few hours. But me, I was hiding away in a corner, my back to the room, on high alert for any word that sounded like "elf". I'd just made a Year 7 cower with a dirty look only to realize too late he'd said "shelf". I would rather be anywhere else but here. But I was meeting Zaiynab and Matt, and with Grace off at her final practice of her *Nutcracker* routine for the end of term show later, I had to stick this out on my own.

"Long time no see!" Zaiynab pulled up a chair. "Sorry!" She was almost shouting. "It's hard to hear a thing in here."

"Hi," I said, hardly looking up. It was annoying – I'd dreamt of this conversation since I'd first heard The POWR, and now it was happening I was just trying to hide and not look too elfy.

"We're SO vibed to have you on-board." Matt sat next to her. Did this mean they hadn't seen the pictures of me on the internet? I studied his face, but he was smiling. "Your lyrics were fire."

"Thanks." I blushed. "I wasn't sure if, y'know…" Where was I going? "There had been any last-minute changes or anything?"

Zaiynab's eyebrows lowered. "As *if*. Unless you're

about to, I dunno…" she laughed, "share some kind of big, bad secret or something…"

She laughed some more. Matt laughed. I gulped.

"Yup, any secrets – declare them now." Matt paused. I knew I'd gone cranberry-sauce red, but there was no way I could tell them. *C'mon, me.* Focus. Breathe. You only have to survive today and this will get easier. "Mine is … I keep Tangfastics in the freezer."

Actually, that sounded like a great idea. I laughed, my mind scrolling through the one million things I didn't want them to find out. "I've got nothing."

"Great. So, we wanted to fill you in on that gig we told you about. Some record label people are coming – we're actually looking for a bass guitarist if you know of anyone…" I said I'd let her know, and absolutely did not say it was the main thing I played in the safety of my own room. Way too risky – what if they asked me to play? "If you're OK with it, we thought we could play the new track with your lyrics?"

"You can come onstage if you want? Do some production?" Matt pretended to be listening to one headphone and pressing imaginary buttons on the table. "Make Zaiynab and me look way cooler than we are."

I laughed. There was no way I'd be setting foot on a stage. Ever.

"Think I'll leave you to it. I'll be in the audience though!"

OUCH.

Something flew between Zaiynab's and Matt's shoulders, hitting me square on the head. It bounced into my Christmas Yorkshire pudding (a unique invention by our canteen) and gravy with a splat.

I didn't look down. If I ignored it, maybe it might be like it never happened.

"So are you looking forward to the end of term entertainment?" I said, trying to waffle on about anything.

But Zaiynab was staring at the paper plane going soggy on my plate.

"You going to do something about that?" Was she disgusted at me or the soggy brown plane?

That's when I heard the shout. We *all* heard the shout.

"OPEN IT UP, LITTLE ELF GIRL!"

I pushed the paper plane under the side of my plate and grabbed my bag.

"Think I might need to head actually…" I stood up.

"YOU SHOULD GO AND LOVE YOUR ELF!?" a different voice yelled. Simon? Whoever it was made the whole canteen laugh.

"Molly?" Zaiynab looked confused. She'd flicked

the potato clumps off the paper plane and opened it up. In big green writing it said "Why did Molly Bell go to therapy? To help with her elf esteem." "What's going on?"

My eyes felt prickly. Don't let me cry. Please don't let me cry.

"Just a class wind-up." I shook my head, trying not to think about the zillion Will Ferrell stickers that had greeted me on my locker this morning. "Who knows what goes on in their tiny minds." I looked over at Simon and narrowed my eyes.

I HAD to stop Matt and Zaiynab finding out. Being an elf was bad enough, lying to their faces about it was even worse.

"You sure everything's OK?" Matt looked worried. "We normally avoid the canteen like the plague."

AND NORMALLY I WOULD AVOID HAVING A FAMILY WHO DRESS UP AS CHRISTMAS FOOD ITEMS AND SING ABOUT ELVES, BUT HERE WE ARE, GUYS. HERE WE ARE.

But I didn't know what to do other than escape, so I said bye and ran out of the lunch hall before anyone could shout anything else. I stayed in the loos until the bell went for the start of the end of term entertainment. I snuck into our assembly hall with my head down and grabbed a chair by TJ from netball. Only ninety minutes left to survive. It was usual end of term happy chaos and I felt like a miserable Halloween skeleton who'd wandered into a Christmas party. But luckily no one around me noticed my complete slump, as they were too busy chatting and weaving tinsel into each other's hair and singing along with our music teacher's piano rendition of "Underneath the Tree".

But I just wanted it to be over. I didn't even smile when our geography teacher came onstage dressed as a Christmas tree and apologized for flashing. He meant his lights, but the whole school burst out laughing and he ran offstage clutching his baubles.

And I didn't laugh when the sixth formers did the annual comedy sketch about our teachers.

The only thing that made me smile was Grace doing her amazing *Nutcracker* dance. She got a standing ovation, and I clapped so hard my hands hurt. But the second she ran into the wings I collapsed back into my chair in more of a slump than ever. Thinking of how excited she was to perform the dance in front of her dad at Grampy G's Grotto made my heart hurt. And my head spin. I needed to find a venue. Fast.

I still hadn't found one that was available, and time was running out.

"And now for the grand finale!" Ms Allen, our head

teacher, shouted into the mic. "Something to start the holidays off with a bang. So, let's welcome to the stage, a last-minute entry ... who only put their name forward today ... St Augustine's very own ... Adele!" No one moved. I got back to thinking about the venue. Should I try the yurt place again?

Ouch! Why was TJ prodding my knee? "Go you!" she said, looking at me.

In fact, *everyone* was looking at me. And clapping.

"I said ..." Ms Allen cleared her throat. "Let's welcome up MOLLY BELL! Or as we now know her ... LITTLE ELF GIRL!"

The blood drained from my body.

What was happening?!

I put a hand out, the room suddenly spinning.

Elf Girl, Elf Girl, Elf Girl.

I looked left, right, behind me. Everyone was chanting.

Was I walking to the stage?!

Elf Girl! Elf Girl! Elf Girl! The Year 7s were screaming.

This couldn't be real?! But I was staggering along the hall towards the stage. And up the stairs.

Ms Allen pushed the mic into my hand. Was I really going to sing that stupid song? For the first time in seven years?

The music teacher played the opening chords.

I scanned the huge hall. All the faces I knew so well. Some smiling, some laughing, some excited to see how bad this would be. Simon was sneakily filming on his phone. Was this his doing?!

The students, the teachers, everyone was clapping along. Except for Zaiynab and Matt. They looked almost as shocked as me.

But then the big wooden door at the side of the hall swung open. And through it ran Grace. Her hands held up in a heart.

I smiled at her. Leant into the mic. Opened my mouth. And…

"I'm sorry, I can't!" I spluttered. The piano immediately stopped. The clapping too. "But, happy Christmas!" Oh no. Was I crying? I was crying. "And Grace, you were amazing." I sniffed, but I was too close to the mic and it echoed round the hall. "A-a-a-nd make sure you ask her for raffle tickets for the *Sleigh Another Day* auction for Grampy G."

And that's when I ran out.

I'd never made hundreds of people go silent before.

But I guess I could add that to my list of achievements for this year.

Make a complete fool of myself in front of entire school. TICK.

Bonus points for being bright red as I did it. TICK TICK.

Kiss goodbye to my dream of being part of The POWR. DING DING DING – JACKPOT.

I was running. Sprinting down the corridors, jumping down the stairs four at a time until I found the perfect place to hide. The tiny art room cupboard. It was packed with reindeer and tinsel but there was space for one small sad person. One small sad elf. One small sad elf who needed a proper big sob.

I only stopped ugly crying when Grace rang to check I was OK. I told her I was researching divorcing my family, changing my name and signing up for a one-way flight to Mars. And she said that was fine, and she'd always wanted to visit Mars anyway.

Which stopped me crying for a bit, so she tried to cheer me up with her big news. She'd been messaging Harry (which cheered me up quite a lot tbf) and he'd said yes to Grace's ideas – asking Elijah if he could get one of the cast to donate a meet and greet as an auction prize. I said it sounded awesome. I didn't say that I didn't hold out much hope considering what he'd said about Maeve and Joseph hating press events. And I definitely didn't say that thinking about Grampy's Grotto and the mess I'd made had instantly dissolved any speck of cheer all over again. Instead I said bye and left messages for every single venue I hadn't heard from and waited.

Waited until I couldn't hear any more footsteps outside and the coast was clear.

But when I trudged outside, bags dangling off me in every direction, there was one person still there.

My mum. Pulled up by the gates. In Cara.

The passenger door was already open and for once, the Christmas lights weren't turned on.

"Come on, you." Mum leant over. "Grace rang me." And for once I didn't care if anyone saw me get in. My first ever lift home from school. She hugged me. "I promise no talk about Christmas, Christmas songs, or what just happened ... OK?"

I smiled. Sometimes, when Mum wasn't leading a banjo chorus or moving light-up reindeer a few inches towards our front door in the middle of the night like a reverse burglar, she knew exactly what to say. She let me sit in silence the whole way home.

And at dinner Mum and Dad didn't say a word about how I wasn't saying a word.

And they didn't tell me to put my phone away as I checked for the millionth time to see if a venue had replied. Or if Zaiynab or Matt had been in touch. Or to get the latest song on the "I Wish Christmas Could

Be Cancelled" playlist Ru was sending through track by track as I'd told him I was having a rubbish day.

And they didn't say it was a bad time to start baking when I whisked up a batch of biscuits at ten p.m. And even Tess, who had finished uni for the holidays, didn't comment when I got excused from chores so I could go and "tidy my room". Which we all knew meant get in bed. And when I got there, Tess had put her iPad on my pillow, a hot chocolate by my bed with the chunk of chocolate from her advent calendar melting in it. As I clambered under the duvet, Billy ran in.

"I was going to wait to tell you but I hate waiting, so is it OK if I tell you now?" She looked super cute in her reindeer onesie, and jumped straight on top of me. I gave her a smile. None of this was her fault.

"Tell me what?"

She clapped her hands – and all around my bed, fairy lights lit up. "I did them today! And you can't shout at me because they're not Christmas lights. They're just lights. Really small ones. And they make everything look amazing."

They really did. I gave her the biggest cuddle and let her fall asleep nestled into me as I propped up my laptop on the other side and typed with one hand. She didn't even wake up when a screaming Grace called to drop the bomb that Elijah had said that Joseph D Chambers had agreed to doing the meet and greet auction! Harry said that apparently he'd recently lost his grandma so it "struck a chord". Elijah even said we could do it online to raise more money. Guess if he couldn't get a press story about Joseph and Maeve dating this could be the next best thing?

But I wasn't moaning – for the first time ever I felt we really could hit our fundraising target, and that thought powered me on to google even more potential venues, sending out email after email. But as my eyes started to dry, I had to be realistic. No one was going to reply at 1:07 a.m. Maybe I should sleep and get up early? Yes. Sleep. I closed my laptop and flicked a leg out of the duvet. Then sneaked my arm out from under Billy. Then rolled over. Then counted sheep.

Sheep … like in the stable with baby Jesus.

After Mary and Joseph couldn't find room at the inn.

Like I CAN'T FIND A VENUE!

This was ridiculous.

I opened my laptop back up and carried on the hunt. If today had proved anything, it was that I'd been right all along – only one person at school liked me for being the real me. Only one person would be there for me no matter what. Grace. And there was NO WAY I was going to let her down, even if my eyes were leaking in protest at me still being awake.

I typed away, feeling like I was the only person awake in the world. Well, and Ru – who was now adding motivational you-can-stay-awake songs to the playlist.

But eventually I drifted off. Thoughts swirling that Ru was kind of awesome, even if it was Harry who had come through with a prize for Grampy G's Grotto and not him.

Even if I was a Jingle Lady who was never going to see him again.

CHAPTER
15

TO DO:

- *Venue!!!!!*
- *Venue!!!!!*
- *Venue!!!!!*
- *Venue!!!!!*
- *Venue!!!!!*
- *Venue!!!!!*
- *Venue!!!!!*
- *Venue!!!!!*
- *Research catchment areas for new schools*
- *Or would homeschooling be better?*
- *Help Grace put JDC meet and greet auction online*
- *Make Ru a playlist – British bands for his flight home?*

- *Venue!!!!!*
- *Make 121 snowflakes*

Why was Mum shaking me?

Why was Billy snoring in my face?

Why was I clutching Mr Nibbles, her toy horse?!

Why did I feel like a leftover Brussel sprout on Boxing Day?!

I sat up, panicked. "Has the penguin light set the house on fire?"

Surely that was the only logical reason Mum could be waking me up at whatever ungodly time this was?!

"Molly. It's half ten," Mum whispered. I rubbed my face. There was a Quality Street wrapper stuck to it. "And you've got a visitor."

Visitor? But Grace would already be at her *Nutcracker* rehearsal? And … well, I didn't know anyone else.

I rolled out of bed, semi-slid downstairs, then ground to a halt in the kitchen doorway. Why was there a life-sized, gift-wrapped present filling the kettle?!

"I ducked out of dance." Grace lifted her arms up to shrug. "Ouch." The huge decorated cardboard box over her shoulders that covered down to her knees whacked her in the chin. "I needed to tell you the news in person. I ran straight here!" She wasn't even pausing to breathe.

"And let me tell you! A box is NOT a streamlined running outfit." Even if my brain wasn't still powering up, this would be a lot to deal with. "To be honest, I wasn't enjoying dance anyway. The only thing anyone wanted to talk to me about was you." She huffed, some glitter from the top of her cardboard box raining down over Sosig, who was just blinking up at the talking present in shock. "I've had a glimpse into the world of elf fame, Mols, and I did not like it. Not one bit."

I couldn't love my best friend any more than I did.

"Sorry." I rubbed my face. "I'm still half asleep. And my best friend is a Christmas present. Is it OK to ask, er, what news?"

Grace tutted like it was obvious. "The date!"

"Thirteenth December?"

"No! The date, sorry 'meet and greet' with Joseph D Chambers? For the auction?" Oh yes. She took a deep breath. And another. "And the fact that I put it online this morning and it's already raised…" She paused. We'd hoped it could add a couple of hundred pounds to the total. "One. Thousand. Pounds." She grabbed me. "ONE THOUUUUUSAND POOOOOOUNDS, MOOOOLLLLLYYYYY?!" She tried to hug me but her arms could hardly reach around the box, and I just staggered back into the fridge.

"Did you really just say ... ONE THOUSAND POUNDS?"

"So liitttt!" Dad said, popping up from behind the worktop. Had he been there the whole time? He circled his arms in front of him. "Go Grolly! Go Grolly!"

One. Thousand. Pounds?!

This was HUGE!

And once it finally seeped into my brain, Grace and I both screamed. And jumped. And screamed all over again.

We'd done it. Hit the fundraising target. Mr W was going to freak! Holly Hospice too!

Once we'd got our breath back, Grace decided to ditch rehearsal and plot how we could raise even more, so we headed up to my room. She had to pull off the box to fit up the stairs.

"Not sure why I didn't think of taking it off before I ran a mile here. Guess I didn't think outside the box, lol." She laughed at her own joke as we sat on my bedroom floor. "Seriously though, can you believe Harry and Elijah made this happen?" I already had a suspicion Harry would do anything for Grace, but Elijah was a surprise. "Joseph too, I guess? One degree of separation and all!" She fanned her face. "Hang on. This means Joseph D Chambers knows about Grampy G. Which means" – she

clutched my arm – "Joseph D Chambers knows I exist!"
I let her do an adequate amount of swooning before I
moved on to actual details and asked if Elijah had been
in touch.

She nodded.

"Yup. He let me know press would be covering the
actual meet." Nice – more publicity for Grampy G's
fundraiser! "Or 'intimate meal for two' as I called it online,
as Elijah's sorting some kind of meal on a boat. Oh and
he said he's going to have to vet the winner before it gets
announced to make sure they're 'not a weirdo'. His words."

"Fair enough!" I had given Elijah all the out-of-control
fan stories this film needed with my antics on the red
carpet.

"My suspicion is it's Maeve's who is the high bidder.
Getting her man!" Grace cackled. It was lovely seeing
her this happy. "Elijah's so great, isn't he?" I said nothing,
feeling super guilty that Grace didn't know the full story
about Elijah. "It's such a shame he didn't invite you, *us*,
to London…" said Grace. "Just seeing London this close
to Christmas would be awesome, tbh."

Would be nice to see Ru too?! Nope! Why did that
thought just pop up?

"Well, Elijah did kind of ask…" I fiddled with my
dressing-gown belt.

"Sorry." Grace leaned right up to my face. "Did I hear that right?"

I had to keep this casual.

"Well, yeah. But I said no, cos of keeping the whole Elf Girl thing under wraps."

"But we figured out every other event?" Grace winced. "Well, *almost*. And now if everyone at school knows anyway" – I involuntarily shuddered – "you should at least *try* and have some fun? Edinburgh and Liverpool were cool! Admit it. And no little green elf should take that away from you." I saw her point. "And Elijah would love you for ever? We could try and friend adopt him?! Think of the film perks!"

But I didn't smile. And she noticed.

"Bit harsh, Mol?"

That was it. I couldn't do this any more. I had to get the Elijah thing out in the open.

"OK. Look, don't get mad. But there is something I didn't mention..." Grace folded her arms. "When I first met Elijah, I didn't just say yes to the events. I sort of … *had* to." And as shocked as Grace was, I told her all about Elijah threatening to release the clip of me on the red carpet, and me having to go to the events. She made me go through what had happened in Pizza Express three times, sentence by sentence.

I sighed. "Honestly, I still cannot work him out. He does all that, but he also comes through with prizes, and hotels, and…" I sighed. I'd thought about it too much, and still had no answer.

"Blackmailing you though, Mol? That's not OK. *Although*…" She prodded me accusingly in the ribs. "WHY DIDN'T YOU TELL ME SOONER?!" She sighed and shook her head. "And all this time I thought Simon was the worst person I knew!"

"Please forgive me, oh great cardboard-boxed one." It was a genuine plea. But Grace was still smiling. Phew. "In my defence, you did have some *stuff* going on."

"Hmmm," she said, fake-annoyed. "I thought the deal was we Jingle Ladies told each other everything? No secret left unshared?!" But she'd already shuffled across the floor and was yanking the big box of prizes out of my cupboard. "Anyway, I was thinking. Now Elijah's helped with the meet and greet, we could ask if he's changed his mind and will let us auction some of this stuff online too?"

But I was staring at the box in shock.

"Oi … what's that face?" Grace wriggled towards me. "MOLLY, WHAT *IS* THAT FACE?!"

But then she saw it too. On the side of the box.

"It's … it's … the same … as … the popcorn

container!" I pointed at the drawing. The bad, very bad, outline of a dragon with a nose ring.

"A reindeer, unless I'm very much mistaken," Grace said immediately. "A reindeer, most probably called … RUDOLPH." She sounded like one of her murder podcasts. "Mol, what is going on?! Cos right now I'm putting two and two together and getting a full sleigh."

I thought back to when Elijah gave the box to us…

"Elijah didn't actually say they were from him, did he?" My voice was shaking. Could this mean…?

Grace shook her head. "Nope."

We both said, "Very Elijah," in perfect unison.

Had Ru done this?

"So… What's going on?" Grace asked, but I didn't know what to say. "Fine! If you want to do it the hard way." She got her phone out. "Let's assess the evidence. Not only do we have this mega prize haul, which as we can see from the artwork" – she traced the drawing with her finger like it was dramatic evidence – "is clearly from Ru, yet he took zero credit for it. We also have this." She opened up a photo taken from the hotel room of Ru and our dads on the hotel steps after we all bumped into each other. "*Exhibit B!* Eyes-on evidence that – after you failed to even say thank you for the prizes – not only did Ru buy us both hot chocolates but he didn't spill A DROP when your dad lunged." Yup, that was quite impressive actually. "And, exhibit C." She started to quote the hot drink reviews I'd told her about that he'd been sending me since Edinburgh, along with a picture of his hand holding up random cups. "Mol, this guy must be spending all his usherly wages on heated beverages. All in the name of making you laugh."

"Make it stoooooop." I slid my hands forward and dropped my head down. I was a Jingle Lady! Not a Ru-liker. Grace didn't even know about all the other stuff. The ideas he'd worked on for the fundraiser. The playlists. Making fifty snowflakes to post. Sending me venue links all week. But that what friends did, right?

"I'm a Jingle Lady!" Why was I wailing?! "There's nothing going on."

"So why," said Grace, forcefully lifting up my chin to study my face, "are you smiling like that?" I tried to stop smiling. She leant forward. "Ru," she said. *Ow!* My smile wanted to come back SO BAD. "Ruuuuuuu." *Owwwww!* The smile was trying to break out. "RU!"

Too late. The smile was out.

"AH HAH! MY FINAL PIECE OF EVIDENCE, m'lud! How can this little reindeer be 'just a friend' when he makes Molly Bell, Molly of 'I'm dead to romance' fame, smile like *THAT*!"

I lay back flat on the floor. Was Grace right?

Did I like Ru?

I pictured him crashing into the door in the cinema in London. Offering me a mechanical robin in Liverpool. Searching around for my imaginary badge in Edinburgh.

I thought how even though I'd been having really bad days recently, he'd made me have fun in the middle of it all.

Eurgh.

Grace was right. Grace was always right.

Maybe, maybe I did like Ru.

And maybe, just maybe, for the first time in my life, I really did want to give a happy ending a go. But how could I, when I was a Jingle Lady?

I stretched my arms out. I needed to shake this all off. Get back to normal.

"This is stupid." I sighed. "I'm never going to see him again. And I made a promise to be a Jingle Lady. And you're more important than anything. And he doesn't know anything about 'Love Your Elf!'. And did I mention he thinks I have a reindeer called Derek?"

"OK. A lot to unpack there…" Grace's face looked serious. "And, not gonna lie, I'm a bit sad—"

"Grace, don't be sad! I'm sorry. I promise you can count on me. Even a Jingle Lady can have a wobble, right? But that's all it is…"

But Grace's face fell. For a second there was total silence.

"You *really* think that's what I'm sad about?"

Nervously, I nodded.

But Grace ... well, Grace laughed. "You absolute banana. I was sad you've been keeping this all to yourself. The Elijah thing. Now this. If you'd just told me, then I could have spent the last few weeks loving that my best friend had the cutest Christmas romance ever – which would have cheered me *right* up!" She shook her head. "Imagine all those funny yet spicy messages we could have written together! You've deprived me. DEPRIVED!" She howled.

I couldn't help it. I had to hug her. My best friend was the very best.

"So, you don't mind about the Jingle Lady thing?"

"What I *mind* is that you should have been having hot snogs at Edinburgh Castle but instead you were skulking around pretending to have a reindeer called Derek."

"And he's leaving the country in ... less than a week. Ru. Not imaginary Derek."

"For one so brilliant, you can't half be a total wally." She sighed, clutching her hands to her chest, a dreamy look in her eye. "London. At Christmas. My best friend falling in love."

"Too far."

But she ignored me. "Dasher and Rudolph. Two star-crossed reindeers—"

"Erm, before you get too carried away…" Maybe too late, but it was time for a bit of reality here… "Can we remember that this is *me* we're talking about. Me, Molly Bell, who hasn't ever snogged anyone let alone 'fallen in love'." She waved that sentence away. "Who even knows if he likes me?" I paused. "I mean, I did tell him I was all about that Jingle Lady life."

Grace shook her head. "I actually despair."

But being a Jingle Lady had felt nice, safe. If I wasn't one any more it meant facing up to scary new things. How much I liked Ru. If he liked me. If this was all a big stupid idea. If I really knew him at all.

"There's definitely something I don't know about him, though."

I had never got to the bottom of that weird phone number, and his grade-A ability to swerve questions.

Grace raised an eyebrow. "Says … Dasher the imaginary-reindeer-looking-after Elf Girl?"

"And your point is…"

"My point is you can't write this guy off for keeping secrets, when you've been doing exactly the same."

"But!" Eurgh. She did make a great point. And from the little grin on her face, she knew it. "But … mine was for a good reason."

"It's fine. I know how to fix this." She held her hand out. "Phone?"

Grace was the only person I'd hand it over to unlocked. She tapped the screen.

HOLY JINGLE BELLS! SHE WAS VIDEO CALLING RU!!!

Grace jumped up on my bed and held my phone in the air.

"Say you're coming to London and ask if he wants to meet." I WAS VIDEO CALLING RU! AND I STILL HAD SLEEP DRIBBLE ON MY FACE AND YESTERDAY'S MASCARA ON!

"Grace!" I leapt up for the phone.

But she bounced off the bed, yanking it away.

With a wail like a banshee, I hurled myself at it. But it flew out of her hand and slid under Billy's bed.

And it was still ringing.

We both looked at each other. Oops!

"Dash?"

Ru's voice came from under Billy's bed. I dived towards it.

"American accents are so hot…" Grace hissed, fanning herself. She was loving this. But I was flat on my front, scrambling around to find my phone. What was Ru seeing right now? What on earth must he think?!

"One sec, Ru!" I yelled, flinging rosettes and horse magazines and forgotten about My Little Ponies out behind me.

"You OK? Are you calling me from a cave?"

Where was the stupid phone? "No, no, I'm all good!"

"Asssk himmmm," Grace whispered. She was sitting calmy on my bed, like this was totally normal and she wasn't in the middle of a storm of flying plastic horses. "Or I will?"

Fine!

"I just wanted to ask…" Was I really asking my first ever person out by yelling at my little sister's collection of grooming brushes? "If…"

"You're cracking up a bit," Ru said back, not knowing I really was, in more ways than one.

"Just do it!" Grace pummelled both her feet into my bum as I rummaged about on all fours. "Grow some Christmas baubles and DO IT."

FINE!

"If you were free before the event in London?" Had I really said it?! "To meet up." I didn't have a second to even take in what I'd just done. But he answered straight away.

"One hundred per cent."

And then the call broke up.

CHAPTER

16

TO DO:

- *Email yurt place! DO NOT FORGET*
- *Google "funny things to talk about on first dates"*
- *Book cinema tickets*
- *Buy dental floss, new mouthwash, chewing gum*
- *Make 69 snowflakes*
- *Persuade Mum to change Cara's ham air freshener for ... anything else*

I stood back and glared at my wardrobe, Billy watching from her bed.

Yes, I'd once chosen all of these clothes, so how come I hated them all?

"You can borrow my reindeer dressing gown…" Billy wriggled out of it. It was ginormous and fluffy and had a light-up nose. And had never been washed. Not *exactly* the first date hot look I was hoping for. "I don't mind not wearing it. For one day."

"Bils, you're the best." I tried to look grateful. "But no one can rock it like you, so you better hang on to it." But what *could* I wear for the date? Or for a meet that might be a date? HOW WAS I MEANT TO KNOW?! I'd never been on either?! And I only had seven hours to mentally prepare. I needed another fifteen years at least.

Grace had to intervene and choose my outfit over video call. Converse, black jeans and a red fluffy cardigan with gold tree-shaped buttons that she'd left at mine "in case". Festive, but not too "walking decoration".

Thanks to a pep talk from Grace last night I was ready to dip my toe into the festive water. Talking it through had been terrifying, but I had to accept I couldn't hide things any more. Elf Girl was out of control. "Love Your Elf!" was in the top ten. My private profile was getting more and more tags every day. Even the old man in the Post Office had sung the song when I'd popped in to get loo roll.

So, we'd decided if Elf Girl was getting out of control, it was time I took control of Elf Girl.

No more hiding. It was time to live my best elf life – Christmas jumpers and all.

But … one small pointy-shoe step at a time. I wasn't ready for the *whole* world to know, so I was starting with people who already did. First up – The POWR. I still hadn't heard anything from them so I'd messaged Zaiynab to apologize for not telling them about the whole Brussel Shout situation and asking if I was still in the band. And … I hadn't got a reply. Or a reply to my follow-up checking she got the message, even though we both knew she had.

I just had to hope Ru might be a bit more understanding. Grace was right. I couldn't be cross about him not being that open about his life when I was doing the same. Today wasn't just going to be about finding out who the real Ru was. Dragging him into the Christmas spirit with me. It wasn't even about Grace's suggestion (*repeated* suggestion) of engineering a Christmassy snog in Trafalgar Square by the tree.

Today was the day I came clean about my elfy truth. No more Dasher. No more hiding who I really was. It was time for Ru to meet Molly Bell. Lover of crisps and dogs in outfits.

My heart sped up just thinking about it. And if Ru didn't want to see me again? I'd at least I know he was just a massive Simon after all. And have a big cry into my very absorbent Christmas jumper.

NO!

I meant … walk away, head held high, and never think of him again, because he didn't deserve someone like me. *Yes*. That's what Grace had said.

I packed my outfit carefully in my bag. I never folded anything, but today was special. Today required folding. Today was a gooood day. This morning I'd finally had a breakthrough with a venue for Grampy G's party. The yurt place had said it was looking possible and I should give them a ring and confirm tomorrow morning. FINALLY. In the nick of time, we had a venue! Tomorrow I could tell Grace the new plan and let the guests know.

My phone lit up. Who was messaging me at 8 a.m. on a Saturday?

Ru: *London says hi…*

I grinned.

"Did Dad send you another picture of his big toe hair?" Billy asked innocently. She was the cutest.

"Even better."

It was the view from Ru's room. A perfect snapshot of lights down an empty Carnaby Street, a huge Christmas tree at the end and … *humble brag much!?*

Fine. Two could play that game.

Me: *So does Bromster.*

I snapped the view from my window. Cute cottages with every window decorated, our village green with tiny Christmas trees dotted about, the village lights designed by the primary school kids ... oops ... and Mum in her dressing gown, inspecting the herd of mini reindeer which had now inched all the way to our front door. Hope he didn't realize they were ours.

Ru: *Hell-oooo! You didn't tell me you lived in* Sleigh Another Day.

Me: *You didn't tell me you'd seen it?!*

Ru: *That's cos I haven't. But tell me I'm wrong?!*

But Mum was beeping Cara's horn and I'd been so busy doing motivational speeches in the mirror, I'd failed to actually get changed. Or showered. I was just going to have to travel down in my Christmas pudding PJs and matching slippers and get ready in our hotel. Mr W had given the slippers to me and Grace as a thank you for all the money we'd been raising for Holly Hospice. With the auction we were up to almost one thousand five hundred pounds, and it was closing this afternoon just in time for the meet and greet tonight!

Much to Billy's delight, I took her up on the offer of her dressing gown after all, threw my suitcase in the boot and jumped in the front seat. Mum gave me a proud look. What had I done?

"Well, doesn't my middle daughter just look perfect for her 'friend'."

Shudder. For days now she'd been using air quotes whenever she said "friend".

I stared out my window, already feeling sick with nerves. I wished Grace was travelling down with us, not catching the train tomorrow after dancing. Trying to calm myself, I ran through the plan we'd made.

- *2 p.m.: Arrive at hotel*
- *3–5 p.m.: Unpack, destress, listen to calming rain sounds, get ready, motivational mirror talks*
- *5 p.m.: Meet Ru at hotel – calm, relaxed and full of excellent chat (or ready to look at list of excellent chat ideas)*

Perfect. And the long journey meant time to work on the conversation topics Grace and I had come up with last night. I looked in my notepad.

- Is American school like on Netflix?
- Best festive thing he's seen in the UK so far?
- ~~Do you love Molly?~~

- What do his parents actually do? (**good
  chance to bring up The Brussel Shouts???)
- ~~Do you want to kiss Molly in Trafalgar Square,
  hopefully in the snow? It would make Grace
  really happy. No pressure.~~

I had to not let Grace's suggestions get lodged in my
brain in case they popped out.

It was weird. Ru and I had hung out loads. But today
felt different. Could I really do this?!

But we were off. Mum was pulling out of the drive,
Cara's outside lights flashing and Santa FM blaring. And,
for once, I didn't mind. Who cared who saw? Everyone was
already laughing at me anyway. And I was off to London.
All expenses paid. Mum was drumming on the steering
wheel. Billy was singing all the wrong words to Christmas
songs. And Cara was packed with festive snacks.

Even Elijah had been really happy when I asked if
we could come after all. I was expecting some really big
condition, but he said he had spare hotel rooms and all
I needed to do was come down to the final influencer
event on Sunday. I really didn't get that guy.

But as we turned towards to the motorway, Mum
glanced at me. "Shall I?"

I looked to where she was pointing. Eurgh. Simon.

Hand in hand with a girl – not even the girl we saw him with the other day. Simon who had bragged about putting me forward for the end of year show. I gave a small nod – and Mum let rip with Cara's horn. Simon positively leapt into a slushy brown puddle. I laughed even harder when Mum wound down the window and yelled, "Behave your elf!"

Oh well. Christmas karma.

I gave him a merry little wave just as my phone vibrated.

Ru: *Got to switch my phone off.*

Ru: *Still on for five? I'll bring the hot drinks.*

I typed back, a stupid smile on my face.

Me: *Plan* ☕

I'd become a gooey Christmas cheese ball.

And … I kind of liked it.

I stretched back and cranked up "All I Want for Christmas", the three of us belting it out. Who cared if everyone at school thought I was an elf? Or was related to singing Christmas dinner and half-horse-half-human sister?

I had Grace. I had my family.

And it had just started snowing just like in the movies. I grinned. After all these years, maybe *this* is what it felt like for my Christmas frost to thaw.

And an hour into the journey, Grace messaged

with the best news. The auction had hit two thousand pounds!! I rang her immediately, but no answer.

I sent a voice note of the three of us screaming.

Which I had to follow up with one explaining we hadn't been in a crash.

Today was the best!

I love snow! I love the auction! I love life!

But two hours later, the snow was so heavy the traffic was down to two lanes and Billy was needing to "maybe be sick" after eating two chocolate oranges … and we'd only moved fifteen more miles.

I HATED THE SNOW. Life-ruining, waste of frozen-water space.

My getting ready for my meet-or-date minutes were disappearing into this traffic jam?!

"Lucky we all had a wee," Mum said cheerily, like she hadn't been stuck driving for four hours and we weren't still one hundred miles from London in standstill traffic. "I'm sure it'll clear soon."

But two hours later, we'd only just reached the centre of London and I was freaking out! I'd messaged Ru to ask if we could make it later, but nothing was getting delivered. Sure, he'd said he was going to have his phone off, but I didn't know he meant *off* off. Not just "not replying within a minute"-off like normal people!

ARGH.

4:45 p.m. Fifteen minutes till we were meant to be meeting and the satnav said we were still thirteen minutes from the hotel car park. One and a half miles. Could I run it quicker?

I looked down at what I was wearing. Sprinting through London looking like a fluffy Christmas pudding probably wouldn't help the whole "Don't worry I might have a secret identity as an elf, but actually I'm quite normal" thing.

"We'll get there…" Mum said, rubbing my knee, as we crawled down a main road with huge white mansions either side. "I'm sure your 'friend'" – she still did the air quotes when she was driving! Probably illegal – "won't mind waiting a few minutes."

Few minutes? FEW MINUTES?! I hadn't even showered! My nails were half chewed off. I had bits of yesterday's biscuit in my hair!

"I can't get hold of my 'friend'." I was so stressed, I did air quotes too. "So, if he turns up…" pleeeease let him be a late person… "you might have to stall for me?" How bleak were things if I was seriously suggesting leaving Ru with Mum and Billy? My mum, who was wearing a jumper that said "Jingle my Baubles". And my little sister who he thought was called Tilly and was plaiting Mum's hair through the headrest, effectively knotting her into the van for life.

"Well, I'm sure a 'friend' wouldn't mind you wearing such a lovely festive outfit for your 'friendly' meet," Mum said pointedly.

"Well, I'm sure I'd 'rather'" – air quotes were officially out of control – "see any 'friend' after a 'shower'."

"At pony camp." Billy put yet another elastic band on Mum's hair. "My best friend wore the same jodhpurs all week. And she just smelt of horse! Which is yum." She shrugged. "So don't worry, Mol."

My phone vibrated. Grace. Phew! Finally a sane person.

"HELLO?" I scrabbled to plug in my headphones. But there was silence. Nothing on the screen except … ceiling. "You OK?" Talking to her was the only thing that could stop my descent into full freak out.

"I … have … news." The camera panned slowly down the ceiling, down her bedroom wall, past the posters of Harry Styles … and on to Grace, who was lying on her bed, her face totally blank.

"About the auction?" Had it gone up again?

"Kind of…" she said. But she didn't look excited. She looked like she'd seen Father Christmas buying a Pot

Noodle in Tesco. "I just got off the phone to Elijah." She gulped. "And I … I … have something to tell you."

"Grace?" My stomach was twisting. This didn't sound good. "What kind of thing?"

"Uncategorized," she said, blinking. "I only found out four seconds ago."

"Do you need me to say reassuring things?" She nodded. "OK … puppies exist. I dropped fresh biscuits off at your house. And whales … just, whales." Not sure why, but they always seemed quite chill.

"Thank you." She nodded. "I needed that." She took a deep breath. "So, the auction just closed. Elijah rang. Then I rang you. And now … well … no. Still processing." Grace didn't even get fazed by my parents throwing half-birthdays. For Sosig. The fact she needed to process was worrying. "You know your plan?" I nodded. We'd made it together. Meet Ru at five. Walk around South Bank, then Trafalgar Square and up Regent Street till around seven. Then my big idea. My big scary idea. "How much would you be up for making it a slightly different plan?"

Huh?

"What's happened, Grace?"

She gulped. "Don't freak out." Too late. I already was. "But you know I said the auction for the meal with Joseph D Chambers just finished." I nodded. "It went to a bid of…" She closed her eyes and bit her lip. "THREE THOUSAND ONE HUNDRED AND FIFTY POUNDS. AND NINETY-NINE P."

Oh.

My.

What. WHAT?

That was enough to redecorate the whole of Holly Hospice social hall AND start a party fund that should last years!

"Seriously?" I whispered. Grace nodded, her face still in shock.

I pulled out a headphone. And yelled. Really yelled.

"WE JUST RAISED THREE THOUSAND POUNDS FOR GRAMPY G!!!!! AND ONE HUNDRED AND FIFTY POUNDS AND NINETY-NINE P." Billy, Mum and I cheered so much a man in a suit gave the bright orange rocking screaming camper van a very suspicious look. But, THREE THOUSAND POUNDS?!! Harry and Elijah had come throuuuuuuugh!

But there was one person not leaping about. Grace. She was lying still, looking concerned.

"Grace?" I put my headphone back in.

"But that's not the thing. Elijah said the bidder had a specific request…"

Oh no… Was the winner some kind of creep? Was

Joseph D Chambers going to pull out? Had we actually not raised the money after all?!

"They're not a weirdo, are they? They didn't ask if they could..." I tried to think of something. "Lick his hair?"

But Grace shook her head.

"No, Mols. Weirder than that. The winner had one condition." She paused. "The condition was..." She gulped. "The person that has to go to the meal with Joseph is ... you."

CHAPTER
17

If I'd been wondering what was worse than wearing furry Christmas pudding pyjamas for the only date I'd ever been on.

Now I knew. Wearing furry Christmas pudding pyjamas for the only date I'd ever been on THEN meeting a movie star.

I didn't speak the rest of the journey. What was happening? Was Elijah playing a joke? Maybe even Harry?

And I didn't speak as we crawled down Regent Street under the huge Christmas lights, twinkling away in the dark evening. Nor as Billy waved at a police horse that was mid arrest. Not even when we pulled into a tiny side street with our hotel at the end. It was HUGE and had baubles and canes pouring out of every window and round the pillars at the front.

It looked gorgeous.

No … it looked AWFUL!

Could we turn back?

Because outside the hotel wasn't just a doorman in a top hat.

Outside the hotel was Ru. *Five minutes early.*

Who on earth turned up early?!

I pulled Billy's dressing gown over my face. Please don't let Ru notice me. Cara. My family.

"Put your foot down," I hissed to Mum, like she had a side hobby as a getaway driver.

"Mols, they park your car-slash-beloved-camper-van for you, you know?" She shimmied her shoulders. "So posh!"

"Can we not park it ourselves?" I spat. This could not be happening. "In fact, let's go back a street. I'll get out. Check that it's the right hotel?!"

"But it says 'The Strand'." Mum waved at the doormen. Then flicked Cara's lights on, illuminating the front of the hotel like a school disco.

Everyone turned to look.

I slid down in my seat.

And now Mum was beeping and Cara was blaring "We Wish You a Merry Christmas" to the poshest street in London.

And Ru was…

I could hardly bring myself to look.

I peeped out from under the dressing gown.

Ru was … smiling. And waving. At me?

There was nothing for it. I pulled the dressing gown off my head, pretended I'd only just noticed we'd arrived and waved back.

"Is that your *friend*?" Mum said. "Now I can see why you didn't give us more details!"

She laughed in a way that I wasn't a hundred per cent OK with. Nice to know my own mother thought Ru was out of my league. I jumped out.

Ru looked even better than I remembered, even if he'd failed to bust out the merest smidge of festiveness. Still, I hadn't warned him what I had in store. He was in a long black coat, grey scarf, black baseball cap, black hoodie.

Think positive, Mol. Maybe I'd remembered my outfit worse than it was? The doorman saw me and tumbled backwards into a Christmas tree. Not the confidence boost I was after. He scurried over to help Mum unknot herself out of Cara, and Ru walked towards me. I tightened the belt on my dressing gown. This was happening. I'd rehearsed and rehearsed what to say. The perfect witty, hilarious, seeming-as-if-I'd-just-come-up-with-it greeting to go with.

Which I'd completely forgotten.

"EYES UP!" I yelled. "Do not look down," I said, pointing – which made him instantly look. "I said, don't!!!!"

"Hello to you too," Ru laughed. "And don't worry, I completely haven't noticed the raisin print pants. Or exceptionally fluffy Christmas slippers." Cringe. Die. Mortification. "Although…" He flicked out the lapel of his coat – there was the tiniest, teeniest enamel reindeer pin on it. "Look! New purchase! Festiveness! I got you one too, to replace the one you lost in Edinburgh."

What? I looked at him blankly! Oh yes! The imaginary one!

"Thanks," I said, after too long a delay. But my pin was really cute. Two little entwined smiling candy canes. I pinned it on. "Also, did I mention that's not our car? Had to borrow it from those neighbours I told you about."

Too late. Ru was looking at Cara like she was a limited edition sportscar.

"Wow, it's a Christmas wagon!"

Billy bounced over before I could reply.

"Do I know you? I think I know you… Did you ride a really big Lipizzaner?" she said in full interrogation mode.

"It's a horse," I said, putting my arm around her. Ru

didn't even do a double take at my little sister clutching a fake horse's tail with a boiled sweet stuck in it.

"And I know you too?" Uh-oh. "You're Tilly?" I went full coughing fit. Did I cover it? "Who won best in show with … Spud? Did I get that right?"

He even remembered to say pony, not horse. Billy blushed. I was today years old when I discovered she was capable of this.

"Oh." Ru reached into his tote bag. "I thought you might like this."

He passed Bil a chocolate, gold-foil-wrapped horse. Billy didn't say anything. My sister was speechless. A WORLD FIRST. I could *not* wait to tell Tess.

"Next time I need to silence her, I know what to do." I ruffled her hair. "And what do you say, B-Tlllmmmy?" I mumbled something incoherent. But Billy was staring at the horse like Ru had passed her actual baby Jesus.

"And I got these for your mum. For when she's done checking in." Ru passed me a metal tin that said "Biscuiteers". His presents were so posh! Inside were the most perfect iced biscuits I'd ever seen. Little presents, Christmas trees, sleighs, even polar bears in Christmas hats.

"Thanks," I said, overwhelmed. Was this boy for real? He'd turned up with thoughtful gifts for my family – and

I hadn't even worn outside clothes? I was SO out of my depth. "You're basically the three wise men right now. Except one. And with better gifts. I mean, who wants myrrh?" What was I talking about?! I needed to get in, get changed, reset. "Look, I'm really sorry, but would you mind just giving me fifteen minutes to…" Check I don't smell of BO? Brush my hair for the first time today? "Freshen up?" I winced. "Long journey."

Of course, he said it was no problem, so I did my most confident walk into the hotel – then ran as fast as I could as soon as he was out of sight. I don't think the conference room of business people in suits expected to see a Christmas pudding sprint past, but it wasn't my fault I had a hot wise man waiting for me. And fifteen minutes later, with dripping wet hair, make-up sliding off over my moisturizer and a damp T-shirt, cardi and jeans on (no time for the towel stage), I was in the lift back down to the lobby, trying to catch my breath.

I stared in the mirror.

It was fair to say today's look was "right mess".

And – I full-body shuddered as I remembered – I was also meeting Joseph D Chambers looking like this?! If I looked a state now, what would I look like in a few hours?! When I was meant to be going on a private boat trip on the Thames with the world's sexiest man (not Grace being dramatic, he'd actually picked up an award). GULP! I'd forgotten there were going to be photographers too?!

The lift doors pinged open. Ru was sitting on one of the sofas scrolling his phone. For a second I felt calm. In all the worrying, had I forgotten that this was going to be fun?

But then Ru looked up and made eye contact – and every single bit of calm pinged out of me and got replaced by pure panic.

What was I going to speak to this specimen about? He lived in America! Travelled the world! Bought classy gifts!!

And me? I was wearing socks that said "Molly's Mistle-toes" with tiny bells sewn on. Tess had made them. And in my pocket were the pair we'd made together for Ru.

Time to be brave.

"So, I've got a question." I sat next to him. "You know how you and me don't like Christmas?" He nodded. "Well, how about we don't? Not like it. Just for one day."

"Hmmmm." He dropped his head to one side, not convinced.

"Being stuck in traffic meant I had some time to look

273

up some stuff we could do?" Truth was I'd been working on this plan every single spare second since we'd agreed to meet and had ten pages of notes ready to go. "For one day only. Go hot turkey." He looked confused. In fairness, I didn't know what I was talking about either. "Like cold turkey, but hot. *All* the Christmas. As in, even Father Christmas would be like, 'Whoa, that's a bit Christmassy, isn't it?'"

But Ru didn't laugh; he looked … scared.

"What *exactly* do you have in mind," he said, quieter than I'd heard him before.

Just when I thought I was getting to understand him, he reminded me all over again I only knew one small bit of him. One tiny Chocolate Orange segment. But I needed the full fruit! And today I was going to get it.

"First up, there's this festive lights walk down to the river. And then at South Bank, there's a Christmas market where we can get drinks in a little igloo pod. And as we know, you are now London's leading expert on all heated drinks." Ru smiled nervously. Maybe he hated Christmas more than I realized? "And, this might be weird, but there's outside curling you can do…"

"Curling?"

I shrugged. "I don't really know what it is either. But it involves ice, and sliding things and brushes, and it *could*

be fun. *Could*. No promises. And we could swing by…"
But I stopped. It sounded so cheesy now he was sitting
next to me, looking all cool. "Well, you might hate it …
but a candlelight carol concert thing." I said it as quickly
as I could, deeply regretting it already. I changed the
subject before I could get a reaction. "And I have an idea
for later. A big finish. Which involves being at Leicester
Square for 6:30 p.m." This was the thing I was most
nervous about. I took my phone out to show him what I
had planned.

"Does it have to be Leicester Square?" Ru looked
deeply unimpressed. "Just with work and all…"

"No no…" I flicked my screen off, trying not to
think about how expensive the tickets had been – the
Christmas wind rapidly going out of my sails. "We could
just see how it goes?"

"Yeah. Maybe that's the best idea," Ru said, with
all the enthusiasm of me when Dad suggests a family
trip to the DIY store. Eurgh. I hadn't even told him
that although we'd arranged hanging out all evening, I
was going to have to dash at 8.45 p.m. I'd understand,
wouldn't I? If he left our meet-maybe-date to go have
"an intimate meal" with Maeve Murphy… Really funny,
really clever, stylish, beautiful Maeve.

OK. Maybe it wasn't best to think about that.

And I still had no clue who had nominated me to go.

There was no way my family or Grace could have made a bid that high. It was seriously weird, and I was hoping Elijah could fill me in.

But at the reception desk, a family was checking in. And a little boy, about Billy's age, was waving. At me! Oh no. This was NOT in my sixty-two-step plan! The plan was to keep the whole Elf Girl thing under wraps until I had a chance to tell Ru later. When we got to Leicester Square. *If* we got to Leicester Square.

I waved, muttered something about kids being weird and ran outside. And by the time Ru caught me up I had Google Maps open. We needed to get going.

"Let's head here. The start of the Christmas trail in … Covent Garden, which isn't far. We could walk down the Strand," the huge main road, with zillions of tourists. Zillions of people who might shout Elf Girl at any moment! "Or … no. Let's go THIS WAY." I traced a route through back streets.

"Y'know what?" Finally, he smiled. "That sounds like a plan. It just took a sec. Adjusting to new non-Grinch me." He nudged me with his elbow. "How about we get some hot drinks for the walk? I don't know if I mentioned, but I might know a little spot…"

And he really did know the cutest place, in this tiny hidden courtyard, where we got two mint hot chocolates, and a marshmallow polar bear to share. We strolled the back streets, chatting about what he'd been up to in London, and the status of the neighbour's outside reindeers (he was delighted to discover they'd made it to the front door and I still wasn't ready to admit I meant our front door) until we sat down on a big empty step.

"You never said, by the way. Did you hear back about the band?"

I dunked the polar bear head in my drink. It got too soggy and flopped off. I knew how it felt.

"Sort of… It was a yes." Ru drummed on his leg, his face lit up like he was preparing for good news. "But now it's a…" A what? A "they seem to be ghosting me since they discovered I'm an elf"? "It's a … it's a, I'm not so sure."

"How come?" Ru looked confused. But I couldn't explain, not just yet.

"Who knows, but that doesn't matter. Because I wanted to say in person. THANK YOU! For that mahoosive box of stuff for the fundraiser!"

He grinned; his secret was out.

"Ahhhhh." He raised an eyebrow. "Is *that* why you finally came around to the idea of a date?"

OK. HE JUST SAID THIS WAS A DATE!

Brain. Words. Find.

"Hahaha, very funny. Funny. No." But he laughed. His soft laugh that I think I liked even more than the marshmallow polar bear.

"Sorry." He stopped. "I mean *friend meet*. Jingle Ladies don't do dates, right?"

Ah. Here it came. Instalment one of truth bombs. The perfect time to tell him my new non-Jingly status, however awkward it would be.

"I'm not actually one any more." There. I'd said it. "Grace wanted to, er, Jingle solo." I tried to hide any trace of emotion.

I snuck a look at him. He'd raised an eyebrow. And was grinning.

"Interesting."

Was it?! And was he blushing?

I was *definitely* blushing. But some literal Christmas angels came to my rescue. A group of women, dressed as angels, turned into our street, cackling and throwing glitter. Ru pulled down his cap like we were under attack. I cheered when they threw some in our direction, but they did a double take at the grinch next to me. Yup, definitely still had work to do on the whole "Christmas spirit" thing.

"The first rule of Ru and Dash do Christmas." I

flicked white glitter out of my hair. "Is you say yes to all things festive." I tried to look stern. "Must. Try. Harder."

Ru laughed. And out of nowhere I felt a weird fizz of happiness.

Like I was the main character in one of Grace's loved-up Christmas films.

Which was brilliant. And amazing. And absolutely, totally terrifying.

"So, we should be off." I stood up. "It's getting dark."

"It's been dark since we met?"

True, but I didn't know what to say, so instead waffled on about why no one got emotional about torches, and if festive yurts were a thing, and wandered down through Trafalgar Square. London looked even more amazing than in the films. From the bridge we had the perfect view of the Houses of Parliament, Big Ben, the London Eye…

"C'mon then." Ru got his phone out but it was so cold it immediately died. He grabbed the other and checked no one was around. "Would it be too cheesy to ask for a selfie?"

Face please serve: ew, how un-imaginative. Because my brain was full: I ALREADY KNOW I'M PRINTING THIS OFF AND STICKING IT TO MY WALL.

"Just for me. Promise I'm not the sharing type."

"Sure." My voice wobbled like when Mum gives me a way-too-tight hug. Had he just put his arm around me? AFFIRMATIVE! RU'S ARM WAS AROUND ME!!!

And that's the moment he took the photo. And that's what got immortalized. Him smiling, head tilted at the perfect angle, cap in his hand, light bouncing off him like a supermodel and me. Standing pole straight like I'd been stuffed more than a Christmas turkey, my mouth hanging open.

"And *that's* why I say no to photos." He sent it to me anyway, and we headed over the bridge into the market. After checking out some of the quieter stalls, Ru leant over the railings by the river.

"Verdict so far? I'm not hating Christmas." He turned and smiled at me. "Not hating it at all… But." He bit his lip. "You've done all the hard work. Do you want me to take over the sleigh reins, little elf?" I did a double take. Was that just an elfing-bad coincidence? I did need to tell him. People had definitely been giving me funny looks. "Or do you have a plan for what's next?"

I knew what I needed to say, *"Yes, I do, but first I need to tell you something that might change everything, and also do you mind me ducking out of our date later to go eat an "intimate meal" with a movie star? Potentially on that posh-looking yacht thing over there?"*

Instead, I said, "Curling." But we had a fifteen-minute wait before my booking, so we grabbed a Christmas waffle, headed away from the crowds and sat on a bench opposite a pub with steamed-up windows.

The time had come. Time to reveal my elfy past. The conversation I'd practised over and over with Grace.

My heart was thumping so hard my enamel pin was shaking.

"We've got time to kill, so how about a British tradition? Christmas truth or dare."

Ru lowered his eyebrows. "Can't say I've heard of that one."

"Oh, in the UK, no Christmas Day is complete without it." We both knew I was lying.

"Okaaay." He pushed his lips out. His really gorgeous lips. OH GOD, I WAS STARING AT HIS MOUTH. I stopped. And switched to staring at his eyes. His really gorgeous eyes.

OK. Nowhere was safe.

"Is it negotiable?" He wiped some snow off his nose. "Cos you look kind of serious right now and I'm getting scared…" But he laughed.

"Nope. It's not optional. That's also part of the tradition." I felt so sick. "But to make it easier, you can go first?"

"Sure. Truth or dare?" I answered "truth" and he

looked at me like he was trying to dredge up the most amazing question of all. Uh-oh. "Total honesty, right?" I nodded. That's *exactly* what today was about. "What did you *really* think about *Sleigh Another Day*?"

I laughed into my waffle, some of the squirty cream spraying out on to my jeans.

"*That's* your question?"

But Ru nodded, no hint of a smile. "Yup. And your honest answer is…"

"My honest answer is – I haven't seen it." Hadn't I told him that? "In fact, I haven't even seen a single poster for it. That's how much I haven't seen it."

"Whoa." He looked shocked. "Kind of wish I'd asked another question now."

"It's fine, you're a novice. There is *something* I could tell you about the film though…" If I opened up, maybe he would too? "Something about Maeve."

Ru pulled back. "Maeve Murphy?"

"Uh-huh. Although you have to promise to tell NO ONE."

He zipped his lips shut. OK, here it went. The second Molly secret.

"I was the one that tripped into her on the red carpet."

His eyes went so wide, for a second I worried they might pop out. "YOU?!"

"Yup. I'm Dread Carpet girl."

"The one with the sign?" He looked horrified.

"Oi!" Was he edging away from me? "Panic not. It's not what it seems. I was actually trying to leave *somewhere* quickly, and I was holding on to this random guy's sign but then I tripped over a dog lead, and one thing led to another."

Ru just blinked. And blinked. OK, this wasn't even the big secret. How was he going to cope with the actual weird one?!

"Earth to Ru…"

He shook his head. "Sorry … that just … took a serious turn." He laughed. Really laughed.

"Indeed. So, I think we can agree I set the bar high? So, your turn. Truth or dare."

He chose "truth" straight away.

Deep breath, Mols.

Just ask what you want to know. What's been bugging you?

"Are you…" Be brave. "Cold?" OK, I was a wimp. "We could go inside if you are?"

He grinned. "That wasn't it, was it?"

Eurgh. It really wasn't. I wanted to check he wasn't doing a Simon. That the Better Half call really had been nothing to worry about. I took a deep breath. "Fine

then… I've told you I'm an ex-Jingle Lady. But are you …
are you seeing anyone?"

He looked confused.

"I'm seeing … you?" Now was NOT the time for
a language barrier to get in the way. "And them." He
pointed down the street then shook his head. "This game
is really not what I expected."

"No, I meant…" This was SO awkward. *Do you have
a girlfriend? Or a boyfriend? Or both?*

"I meant … is there anyone who, y'know, wouldn't
like you being here…" Gulp. "On a…" Just say date…
"Bench?"

After what felt like hours, but was probably nearer
ten seconds, he looked up.

"Dash. Do you really think I'd do that?"

But that was the problem. I *hoped* he wouldn't. Just
like I hoped Simon wouldn't have done that to Grace.
And look how that had turned out. "To be honest, who
knows? We don't even know each other's names."

I knew his name was Kyle, and I guess he knew mine
too, but finding them out by accident didn't count.

Ru sighed. "I guess that is something we should
have covered in the last twenty-one days." He'd been
counting?!

"Fine then." Here went nothing. "I'll start. I'm Molly.

As in, 'tis the season to be Molly." That's why my parents had chosen my name. "Although I think you heard my dad yell it in Edinburgh. My parents probably would have called me Jolly if it wasn't a criminal offence. Do you know in the UK it's illegal to call a baby 'Martian'?" Oh hello Nervous Gabble. Nice to see you again. "And in France, you can't call one Nutella. But things like Apple or Beverley are fine."

"Pleased to officially meet you, Molly." Ru held out his hand. "I'm Kyle Apple ... and I am deeply offended." He laughed through his nose. "Sorry, no, bad joke. I'm actually Jay. Did I mention that wasn't my name badge I had on when we met?" He hadn't. But it didn't matter. HOUSTON WE HAVE A CONFIRMED NAME. Jay. Jaaaay. Molly and Jay. May. *Jolly?!* Was this fate? "And what else can I tell you? Oh yeah ... I'm a recent Christmas convert. Very recent. As of today really."

He paused.

"And..." I willed him to tell me something more. Anything more.

"Let's see ... I tell everyone I love snowboarding, but I've never been. I hate heights. I'm totally flunking math." Flunk or not, why did saying it without an "s" make it hot?! "Which sucks as I used to love space stuff, my parents are obsessed with it too. I was convinced I'd be an astronaut.

Although I guess, space is kinda high." He thought for a second. "I've been travelling on and off for almost two years now, and I really miss my bed. And our weird old neighbour who is convinced Elvis is hiding in her yard…" But he still hadn't said anything about the seeing-someone situation. "And one time, when I was twelve, I broke my nose" – he pointed to the scar – "trying to prove to my best friend that our truck window was made of shatterproof glass." BUT WAS HE SEEING SOMEONE?!

But I said nothing. He noticed that I wasn't reacting. Waiting.

"Oh, OK. It's like that, is it." I nodded. "Fine. To answer your question. In the most suspicious game of British Christmas Truth or Dare ever…" I braced for impact. Face – stay calm. Whatever he says, stay calm. "If you really want an answer. There *is* someone I liked. Well, like." Ouch. And that, right there, was exactly why romcoms should be banned. "But that someone … is you." What?! "And I swear, on the world's supply of gingerbread-without-coffee drinks and polar bear marshmallows, and all the pickles on all the Christmas trees, there is *no one* else. No other person. Not here. Not in the US. Not anyone." Gulp. "Just you. Who, until two hours ago, I thought was a complete and utter Jingle Lady." He stopped. "And yes, I still can't make that sound cool."

I felt like a Christmas cracker that had been pulled; all the feelings I'd been tucking away, bursting out.

I did like Ru. Really really like him.

I'd always thought happy endings weren't possible. But maybe they were? Even for someone like me. Because Ru – who had made me laugh, made me not worry, made me the very best playlists – liked me. Molly Bell.

And that made my mind up.

There was no way I was cutting this night short to go and see Joseph D Chambers. I was going to have to speak to Elijah. See if it could be rearranged.

"This silence … not super relaxing, by the way." Oops. But Ru laughed and started tracing shapes in the snow with his shoe. "Especially as I have no idea if you like me back. I mean, I thought you definitely didn't. Making the whole Jingle Lady thing clear. And blanking my messages. But then out of the blue you asked to meet. And I don't know what's going on, and maybe it was the prizes for the fundraiser or maybe it's not and maybe I shouldn't have said any of this…" He chewed his lip. Did he really think my silence was me not liking him? Did he not know I was knee-deep in a total meltdown? Did he really not think it was him who had been giving mixed signals?!

It was time to be honest. Even if my brain was one big jumble of words. The biggest one being "ELF".

"OK, if you want the truth…" He nodded. I wasn't sure he'd feel the same once I'd got it all out. "I'm Molly, Molly Bell, and I've got two sisters. Billy, who you met. And Tess." He looked confused. "Yup. Sorry about that. *Kyle*. And it's not my neighbours who have ridiculous Christmas decorations. Or move plastic reindeer every day. It's my family. And that *was* our car. Aka Cara."

"Whoaaaaa." He whistled.

"Oh, there's more. I love playing bass guitar, but only ever play it in my room. And I also play banjo, but wish I couldn't." Had he moved nearer to me? "Half of my bedroom is covered in horse photos, thanks to Bil." I had way too much to work with. I'm sure an edited highlights would have been fine? "And that bad day I had last week?" Were our legs touching?! "Well, I totally humiliated myself at the end of term awards and may have to feign illness from January through to July. And just stay inside making these with Tess…" I pulled the socks out Tess had made and I'd sewn "R" and "U" on. He immediately flicked off his shoes to put them on.

"Molly," he said. It sounded so nice when he said my real name. "You are a bass guitar, banjo-playing legend?! These are" – he wiggled his toes – "my new favourite thing. And you HAVE to show me a photo of your house.!"

But I had to get my final secret out in the open. All this time keeping it secret hadn't protected me after all. It had just stopped me living my life.

"Wait. There's one last thing. And I really don't want you to freak out." Please don't let him react like Zaiynab. Or Matt. Or Simon. Or all those people who had left mean comments online. "I don't herd reindeer." Weirdest confession ever. "And nor do my parents. I'd never even met Derek before that day." Not getting any less weird. "My dad works in insurance. And my mum's a librarian. But years ago… Erm … you know how much you hate that song by The Brussel Shouts?" He nodded, confused. I got out my phone. Opened up the photo of me and my family when I was little. "Well, that little elf girl that makes you cringe…" I turned the screen. "It's me."

CHAPTER

18

Ru didn't laugh.

Well, he did, but only the totally appropriate amount when he saw the picture of bright-green-child me in full elf mode.

But, more importantly, he didn't run.

"Molly. This is adorable!" *Adorable*?! No one had ever said that before! "*This* is your family? They're incredible. Although I'm kind of sad about Derek." He dropped his head into his hands and groaned. "No wonder your dad gave me that look in Scotland."

"Please can we never speak again of what happened with my dad in Scotland?" The lunging image lived in my mind rent free, and I seriously wanted it evicted.

"Deal." Ru looked back up. "Although why on earth didn't you tell me sooner? All this time, I've been hanging out with the world's most famous elf? No wonder you didn't return my calls. Or messages. Or…" But he was grinning.

"OK, OK, I get it!" But I was laughing, a huge green-and-red weight lifted off me. All this time I'd been trying to hide who I was, and now Ru, no, Jay, knew and … he didn't seem to care. "I just thought it might be weird. That you might not…" But I shrugged, too embarrassed to say, "Want to hang out with me".

"Seriously?" He shook his head in disbelief. "Being the elf girl just makes you even better." *Even* better? That sounded nice. "And anyone who doesn't agree should probably hide, as I've seen what you can do with a wooden sign."

"Oi." I bumped my knee into his. "It was an accident."

"Course." He grinned. "Wouldn't dare say otherwise." He held his battered phone up. "So how about a photo? Me and Elf Girl. On this momentous bench… Maybe you could even not look petrified this time?"

"I can't make any promises." I laughed. But this time, squidged together on the bench, the snow falling, we got a photo of me laughing my head off and Ru grinning next to me.

It looked amazing. Like … we were a couple at Christmas. A perfect romcom moment, even better than the bench in Liverpool.

"Who needs Elijah's photobooth, right?" Ru

airdropped the photo over to me. I couldn't help but see who I was in his contacts. Smiley Girl aka Dasher.

OK. That was cute. That was *very* cute. And I didn't know what to say. And neither did he.

And erm…

"I think I need a wee," I said, shattering any illusion of me being able to have cutesy couple moments. "Be back in a sec…"

As soon as I was out of sight I rang Elijah. He picked up immediately.

"Elf?"

"Oh, hi, Elijah."

"Please don't tell me you're here early? Is that you on the jetty? Molly! We're not set up yet."

I bit my lip. This was going to go down like a lead balloon. But I thought of Ru, and him waiting on the bench, and, well…

"Hypothetically. If I couldn't make the meal with Joseph D Chambers later … could we maybe, reschedule it?"

"You what?!" Elijah then made me repeat it. Twice. Before he went silent for about thirty long seconds.

"*Hypothetically*, I don't even want to discuss it, Molly." Elijah swallowed hard. "We pulled some serious strings to make this happen. Joseph NEVER does stuff like this. And we're guaranteed at least twelve publications running the photos?!"

He really did only care about stupid press stories.

"So, is that a maybe?"

"It's a 'you better be joking' silence. And what about your friend who paid all that money?"

Could I find out who?!

"Friend?"

"I'm not at liberty to say, but I'm sure they'll tell you in good time."

Who could it be?!

"But the bid would still stand if we did it another time? Like at the event tomorrow?"

Elijah gave a furious sigh. "We're not talking about any old person here. Joseph's got no availability after tonight." My heart sank. If it meant losing money for the fundraiser of course I'd go. "Molly. Really. Even Tim liked the auction idea. Even more when you were the winner. Little Elf Girl and the lead." So Elijah was going to use the photos to get his reveal of my Elf secret? Nice of him to tell me! "A perfect little story about Joseph for once!" Not sure how cute a set-up meal was, but it didn't seem like the time to argue. "In the MOST CRUCIAL week for getting Christmas number one!"

"So is that a no then?"

Elijah actually growled. "It's a 'I'll see what I can do'."

But he'd already put the phone down.

I felt bad. But minutes later, as I was drying my hands, a message from Elijah pinged through.

ELIJAH: *Meet is cancelled for tonight. Still looking for another slot. Bid still stands. Can't talk. Too busy waving bye to chances of me getting that job.*

ELIJAH: *Merry little Christmas.*

He was taking it well then. I felt bad, but had to remind myself this was the guy who'd been threatening to release that red-carpet clip of me. Thank goodness I'd made sure it was deleted. I quickly messaged Grace to tell her the meet was getting rearranged, and that the bid was still OK and pinged over the selfie of me and Ru. I knew if she saw it, she'd understand why I'd asked to postpone.

I tried to push all thoughts of it out of my mind, and slid back next to Ru on the bench.

"So, Ru, I mean Jay." It was going to take some getting used to. "Now that you know my deepest darkest secret…"

"You play the banjo?"

I gave him my best withering look. "No, about the whole *elf* situation. And I know yours…"

"I never mastered long division?"

"No, that you actually quite like Christmas."

He went to protest, but stopped. "Fair, actually."

I grinned. "It's time to unveil the final part of the

294

plan." I opened the booking confirmation email I'd got when I was feeling brave with Grace. "I thought we could finally see it. Rip off all our festive plasters at once."

His face fell. "Is *this* why you wanted to end up in Leicester Square?"

I nodded. But Jay was rubbing at his forehead, like I'd shown him tickets to one of Mum's banjo recitals. And Grace was ringing. I never didn't answer, but for once I cut the call. I knew she'd want me to make sure our plan happened.

"We don't have to..." But the tickets cost me twenty-eight pounds so we kind of did.

Grace rang again. I clicked "Give me a sec".

Jay cracked his neck. Did he hate the film that much? Or was there someone he really didn't want to run into?

"I made sure I didn't choose the cinema where you worked. Thought we could mix it up..."

But he shook his head. "Sorry, Molly. Ignore me. I'm being weird." He picked up his bag. "It's fine. Although, I might have to run straight after." Oh no. After all that, could I make the meet and greet after all?! "And if there's any way I could persuade you to do literally anything else..." He did know we were going to see a film, not go to the dentist? And why had Grace sent a minute-long voice note? Guess she wanted a full debrief on the call with Elijah.

"Well, it's up to you. But, no pressure, I just cancelled a date with actual Hollywood royalty for you."

He leant forward, his eyes narrowed. "You what?"

I shrugged. "Probably should have added that to the 'things I haven't told you' section."

"You want to explain?"

"Nah. I can fill you in later." Once I'd told Grace.

"Never not confusing." He grinned. "But let's go. See this ridiculous film. Although there's one condition…" I froze. "I hold the popcorn this time."

And he reached for my hand. And I took it.

And it felt amazing.

And we were still holding hands as we buried our heads into our scarves, trying not to freeze as we walked along the river. And we were still holding hands as we cheered and laughed at our attempts to score points in curling. And we were still holding hands as we walked past the huge Christmas tree in Trafalgar Square. And we were holding hands as we threw snowballs at each other. Which actually made a snowball fight really hard. Fun though. And we were still holding hands as we walked through a tiny alleyway, lights strung above an old man roasting chestnuts.

Yup, we were holding hands as I realized I'd become one half of those couples I used to side-eye. But I didn't care. I was done hiding things. And as we slid and skidded our way to Leicester Square, I was grinning so hard snow kept landing on my cheeks. But as we walked into the hot air of the cinema, the bright lights making us readjust, my laughing twisted into nerves.

This suddenly felt like a proper date date.

What if Ru, argh, Jay, thought my film laugh was weird?

Or I choked on a really dry unpopped kernel?

Or I needed an above average amount of toilet trips?!

"You OK, Mol?" Jay stopped as we got to the doors of the screen. I must have looked as stressed as I felt.

"Just wondering whether to warn you, I'm very bad at sharing pick 'n' mix..."

He grinned. "Well, I might have something to admit too."

"*Now?*" I didn't feel up to any more revelations today. But as a group of people walked towards us, he laughed.

"You know what... Maybe it can wait."

And we headed into the screen. My first proper date.

I felt sick with nerves. Then excited. Then nervous about feeling excited.

My head was spinning. Which is why I didn't think to check my phone.

Because if I had, I'd have seen the twenty-eight messages from Grace.

And maybe I would have had some warning how bad this film was about to get.

CHAPTER
19

Ru had chosen the very back row. The very, very back row. In the very corner. Just like Grace had hoped.

The back row, like where I'd sat awkwardly next to Grace and Simon as they'd snogged all the way through *Hero Horse 3*, when I took Billy (weird, but at least it meant they didn't see my blubbing).

Did this mean Ru was going to…

Was this going to be…

GULP.

Might I be about to have my first proper kiss? With Ru. No, Jay. *JAY!*

Sure, it would be more under "fire exit sign" than "bunch of mistletoe", but *I. Would. Take. It.* And Grace would *more* than approve.

How on earth was I going to focus on the film with all that to think about, though?!

But it was starting.

SLEIGH ANOTHER DAY. RATED 12.

The moment had come. Me and my nemesis were meeting. But it didn't feel half as scary with Jay beside me. The lights dimmed and Jay flicked his cap off and shuffled down in his chair. I'd got the posh squidgy seats. I was glad it was already dark so he couldn't see me breathing him in. MMMmmmmm. He smelt of sweet and salty popcorn.

Oh no. That was the popcorn.

I looked at him and grinned. Here we were, two Christmas film haters, facing the ultimate test. But after today, I had a feeling I might kind of like it – theme tune and all.

But Jay looked kind of nervous.

"Don't worry. You're going to do just fine," I whispered, stuffing my coat under my chair. "These holiday films are always the same." Grace had made me watch so many. "There'll be a meet cute, some kind of misunderstanding, and you'll know from the very first scene the two leads will end up together, but for some reason they just can't be. But ... it'll all work out in the end... With lots of added Christmas. We've got this!"

Did he mutter "I hope so"?

He was really overthinking this. I was the one about to hear myself singing about being an elf. In 3D surround sound.

I took a deep breath, getting ready to hear the first notes of the song and pushed myself back into my chair. All these weeks trying to hide every single detail of this stupid film and now, here I was, watching it in London. With the first ever guy I'd ever really liked. Really, really liked.

Maybe Christmas romance was a thing after all?

And maybe I liked it.

I put my hand in the popcorn and made contact with Jay's. We looked at each other, not sure what the popcorn-hand etiquette was.

He gulped. "Molly. Before it starts…" But a booming narrator's voice cut him off.

I shuffled back into my seat. Jay edged further forward in his, his hands clasped over his mouth and nose.

Then the screen went black.

And the first notes of "Love Your Elf!" boomed round the cinema.

A whoop came from the front row.

People around us started singing along.

Wow. I guess people really did like it.

Jay gave my hand a squeeze in elf solidarity.

Deep breath, Molly. One and a half hours and it'll be over.

Try and think of all the positive things.

Like making Grace happy by finally seeing Joseph D Chambers in action. Was he going to be as hot as she said?

And there he was. In the very first scene. With his plummy British accent.

Holding a mini-Christmas tree in the snow, as he waited for his grandma to answer the door.

Grace wasn't lying. That boy wasn't just hot. He was the hottest boy I'd ever seen.

Well, except one.

The boy next to me. That was sitting with his cap on, head in his hands.

And this time I really did drop the popcorn.

Joseph D Chambers wasn't hotter than Ru.

Joseph D Chambers WAS Ru.

CHAPTER
20

I stood up. No idea why.

Then sat down. Then leant forward. And rocked back. Then stood up again.

This *wasn't* happening. This *couldn't be* happening. WHAT was happening?!!

Why could I see two of Jay? Of Ru? Of whoever this guy was??!

Was I on my first date with…

No, I couldn't be.

NOPE.

"Mol…" Jay put his hand on my knee.

THE NUMBER ONE SEXIEST FRINGE WEARER OF THE YEAR HAD HIS HAND ON MY KNEE.

I opened my mouth. And shut it.

Thank goodness on screen there were reindeer

clattering through snow, cos I think I was making a malfunctioning noise.

"I'm sorry," Jay mouthed. I blinked, and turned back to the screen.

BUT NO. Seeing the exact same face as the one next to me, but this time the size of my house, was not particularly calming.

He leant over. "Want to go outside for a minute?"

Outside? Sure. If he could pick me up and carry me. I couldn't handle walking at a time like this?! But somehow I managed to edge out. I felt like I had a big flashing light on my head. LOOK, EVERYONE! I'M WITH JOSEPH D CHAMBERS. THE INSANELY HOT GUY ON SCREEN! AND YES, I ONCE WAS AN ELF.

No wonder he always wore so many hats and scarves! It wasn't because he had a low body temperature – it was because he was intensely famous and didn't want anyone to know!

I staggered into the foyer, Jay grabbing my hand and guiding me to the seats in front of the huge window overlooking Leicester Square. I stared at the people down below. How were they just walking about when MY WHOLE LIFE HAD FLIPPED UPSIDE DOWN!

I plonked down on the bench, watching the usher do a double take at the person next to me. Jay flashed him a quick smile, with the ease of someone who did the same thing a million times a day. Of course. *OF COURSE!*

I'd really thought all those odd looks, those random waves, were because of me being Elf Girl.

WHAT AN ABSOLUTE WALLY! I couldn't help but laugh.

"OK. Maybe not saying anything sooner wasn't my greatest idea…" Jay fiddled with the Christmas badge he'd pinned on to his jumper. "I thought Billy had outed me when she said about riding that horse." Wait. She meant a scene from the film? "Are you … angry?"

I didn't know? So far, I'd only processed "shocked".

"I'm…" But then I got it. Ah-ha! I looked around for a camera. "I'm on a prank show, aren't I?" Yes, that made sense. "Is this Elijah's work? Or Harry's?"

"Sadly, no." He sighed. "I can promise you this is one hundred per cent real. *Now* can you see why I had my doubts about your whole 'Let's go see *Sleigh Another Day*' plan?" He shook his head and laughed.

"Well, I *definitely* know why the ticket guy gave us free snacks." And that's when I remembered Grace's messages. I pulled my phone out. The words JOSEPH D CHAMBERS in capitals down my screen at least fifty times. "So…" But I had no idea what to say. What did you say to an A-list celebrity? "Erm…" I thought. And had nothing. "Sorry, I just don't know what to say any more."

"How about whatever it was you would have said before you found out what my job really was?" But back then, I thought he was normal, like me. He kicked the faded carpet. "I'm sorry. I should have told you sooner. Once I figured out you didn't recognize me."

"Oh, I *didn't* recognize you," I said, still processing. Did he really think I'd have met WORLD'S SEXIEST FRINGE WEARER for a date wearing a Christmas pudding onesie?!

"Sorry, that sounded rough. Just, growing up with my parents has made me a bit, I dunno – not everyone's as nice as they pretend to be, I guess." He looked more stressed than me. "Anyway. Jay's what my friends call me."

"Jay. I told you I was an elf. You didn't think maybe that could have been the time to mention you were a Hollywood film star?"

It was weird. What I'd loved about Ru was that he was one of the only people I felt comfortable chatting away with about stupid stuff. But now I knew who he really was, nothing I had to say felt good enough.

"You kinda made your feelings about 'Joseph D Chambers'" – Jay cringed as he said it, although Mum would love his use of air quotes – "quite clear when we met." Ah. I thought back. Maybe I *had* said he was a nightmare. And a terrible actor. "Trust me, it's not exactly the best conversation starter." But I was only half listening, my mind scrolling through all the things I'd said. Things that had happened. And the pieces that were slowly slotting together. Travelling with the film. Never wanting to meet when people were about. Not talking about his family. The box of film stuff!

"Oh my goodness, your parents…" Everyone knew his parents were Bry and Cate, the most iconic movie star couple. And he'd met my mum. In a camper van that played banjo carols. And my dad had lunged. "They sent your dog to the moon?!"

Ru raised an eyebrow.

"Nope, they sponsored some space research" – as you do?! – "and the project already had the same name as our dog. But that story wasn't so good for the media."

Was I really chatting about Cate and Bry like they were Mel and Jan from next door?

"Sorry, but your life is epic."

"My life is … really not." He half-smiled. I bet he thinks I'm really embarrassing. But I'd never met a celebrity until two weeks ago. "You're the epic one. With your lyrics. The band. The fundraiser … the whole elf revelation."

I stared out of the window. I needed a second to process everything. This was normal. This was totaaalllly normal.

Totally normal that the cinema opposite had a huge sign up. "This Christmas, Who Will End Up Under the Mistletoe, When the Crew Come to *Sleigh Another Day*?" And there he was. Ru. Joseph. Jay. The size of a bus, smouldering away in a way that could melt snow.

THIS WAS SO NOT NORMAL.

"I can't believe I took you curling." What was I thinking? And how much had I slated the film?!

But Ru didn't laugh. He shifted his body to face me.

"The curling was awesome. And you are awesome. Please don't let" – he nodded out at the poster – "my job, that's all it is, change stuff."

I tried to keep a straight face. "Ditto with my not really working for Reindeers 'R' Us confession."

Joseph grinned. *Joseph*. Ru was Jay. Ru was Joseph. I had SO many questions.

"So, what were you doing that day we met?"

"Honestly?" I nodded. "Hiding. It was my first big premiere and it was all a bit much. Especially with everyone grabbing me for a photo, like I was a piece of set." He shook his head. "Soooo many awkward photos. So when the red carpet was done, I bailed. Swapped into the only spare clothes I could find – Kyle sorted me out – and I went to sit it out. Until…" He shrugged. "Until you arrived. If *arrived* is the word…"

I'd thrown popcorn over the star of the film! Got him locked in a storage room! No wonder Elijah had been in such a mood when he'd found us!

"Can I say sorry once more?"

"Sorry?" Ru looked me dead in the eye. I know Grace thought he was hot in the film, but in real life he really was something else! "Molly, it was the best evening I'd had in YEARS. Even if Elijah was less than impressed."

Elijah! He must have known all along! Why had he never filled me in on who Ru really was? But then it hit me. Probably because he didn't really think there was any point. Someone like Ru couldn't actually like someone like me. Not like that. I suddenly felt so stupid. So, so stupid. Here I was with one of Hollywood's Hottest Twenty Under Twenty, and I'd had to do the drying up for a week to be able to afford tickets to pay for tickets to see his film.

"Well, it's probably best if you get back to your life now." I reached for my coat. "You don't need to hear about me and my horse bedroom any more."

"I don't *need* to, Mol. I *want* to! I've been in from day

one. You're the one, who didn't want to meet up?"

Is that really how he saw it?

"But you kept acting so weird? Like when you disappeared in Edinburgh."

"I got dragged into an interview on some random Belgian TV station." OK, that did sound stressful. "And I thought it would be quite a hard thing to explain considering you thought I was an usher called Kyle." So *that's* why his phone was off? "In fairness, I did try and find you afterwards, but when that failed I had to hope you wouldn't be creeped out if I randomly – not-at-all-randomly – bumped into you at breakfast." He cringed. "Credit to Elijah for helping me out with that one."

Sorry. Was he really telling me that I, Molly Bell, had had an A-list Hollywood star trying to bump into me? But then an even worse thought hit me.

"What about all that Maeve stuff?"

"Maeve?" Ru looked genuinely surprised. "What about Maeve?"

"Aren't you two…" It felt awkward to say. "… y'know?."

Maeve and Joseph made way more sense than me and him. Unless this was just like a fun experiment for him? To see how non-famous people hung out?

"I don't, but judging by the way you're giving me that look, I can guess… And it's a no. All just rumours, I promise." Probably wasn't cool to actually sigh with relief, but that's exactly what I did. He was polite enough not to acknowledge it. "That's why I never say anything to anyone about my personal life. Way too much drama. Although, don't get me wrong, Maeve has been the best thing about this whole film for me. Even if she does annoy me. Like saving herself as 'Better Half' on my production phone cos she was playing my girlfriend but thinks I'm dead inside."

Ah.

"Yeah, I knew you'd seen. But 'my fake on-screen girlfriend thought she was being funny' was also not the greatest explanation at the time."

Ha. That did explain it! And there was I thinking I was the only one making it up as I went along.

"Oh, and I couldn't say earlier, but Maeve thought the whole red-carpet thing was hilarious. Got her out of wearing a dress she hated and hanging out with Stormy, so if you told her it was you, you'd have a friend for life."

Jay as my date. Maeve as my friend.

Someone help. I am DECEASED.

But Jay was looking at me, so I had to rein in my breakdown.

"She did seem really nice when we hung out?"

"You hung out?" He looked confused.

"Yeah, that night in Edinburgh."

"No way." He scratched his head. "She asked me to join, but I was annoyed I'd messed things up with you so went back to my hotel."

I had to laugh. Maeve had said Joseph was in a mood, but I really had no idea it was anything to do with me. I was going to need a long lie down to deal with all of this. Like maybe for a year.

"So why do the headlines always say you're together?"

They would make a great couple. And hadn't Grace said there were rumours about him and loads of amazing celebs? Ewww. I tried to push the thought away.

Ru shrugged. "No idea. Probably because Elijah wishes it was true. If I hear one more thing about 'leaning into some loved-up headlines being the best thing for the film and my career'." He tutted. "He's ob-sessed! Although, between us, apparently there *is* a new girl Maeve's really into and she's being very secretive and un-Maeve about it. But you didn't hear it from me."

"Imagine the donation Elijah would make to the fundraiser for that info…" I grinned, but Ru looked worried. "Don't worry, your secret is safe. Well, although, sort of legally, as a best friend, I have to tell Grace."

"I think Harry knows too."

"Sorry? You've met Harry Styles?"

Ru snorted.

OMG. I've seen a movie star snort. "I meant Harry from Grace and Harry. But sure, good to know how your mind works." Ru shook his head. I bet his famous friends didn't do things like this.

"So, you and Harry are friends?"

"Yeah, although Harry has no idea we've been hanging out. I knew he'd hate having to cover for me. So when he and Elijah asked about doing that meet and greet for the fundraiser, I figured out it was the one for Grampy G and, thanks to your dad, I knew you were the best mate 'Molly' he mentioned, so I said yes." So that's why Joseph D Chambers had broken his rule of not doing press?! He scrunched his nose. It was probably insured for twelve billion dollars. "And when Elijah called to say earlier it was going to be with you, it got even better!"

He knew?!

"But I just cancelled it?"

"That's when I knew you were even more awesome than I thought. Not many people turn down exclusive 'intimate meals' to hang out with an awkward American guy who likes Elvis conspiracy theories and overly descriptive hot drink reviews."

My brain was doing the brain-equivalent of the spinning computer wheel of death.

All these years I hadn't let anyone get to know the real me. I'd been so focused on making sure no one knew *anything* about me. And now I'd let someone in. And that someone was Joseph D Chambers. And he was saying me, Molly Embarrassing-Elf Bell, with no secrets left to hide, was … awesome?!

This was a mistake, wasn't it?

"I'm sorry, Jay… This is just a lot. Like, a lot a lot." I didn't know what to think. If the last day of term had been hard, how full on would it be if people discovered I'd been hanging out with the star of the film? "Maybe even, I dunno … too much."

"I get it. No pressure." Jay sighed, picking up on my folded arms. But was I doing to him exactly what people had done to me? Treating him differently because of something that wasn't anything to do with who he really was? "Although, kinda wish I *was* Kyle the usher right now." He looked me dead in the eye. "Because, for the record, can I say that for once in my life I've met someone that I really like. I *really* like. Who makes me laugh, makes me share stuff I've never shared? Makes me vibe about Christmas." He pointed to his reindeer badge.

"And for clarity…"

"Yup. That person is you."

"But you saw me in my sister's dressing gown?"

"And that's exactly WHY it's you!"

And I liked him. And finding out who he really was shouldn't change that, should it?

"Grace is going to freak."

"Think she might already be…" He nodded down, the words JOSEPH D CHAMBERS still pinging on my phone every few seconds, only broken up with photos of her doing her tongue-out-fake-dead face.

"Can we pretend you're not seeing that?" I bet this would never happen to Maeve.

"We can."

"And can we also pretend that man isn't taking photos?" I pointed outside to where a man was crouched, pointing up a long lens camera. Jay instinctively flicked his collar up and turned his shoulders away. The saddest thing was, he wasn't even bothered. My end of term entertainment had been bad enough for me. But this was his life. I stood in front of Jay and waved. Big double arm wave. And jumped about. "If you want a photo with Elf Girl," I shouted at the window, posing in all kinds of shapes. "Just ask."

After flicking a heavy variety of swears with his hand, the photographer walked off.

"And I refer back to when I said you're epic…" Jay

314

smiled. But we were stuck. Neither of us sure what should happen next. "So…"

"Sooo…." I replied.

"Thanks to him, if we walk out, I can already see the headline."

I filled in the blanks "Joseph D Chambers… Why *do* they always say all the bits of your name by the way?"

He shrugged.

"Dunno, Molly N Bell. But you're right."

I finished off my thought. "*Joseph D Chambers walks out of own film.* Elijah would kill you."

"You're not wrong. And it's Christmas box office in a few days, and I've never seen him so … well … Elijah."

"Well, in that case…" A burst of "Love Your Elf!" drifted in from the film. "If you're up for it. How about we just go back in?"

"You really want to do that?" Jay looked like he couldn't tell if I was joking. It was like he had no idea how much I liked him.

So I did the only thing I could think of.

Grabbed his hand, and went back into the cinema to watch my date pretend to fall in love with someone else while I tried not to fall too hard for him.

CHAPTER

21

TO DO:

- Set alarm for Grace's train
- Go get that yurt
- Update invites & send
- Make 69 snowflakes
- Brush teeth
- Wear Christmas pin
- Brush teeth again
- Remember not to smile like this around Mum!!!!!!

Where was I?

RING RING!

Why were my feet jingling?

I opened my eyes.

RING RING!

Hotel.

London.

JINGLE MY BELLS! LAST NIGHT WENT ON A DATE WITH JOSEPH D CHAMBERS!

I sat bolt upright, sending my laptop flying.

What were the rules around falling asleep while watching interview after interview with the boy you'd just been on a date with?

MUST delete my history asap.

RING RING!

I hit the alarm clock.

RING RING!

Oh, my phone!!!

I dug around in my duvet to find it. I maaaaay have fallen asleep clutching it, but Grace and I had a LOT to message about, as she'd been at her cousin's wedding and her dad wouldn't let her ring.

Her face popped up on screen.

"I want to hear every detail. EVERY look. Every word. Every silence." I shuffled back on my pillow. I looked a big hairy mess on screen. A big hairy happy mess. "Every breath. Every sniff. Every..." She gave what I think was meant to be a brooding look.

I laughed.

"Would now be the time to say maybe I am into Christmas romance after all?"

Last night, during the film, as I'd watched confident on-screen Joseph make Maeve swoon, and real-life Joseph cringe into soda, I'd finally given up trying to control what I did and didn't feel. Given up trying to pretend I didn't like Jay. Given up trying to not enjoy a full-on, big cheesy Christmas dollop of romance.

"Now WOULD be the right time. In fact, the ONLY thing you're allowed to talk about is yesterday." Grace fanned her face. "My bestie is dating Joseph Chambers!!" She took some fast breaths. "MY BESTIE IS DATING JOSEPH CHAMBERS. Bry and Cate are going to be our in-laws. Your in-laws, our in-laws – whatever." She swallowed. "Have not slept one bit. Here I was, excited about just *watching* the film, and you've gone and lived an even more romantic version of it." She looked into the distance, a grin on her face. "*Two main characters. Both gorgeous inside and out. From opposite sides of the Atlantic but destined to be together. Throwing popcorn. Rubbing out phone numbers.* Soz I encouraged that, by the way." I wasn't getting a word in edgeways, was I? "The fundraising prizes?! The thoughtful mum biscuits?!" Genuinely was wondering if she liked him even more than me. "It's all too much!? I mean, THIS is how you take off your boyfriend stabilizers?! With the most eligible guy in the world." I still hadn't said a word. "From popcorn covered lock-in … to true love."

"Erm." Probably should rein this in a bit. "One step at a time, Gracey. We haven't even…"

"Kissed," she said, matter-of-factly. "But that's on the cards. Tonight's plan. And what a location. The final stop of the *Sleigh Another Day* tour. In snowy London. Capital of romance. Molly Bell, waving to Joseph D Chambers' legions of fans as the world realizes she's his one true love, and the shipping begins. HARD." She stopped for half a breath. "Molsephs? Jollies? Either way. I stan!"

I had to laugh. "Not sure it's quite like that." I was still having a hard time believing this was happening. That Jay, Joseph, really might like me. The real me.

I pulled back the curtain. It was still snowing.

Grace's eyes widened. "Are there paps outside? You've got to lie low now, Mol. Girlfriend of the lead? The world will want a piece of you!"

I sat back on the bed, properly laughing. "First up, we've had one date. Sure, one quite eventful date, but only one. And second up, the world is NEVER finding out." I'd made that really clear to Jay last night. One step at a time. I wasn't ready for my life to go even weirder than with Elf Girl. "And thirdly, can you, my best friend, not already relegate me to girlfriend of someone famous? I'm actually a very talented, er, lyric writer, bass player…"

"Music producer," Grace added.

"Why thank you … and, er, elf in my own right."

But … girlfriend did have a nice ring to it.

"You're grinning about being his girlfriend, aren't you?"

"No," I lied.

"You're lying."

"No."

"I thought we said no secrets!!"

"Fine." I couldn't help but smile. "Maybe it is kind of…"

"THE BEST CHRISTMAS PRESENT EVER!" Grace stretched out on her sofa. I wondered if the old Grace being back was all me and Ru related, or if there was something – or someone – more.

"So, does the return of loved-up Grace mean we can stop pretending you don't like Harry? Cos he'll be there later…"

Grace's smile dropped. "Let me stop you there, Molinder. Romance for you, I'm HERE for. But once you've been Simoned, well…" She shrugged. "Harry and I are friends *only*." It sucked that Simon was stopping her from having some Christmas fun of her own, but I wasn't going to push her. "Oh!" She clicked her fingers. "I forgot to say. When I was chatting to him yesterday, he said he loved our photos from the maze. In Edinburgh. Which was suss. Did you send them to him?"

"Nah." I shook my head. "We didn't even use my phone." It had been the production one.

"Weird." Maybe we'd shown him and just forgotten? "But today isn't for investigations. Today is Mol's First Snog Day. And tonight, I'll be there to hear all about it in person."

We ran through what was happening before then. In just over an hour, I was meeting Elijah to board the *Sleigh Another Day* boat. To make up for cancelling the date, Elijah had asked me to do an interview with one of the influencers as it would be good to get a "normal face out there". I'd agreed and kept very quiet about who I'd been with last night. Then I was meeting Grace off her train and at 6:34 p.m there was a huge fireworks display to match the time Maeve and Joseph kiss in the film.

So I needed to get ready. I'd packed something I thought was kind of cool that I'd borrowed (taken) from Tess. But… I looked out at the twinkling lights and giant tree covered in strands of silver and white baubles. And then looked back at the snowwoman jumper from

Edinburgh I'd bought to lounge about in. And ... if I couldn't wear a Christmas jumper today, then when could I? I pulled it on, with my favourite black jeans and DMs, and practically skipped down the road, wishing anyone within shouting distance "Merry Christmas".

Grampy G would be proud. When I knocked on the door of the shipping container that was the press office, Elijah looked me up and down like I'd come dressed as a sausage.

"I did say this was THE most *exclusive* Christmas event of the year."

But I was too happy to care what he thought. "Sure did. Looks awesome, by the way."

He raised an eyebrow. "What's got you in this mood."

There was no way I was telling him. I didn't have a spare four hours for all his opinions. And I didn't want to land Jay in trouble. "Nothing." And somehow I managed to not react as a bunch of big guys in black puffer jackets bundled Maeve and Jay past us to take them to Radio One. Jay and I locked eyes, both trying to not grin and give the game away. It felt amazing. And private. And perfect. Until Stormy ran after them yelling, "It must have been an admin error, my name must have been on the invitation."

"Fine. I don't want to know anyway. I've got headlines

around the world to make. Don't exactly have a spare minute to hear about whatever ridiculous thing made you cancel the incredibly intimate meal with Joseph for. And before you ask. No. I haven't found a new time yet." Little did he know. "And yes, I'm still FURIOUS. So how about you go into great detail about this being THE most magical Christmas forest meets boat meets wonderland you've ever seen?"

"It does look epic." Epic. Like Ru said I was. Uh-oh! Stupid grin was trying to come back. "And with all these people coming," I looked at the long list of influencers and celebs, "I reckon you'll be ALL over the papers tomorrow. Number one in the box office next week. Tim will love you. And you'll get that job." OK, I may have added in a little extra compliment-sauce to make up for the conversation we had yesterday.

"Well, that's the plan." He tutted. "I will NEVER be over *All I Want for Christmas Is Drew* re-releasing today. Did someone say sabotage? Much?!" Maybe that's why he was so stressed. "Still, if they want something to talk about, it's my job to give them exactly that. This Christmas, it's … war."

"Not sure that's going to catch on as a Christmas slogan, tbh."

Elijah raised an eyebrow. For twenty-three seconds.

"And you're still saying no to the music video? We're in the final week we could make it happen – 'last chance' territory for a little lo-fi job? Cos everyone's off for the Lapland trip in a few days, then no more cast and crew."

"It's a forever no, I'm afraid." Telling Ru I was Elf Girl had been a big step. Telling the whole world was not an option.

"Fine! So today. You know the plan. One interview. Tell them how you're a mega-fan … blah blah blah." But he saw Harry run past and rushed off to speak to him, just as Big Ben chimed midday. The boat was leaving any second. I yelled at Harry that I'd come and find him later (he beamed when I added "with Grace") and hurried down through an archway of holly and berries, past the huge screen playing clips of the film and on to the deck. As soon as I'd boarded we started chugging down the Thames, the whole boat flashing away like one big floating Christmas decoration. Speakers were blaring out Christmas songs and back on dry land even the most serious suit-y people were having boogies. And on deck influencers and press were busy getting content about the film, and for the first time I wasn't doing everything I could to hide. I was just enjoying being here. I even waved at all the tourists taking photos.

Three hours. Threeee hours till Jay was finishing his

interviews. And he'd asked if I fancied going to watch the candlelight carols with Harry and Grace, seeing as we'd missed it last night. Which sounded like actual heaven. Grace was on the train so my message about it didn't arrive straight away, but an hour later, when it did, she replied "SNOGGING HEAVEN!", which made my legs buckle so much I fell into one of the displays.

"Getting up close and personal with a snowman? In *that* sweater??! And you said you weren't doing Christmas this year?" Jack appeared, laughing. I brushed myself off.

"Just a trip. No biggie."

"No biggie, sure. I see your face." He pulled a blusher brush out of his belt and circled it around my cheek. "The big grin. The way I just caught you staring at the cut-out of Maeve and Joseph." Had I? "For a full five minutes." Maybe I had. "The way you do THAT face whenever anyone says 'Joseph'…" Jack put his hand on his hip. "Got anything you want to tell me?" He looked up at the huge screen above us. The screen playing the live interview with Maeve and Jay.

The presenter was making them play a game of Christmas charades. Jay looked so awkward. Awkward, but hot. Awkwardly hot.

And Jack was still staring at me.

"Erm, no. Nothing." I'd knew how much privacy

mattered to Jay. But Jack was still staring. And my "nothing to see here face" was disappearing. And my "oh my gosh, I haven't stopped smiling in thirteen hours face" was coming back. "Fine. FINE!" I was hopeless. "Maybe *something*."

Jack grinned. "OK. Well, you didn't hear it from me. But if someone asked me 'has Joseph not been able to stop talking about a girl he met? And I mean. Not. Stop. As in, even when I tried to talk about *literally* anything else.' Then the answer would be yes." Jack bopped me on the nose with his brush. "It's about time I saw him happy."

But he was getting a call over his headset, so had to run. They'd turned the volume up on the screen and a crowd had gathered to watch. There were only ten minutes before we docked, so I thought I'd make the most of it. By staring at Jay on the big screen.

"He's so cute…" A guy next to me leant over. I nodded, hoping he couldn't sense the deeply inappropriate thoughts I was currently having. "Reckon it's true about him and Maeve?"

Molly. Do not grin! Play it cool. "Jury's out." I tried to look mysterious, as Maeve and Jay messed about on screen, cracking up in fits of laughter. "I don't really believe everything I read."

"Totally." He nodded. "But when there's receipts…"

"Receipts?" I snapped.

"Yeah. The pictures SleighAllTheDaysFans posted that have been trending for…" He opened his phone… "At least an hour. Number one worldwide."

As he scrolled to show me on his phone, the exact same image came up on the big screen.

And all the noise around me blurred into one big wall of sound.

Which meant no one heard my heart shatter like a cheap bauble.

Jay. By the Christmas tree in Trafalgar Square. Where we'd stopped on our date.

One arm holding out his phone to take the photo. His other arm around a girl. A girl that very much wasn't me.

And was very, very much the most drop-dead gorgeous, super talented, adored by everyone, Maeve.

A selfie of them looking into each other's eyes, millimetres away from kissing.

"Adorbs, right?" the guy said.

I opened my mouth to reply, but nothing came out. *Keep calm, Mol.*

Maybe this was from ages ago? Maybe it wasn't what it seemed?

Although, it did *seem* pretty bad.

"So, can you guys give us the inside story?" The presenter turned to Maeve and Jay.

And that's when I saw it. On his coat in the picture. The tiny enamel reindeer pin that Jay had only just bought.

This photo *wasn't* old. It was recent. Last two days kind of recent.

Despite everything Jay said to me last night about liking no one else but me.

Promising me him and Maeve were just friends.

There WAS something going on between them after all.

I grabbed on to the boat railing.

"C'mon, guys," The presenter wasn't letting this go. "The world is *dying* to know?"

Me? I was just dying.

I held my breath, willing there to have been a mistake. But all Jay did was look down and laugh.

"No comment." Is what he said. NO COMMENT?! He knew I was at this event today, and he knew I, and the whole world, would be seeing these pictures, but I guess he also knew he'd been caught out.

"So if Maeseph is real" – the presenter looked right into the camera, loving every second. Thank goodness I was on a boat, so I could be sick overboard – "yup, you heard it here first, cos this picture does. Not. Lie! Then does this mean the girl next door you were spotted in London with yesterday is just a friend?"

And that's when it came up. The selfie of Jay and me on the bridge from yesterday, as posted by SleighAllTheDaysFans. My face had been blurred but it didn't matter. Jay knew EXACTLY what it was.

Seeing it somehow hurt even more than the other photo. He'd told me it was just for us, but he'd clearly been sharing it with whoever. Probably laughing about it with Maeve. And now the world was seeing it.

He did a double take. I bet he did.

This almost hurt more than the kiss. And as much as I'd been kidding myself, I knew for a fact I couldn't trust a word he'd ever said.

"We're going to need details," the presenter said. Everyone on the boat "oooohed", but I was silent.

"Oh, her?" Jay looked into the camera with his big brown eyes, and smiled. "She's just some fan."

He really was a much better actor than everyone said.

Forget the boat.

Stop the world. I want to get off.

CHAPTER

22

In my mind, I was at home, under my duvet, crying my eyes out and working my way through a bottomless bucket of Twiglets.

In reality, I was pushing through millions of tourists, trying not to ugly cry.

Stupid Joseph. Stupid Christmas. Stupid me.

How had I been so foolish? Of course Joseph hadn't ever really liked someone like me.

I'd ditched the interview Elijah had wanted me to do. He was going to be even more fuming with me, but if he asked for us to pay for the hotel, I was just going to have to do the drying up for the next ten years to pay Mum and Dad back. But I was DONE. I was never, *ever*, going to have anything to do with this stupid film or that stupid song or stupid Joseph D Chambers ever again.

At least Grace was almost at the station. Her phone had been going to voicemail for a while, which happened last time the train got near London.

Eurgh! I wished everyone would stop taking selfies with the Christmas lights and get out of my way! But I also wished Ru wasn't a massive lying toenail … and look how that turned out.

Not Ru. Joseph. Joseph D-on't-Believe-A-Word-I-Say Chambers.

I did a long blink to try and plug my tears in. But every time I closed my eyes, I just saw that picture of Joseph and Maeve again. And I kept hearing all the thing everyone on the boat had cheered. "Hottest couple", "perfect love story", "Maeseph for ever".

I'd had to stop in a portaloo to have a power cry. What an idiot I'd been to think Joseph really liked me. Had him and Maeve been going on the whole time? Had a single thing he'd said to me been true?

I hated that I'd really believed he liked the real me. He probably found the whole thing hilarious.

Nope. The crying might be about to start again. And I didn't want to be late to meet Grace.

That would be the stupid cherry on the stupid Christmas cake.

We'd planned to have an outdoor river picnic, and I'd

even sneaked some breakfast pastries out of the hotel. Grace loved a mini croissant. And there she was!

"Graceeee!" I yelled, waving from the barriers at the platform. I'd made it in time to see her get off the train. But she wasn't heading towards one of the exit gates. "Grace!!!!!" I yelled again, but she was marching towards the ticket booth – and she didn't look happy.

"Grace?" I yelled even louder. Phew. She saw me and walked towards me. Man, it was SO good to see her. But why did she look so unhappy? Had she already heard about Joseph and this was her solidarity rage? "Everything OK? You need a hand with anything?"

She stopped, and folded her arms.

"I'm not staying long." I knew that – we were only here for one night. "I just got off the phone to my dad."

"Is he all right?" Suddenly all the sadness I'd had about Joseph paused. Seeing Grace like this rugby tackled it way down the priority list.

She shrugged. "Sure. He was letting me know he'd got his work to sponsor some pretty amazing lights for Grampy G's Grotto." Wasn't this a good thing? "And he'd just been to drop them off at the village hall to get a head start." But that's when I remembered. Like a snowball in the face. *I'd never told Grace about the village hall.* "And they said you'd known from the start that we never had it booked?"

Oh no. Oh no, *oh no!*

"Oh my goodness, I meant to tell you…"

She raised her eyebrows. "And?"

I had to explain. I hadn't done it to ruin things. I'd done it so it was one less thing for her to worry about.

"Don't worry. I can explain. I was just waiting until…" Until I had the replacement. Oh no. A shudder went through me as I realized … I was meant to ring the yurt place this morning. Twelve p.m. was the cut off to confirm. And I'd completely and utterly forgotten.

I didn't have a replacement, did I?

"Until?" Grace waited for me to explain. To say there had been a mix-up. That it was all under control.

But the reality was, I'd really messed up – I'd been so caught up with Joseph.

"Grace, I'm SO sorry … I know it looks really bad but I promise, I can explain."

"All I need you to explain" – she was speaking so slowly, so calmly, her voice thick with anger – "is do we have somewhere to hold Grampy G's party? In forty-eight hours' time. Or do I have to head back to Bromster right now to tell everyone – all my family, Grampy G's friends in Holly Hospice that were looking forward to it, all the people travelling down, flying down! – that instead of celebrating Grampy G, I've just wasted their time? And probably money too."

Things with Joseph were bad, but nothing, NOTHING, felt as bad as me letting Grace down... Letting Grampy G down.

"Grace, I'm so sorry. I can sort it. I promise!"

But Grace shook her head, her disappointment so very clear.

"I guess that's my answer then." She grabbed the handle of her case. "My train home is leaving in four minutes."

"Please!" I shouted, as she turned to go. "Whatever you do, don't call it off!"

I was going to fix this!

But when she looked back, there was a tear rolling down her cheek.

"And you know the worst thing?" She stopped and caught her breath. "It's not even that you messed up." Her voice started to break. "It's that you said no more secrets – and I believed you."

CHAPTER

23

TO DO:

- *Find a venue / build a venue / JUST GET A VENUE*
- *Get Grace to talk to me (cookies?? Photos of Sosig in costumes??)*
- *Don't cry*
- *Buy waterproof mascara*

"Anything more from the Christmas Cheer menu?" One of our hotel waiters dressed as an elf offered a tray of reindeer-decorated breakfast muffins and Christmas-tree-shaped pastries. Could he not see I was one Christmas item away from bursting back into tears?!

I hadn't slept a bit. I'd spent the night staring at my

phone, hoping for Grace to read any of my messages, pick up any of my calls. At least let me explain.

All these years I'd thought the worst thing that could happen to me would be everyone finding out about that stupid Christmas song. About my elf past. About who my family really was.

But Grace being mad at me was worse. WAY worse.

Forget being an elf. I was the worst best friend on the planet.

I'd left messages begging her to not cancel Grampy G's Grotto, saying I'd sort it, even though I had no idea how – but I didn't even know if she'd got them.

And Joseph had rung and rung me, but I hadn't turned up to meet him and I think he was getting the message I didn't want to hear anything he had to say. His voice messages said the photo of Maeve wasn't what it looked like. Sure. That he didn't know how anyone had got the photo of us either.

Uh-huh

Blocking and deleting someone had never felt so good. I'd deleted my social apps too.

He'd never cared about me. Why would he? I was just stupid Little Elf Girl Molly. He'd probably shared our photo with someone for a laugh.

"Think we're OK for Christmas cheer," my mum

said softly to the waiter, who was staring in alarm at me stabbing my candy cane croissant like it was personally responsible for Grace not speaking to me. For Grampy G's Grotto being ruined. For me letting my guard down and trusting Joseph.

"Can I interest you in a paper instead?"

Why did I look up? WHY? As he flicked through options, right there on the front pages was that picture of Maeve and Joseph.

MERRY KISSMAS FOR *SLEIGH ANOTHER DAY* STAR COUPLE

I dropped my head on to the table, the expensive silver knives and forks rattling. I bet Elijah was already popping the champagne! Eurgh. Deep breath, Mol. Try not to be a Christmas grouch, not around Billy. But it was so hard when I was mad at everything – most of all myself.

"Think we'll go freshen up in our rooms," Mum said politely, allowing us to escape to the lifts.

"Don't worry, Mols…" Billy put her hand in mine, gluing us together with the chocolate spread that was all over her fingers. "Mum said we could go to Hamleys, and that makes *everything* better."

Oh yes, five floors of toys and bright lights and

Christmas and cheerful people, when all I wanted to do was lie in a dark room and wait till February, or whenever it was that Grace started speaking to me again. *If* she started speaking to me again.

"Sounds ace." I mustered all the smile I could. "You can give me some Christmas present ideas…" Although the only idea I really needed was how to save Grampy G's Grotto.

"Mols…" Mum whispered. She looked concerned. "Don't look now, but…"

Too late.

"I hoped I'd find you here." Joseph?!

What was he doing here?! I never wanted to see his face again, not even on a poster from very far away.

I turned my back as he hurried over, snow still on his hair and coat. "Hope it's OK to interrupt." It wasn't. "Hiya, Mrs B. Billy, cool hairclips."

They were sparkly with unicorns on. Billy normally had beef with unicorns as she felt they tried to steal horses' thunder, but these were cute.

I folded my arms. Read the room slash hotel lobby, Joseph. You're not wanted here.

"Surprised to see you so early, Joseph," Mum said frostily. "Seems you had quite the busy day yesterday." Mum gave him a cool micro-smile. Yes, Mum!

DING. The lift arrived. "And that's our cue to leave." Mum stepped straight in, holding Billy's hand. But I didn't move. I bet Joseph was so used to everyone sucking up to him because he was famous, but I was ready to tell him *exactly* what an idiot he was.

"My sister's the best, by the way," Billy called through the gap. "And you're terrible at riding. And unicorns aren't cool. Everyone knows that."

The doors snapped shut.

Yup. My family were the greatest.

"Molly." Joseph stepped between me and the lift. "Please can I explain? It's not what it looks like."

No comment. I'd give him no comment!

"What, you slipped, fell, landed on Maeve's face?"

Was I more mad about the kiss, that he'd shared the photo and it had ended up online, or that I'd been so honest with him and all he'd done was lie?

"It wasn't a kiss, I *promise*." He kept his voice low, looking round to check no one could hear. "Like I said, it was work?!"

Work? It was a couple selfie of him and Maeve!

Now I knew who he was, I noticed how many people stared wherever he went.

Well, let them look. They could find out who he really was.

"Work. Yeah, totally." I flashed the quickest fake smile. "Come to think of it, that's what all my photos with my *friends* look like too." I rolled my eyes. "Sorry, not friend. 'Better Half'." I was not going to hold back. I couldn't. "Oh, and nice work on sharing the photos with whoever. Nice touch. *Really* private." Joseph took a deep breath in, like he was composing himself. "In fact, why are you even here? Haven't you got some famous friends to hang out with? Not 'fans' like me." He was leaving the country in a few days; couldn't he just leave me alone?

"I'm here because I wanted to talk to you." He paused, his voice serious. "There's nothing going on with me and Maeve. Never has been."

"I was wrong about the acting, by the way. You're actually quite good."

I was done with this. Time to go. I pressed the lift button.

"Honestly, Mol."

I tried not to snort. Honest and him did not go together.

"Sure. I heard you tell the interviewer that." I hated that my voice was wobbling. I hated that I could picture his grin when he'd said it. "Heard you laughing at the 'just a fan' you'd been hanging out with."

"Mols." Joseph grabbed my arm. I shook his hand

straight off me. I wasn't his to touch. I jabbed the lift button on repeat. "It's not like that. That photo wasn't us kissing, it was Maeve and me goofing around. When I said I liked you, I meant it."

Liked me? Was he really so full of himself he thought I'd believe any of this?!

"And the whole 'fan' thing was just to keep you out of it, like I thought you wanted?"

Keep me out of it? Why had he shared our photos them?!

"Fine. Let's pretend for a second you didn't kiss Maeve despite the photo of the two of you basically kissing. For someone who *really* wanted to keep me out of it, sharing our photo was kind of an odd thing to do, right?"

"I didn't give anyone that photo!" He looked exasperated. Where was this lift? "Molly, please don't be like this. This is all a mix-up." He dug his hands in his pockets and looked down. "I really like you. Not Maeve. And I thought you liked me. For me. Even when you thought I was a no one."

And that's when I snapped ... faster than a Christmas cracker. But with no joke, or hat, or even tiny pencil sharpener.

"A no one, huh?" DING. The lift arrived. "Nice to

know that's what you think of people like me." I stepped in. "Have a nice life with your famous friends and all your adoring 'fans'."

The quicker I could get out of here, get back home, never see him again, the better.

I waited for the doors to close, but Joseph didn't leave. He didn't even budge as people pushed past him, getting in next to me. He just kept on looking at me.

"I promise, Mol. I promise I'm telling the truth." The lift went silent everyone loving being caught up in this drama. "This can't be how we leave things…"

But the lift doors shut. Just in time. Because my eyes were prickling with tears.

And I had no time left to waste on him. I had to use every second to fix things with Grace.

Grace – miserable back home. Her home without even a single piece of tinsel.

And even though I was in a lift full of strangers, I burst into tears.

CHAPTER
24

I'd been a terrible friend, so the least I could do was be a better big sister. I stuck out Hamleys, and even pretended to be excited about the furry knee-high horse that did fake furry poos.

But the second we were done, I raced down to the river to say goodbye to Harry and Jack before we headed home. Despite everything that had happened, I wanted to say thanks for all their help – especially the prizes for the fundraiser, even if I'd made one big mess of things.

I spotted Harry first. As usual he was goofing around but when he saw me, his smile broke. Guess he'd spoken to Grace. He left his friends and walked over. Had I ruined things with him too? I couldn't blame him. I'd even blown his last chance of seeing her yesterday.

"Harry. I'm an idiot. I'm going to make it up to her, I

promise. And to you. In fact, that's kind of why I'm here, I've got an idea… Well, that and to say goodbye."

Harry's face looked all wrong when it wasn't happy.

"OK." Phew, he was still talking to me. "I'm not taking sides but … this better be good." He paused. "As in the *idea*, not the *goodbye*. That can be anywhere from average up."

He smiled. And so did I, relieved to have not lost another friend too.

"Well, the goodbye will be adequate and the idea is the best one I have." I had no clue how he'd react, but with Grace not talking to me, it was the only thing I'd come up with so far to try and start putting things right. Instead of just sending her apologies or baking guilt cookies, I was going to raise more money for Grampy G's fundraiser, more money than Grace could ever have dreamt of. "What would you say if I asked you if you knew of a way of getting the login for the official *Sleigh Another Day* social accounts." I paused. I knew Harry had helped Elijah out with them the other day, so had access, but I also knew Elijah had sworn him to secrecy.

"Oooooh." Harry took a sharp breath. "I'd say the only way I can think of right now would very much end in Elijah knowing full well where you'd got it from and promptly telling my mum that I had actually gone to all the secret cast and crew parties I promised her I hadn't, and me being grounded till summer."

Yup. I had a feeling he'd say that. Oh well, it was worth a try. "OK. Well, that sounds awful. Definitely don't do that." I was done with causing problems for people. "I was just thinking of how I could raise shed loads of money for Grampy G and some unauthorized posts on the official accounts was the best plan I had." My idea had been to talk (well, beg) Elijah into letting me put up all the movie stuff Joseph had given us online, making one big public raffle, and promoting it on their social. Guess I'd just have to think of another idea.

"Gotcha." Harry nodded. "If I can think of a way to help, I will."

And, unlike Joseph, I believed him. Harry really was not a Simon. I gave him the biggest hug and said bye. It was weird, all this time I'd been looking forward to putting everything to do with the film behind me, I hadn't stopped to realize it would mean saying bye to some good things too. And it was time to do another. I headed up the steps to the make-up trailer, ignoring a picture of Joseph and Maeve taped up on the wall.

"There are some things concealer can fix." Jack looked up from his laptop, opening his arms up for a hug. "And there are some things that…"

But I'd already run over for a cuddle and stayed there for at least a minute. Jack made me feel like there was no pressure to explain or speak. I could just be sad. And I was really, really sad.

"For what it's worth, I really did think – *do* think – Joseph likes you." Jack leant forward, wiped under my eye and plonked me down into one of his spinny chairs. "Although, let's change the subject as that mascara does *not* look waterproof."

"It's fine." He didn't even know about Grace. "I just came to say bye."

"Already? I thought you coming to the big crew party tonight?" Everyone was having one big blowout before they finished up on the film or headed to Lapland for the final screening event.

"Change of plans. I need to get back ASAP. Sort something out." I sighed. "I kind of messed up with Grace."

Jack raised an eyebrow. "You wanna talk about it?"

I shook my head. "Nope."

He rubbed my arm. "Well, hang in there, Little Elf. Cos cute boys and girls and enbys, well … they come and go. But friends like you two? Sure, you can have bumps but you can also figure it out." He paused. I wanted so hard to believe him, but right now it felt patching things up would take a Christmas miracle.

"You really think so?"

"Course," he said softly. "We all make mistakes; we're human. I mean … I don't even want to show you the spotty trousers I wore to my first red carpet." Jack laughed. I was really going to miss him. "But you two will be OK. I saw those pictures of you posing it up in Edinburgh, and don't even try and tell me they weren't the cutest."

I laughed. He made me feel like maybe it could be OK.

Although…

"What pictures, Jack?"

"You and Grace. In the maze? Being all cute and ish!"

"Did Grace show you?" Jack shook his head. Something didn't feel right. "So how did you see them?"

Jack reached for his laptop. "All right, Agatha Christie. They're all here." He opened up a photo library and scrolled down. There were hundreds and hundreds of photos. From the events. From the red carpet. From Liverpool. Edinburgh. London. Selfies of crew. Posed pictures with the cast. Even ones where Stormoo had stolen the phone and was chewing the camera.

"What are all of these?!"

Jack nodded. "The production phones. They all sync straight to here…" He carried on scrolling. "To be honest, I don't think most of the crew even know, but that's because they don't bother reading paperwork. Still, makes for a good giggle."

He stopped on a selfie of a camera operator doing a full-on pout. But I wasn't laughing. I couldn't.

"Would you mind…" I reached out, my hands shaking.

But there they all were.

The photos of me and Grace in Edinburgh.

The photo of me and Harry from the pod. That had gone on the SleighAllTheDaysFans social and outed me as Elf Girl.

The photo of me and Ru on the bridge.

The photo of Maeve and Joseph that had been in all the papers today.

"And who has access to these?" My stomach clenched.

"Me. Cos I'm nosy and got added by mistake." Jack laughed. "The press team. And…" He shook his head. "No, that's it."

And that's when I knew.

I didn't know what was going on, but I knew Elijah had some serious explaining to do.

CHAPTER
25

I banged on the press door so hard security ran over.

I didn't care if Tim was inside having a meeting with the whole press team. I needed to find out what was going on.

"Molly?!" Elijah spotted me through the tiny window and flung the door open. "We're kind of in the middle of a brainstorm here."

"Can. We. Have. A. Word?" I said firmly. I was not being brushed off. "I think you know what about."

"Not now," Elijah hissed, looking back into the Portakabin to check no one was listening. "This is literally my last chance to impress them!"

Fine. Let's do this the hard way.

"I know it was you who leaked the photo of Joseph and Maeve. The blurred one of me too. And I'm not leaving until you tell me why." He went to speak, but I carried on. "No spin. I want the truth."

Elijah looked up to the sky and with a heavy sigh, shut the door.

"Two minutes, that's *all* I've got." But that's all I needed. I marched us over to an alleyway where we couldn't be overhead.

On the outside I was so cross, I'd switched into icy calm, but on the inside my heart was pounding.

"First up. Did Joseph give you that photo of him and Maeve?" I needed to hear it the truth. "Or the one of me?"

Elijah rolled his eyes. "Not exactly."

"Not *exactly*?" What did that mean?! "I'm going to need exacts."

"Look. I'm sorry, OK? It just got a little out of hand, that's all."

"Out of hand?!" *Deep breath, Molly.* "I've spent weeks doing your stupid events, letting you call the shots, trying to avoid your plan to reveal me as 'Elf Girl'." My mind was racing. "But none of it makes sense. And I know you're up to *something*?!" I thought back. "Day one, I met Joseph. And *someone* gave him my number." Which I didn't message, but then I'd bumped into him. Or had I?! "Then in Liverpool *someone* made him find me to give me my elf hat back. And hinted where I'd be in Edinburgh. And…" A new thought hit me. "Wait. A mysterious friend even arranged for a meal for the two of us, with full press, to happen in London?" Had Elijah been pulling strings from day one? "And not to mention, along the way, thanks to private photos being shared online, my entire town slash world has started calling me Elf Girl again?" Elijah didn't react.

If he even tried to tell me I was overreacting then he would see what overreacting really was. This was messier than a tangle of Christmas lights and it was time Elijah stepped up and helped me unravel it.

"Like I said, it got out of hand."

"*What* did, Elijah?"

He sighed again and sat down on the tiny wall. "You really want to know?"

"Every *single* thing."

"Fine." He sighed again, and rubbed at his normally perfect hair. "It *was* me who put those photos on the fan account. I run it. And that photo was one I made Maeve and Joseph take this week when I was getting the cast to recreate 'movie moments' for some online content we were filming. They never kissed, the angles made it look way closer than it was. I wanted the guys to see how good the shot looked. I got it off the production account." He shrugged. "Joseph seemed to have no idea I even had access to it? But I had all the pictures, from all the phones."

"So…" I let it sink in. "The kiss wasn't real?"

And Joseph hadn't given anyone the photo of me?

Elijah raised an eyebrow. "C'mon, Molly. You of all people should know they're not together. Never have been."

"What do you mean by that?"

"I mean." He cracked his neck. "You're right. I did try and get you two together. Well, at least give you the space to like each other. I could see how much he liked you from day one at the premiere. He thought he was being discreet, but he would not stop hassling me for your number. For what you were up to." Sorry what? Had Elijah really been playing some kind of cupid? This made zero sense. "But I also knew you'd freak if you knew who he really was."

"Sorry, I'm struggling to believe you were bothered about my love life?" Or Joseph's for that matter. All Elijah ever seemed bothered with was that stupid music video. His job. Christmas number one.

"C'mon. The up-and-coming actor, notoriously private, doesn't do press, dating the girl who happened to be the cute Little Elf Girl from the theme tune. What's not to love?"

Could he hear himself?! He did not care one bit. He was just using us to get something to fuel gossip columns?

This guy got worse and worse.

"I'm not a prop, Elijah! Some cardboard cut-out! You do know this is my actual life you've been messing with."

"Like I said, I *might* have got a bit carried away. And I tried to make sure you had the space to say no. I never would have really released that clip." Well, nice to tell me two weeks later. "But" – he shrugged – "if it helps, the him liking you bit was all totally real. All I did was make sure you guys got chances to see each other. Oh, and stop you seeing him when you'd painted yourself green."

He laughed softly, but I was NOT in a laughing mood.

"Chances?" My mind raced through all the weird coincidences. "The winning bid on the meet and greet for the raffle…"

"Three thousand pounds is not much from our budget, especially not if it secured some positive headlines with Joseph in for a change."

My head was spinning. No wonder Elijah had been so furious when I'd cancelled.

"And you were going to fully out me as Elf Girl at the same time?"

"Well, I thought it wouldn't hurt?"

I glared at him. He had gone way too far.

"Wouldn't hurt WHO? Because newsflash, this

whole thing has kind of made my life hell." He just looked at the ground. But it didn't add up. "And if you really wanted us to get together, why release that photo of Joseph and Maeve?"

Elijah looked me dead in the eye. "I didn't, Molly. I wanted a story. And last night, when you cancelled the meal, the nice, neat date pictures went away. And I had to get *something*. Tim had lined up all those media outlets. And then that picture of you and Joseph came through on the production account from his phone. You, looking so cute. It was the picture I needed all along! Way better than trying to get one in that photobooth in Liverpool?" So that had been a set-up too?! "So yesterday morning I gave Joseph a heads-up that someone might have photos of him on a date last night, and it was going to get released. I was hoping to get details. But he just begged me to do what I could to make sure no one would find out who he'd been with. That they were someone kinda special, who valued their privacy even more than him'." Joseph had said that? "In fairness, that's what made me blur your face. He even offered to speak to Maeve about faking some pics of them looking cosy together to offer out, to see if it would be enough to stop the press running any of the date pictures. But I already had what I needed."

So, Joseph had been telling the truth?

He'd never shared any of the photos on purpose. Instead he'd offered to get some of him and Maeve, despite knowing it would get the world talking about his private life, which he'd tried so hard to keep secret? Is that why he'd tried to brush everything off with the fan comment?

This was too much. My brain was overheating.

I couldn't believe Elijah had done this?!

And in the middle of it I kept seeing Ru's face at the lift. As I yelled at him.

"Elijah. I seriously cannot believe you did all of this." He had to know this was NOT OK. "You know you've made everything a trillion times worse, right?!"

"ELIJAH!" Tim yelled out the door. And that's when Elijah crumpled, his whole body, his face, losing the hardness they normally had.

"I just wanted to get that job, Molly. So bad. And it's been SO hard. I've spent every last penny trying to stay in London and hold this internship down. I needed to impress Tim. Everyone knew he was looking for a big story, and I thought what better than a love story as cute as the film. It really felt like my only hope." He was speaking quietly for a change. "And for what it's worth, I'm sorry. Really sorry. And if Joseph hadn't fled to Paris

I'd tell him the same too."

So Ru had gone? And thanks to Elijah I'd ruined any chance I'd ever had with him before he flew to Lapland, and then home to America.

"And you thought all this." I looked at him. He didn't look like the angry Elijah any more; he looked even more broken than me. "Blackmailing people. Sharing photos. Lying. *So* much lying. You really thought it was OK?"

Elijah shifted round to look at me. "You want me to be honest?" I nodded. "I don't think I thought at all. I was just so stressed, and we've been working on this film twenty-four/seven for months, and I'm..." He paused. "I'm sorry, Molly." He rubbed his face with his hands. "Really sorry."

I didn't know what to say. I couldn't believe Elijah had done this. But then I hadn't exactly been making great decisions either.

We both sat in silence for a minute. Until a furious Tim shouted again.

"ELIJAH. This is not acceptable?!"

Elijah stood up. "And if all of that doesn't make it bad enough, Tim's saying I still need to do more."

But maybe, just maybe, I had an idea for a real story Elijah could give him.

CHAPTER
26

TO DO:

- DON'T PANIC
- THINK POSITIVE
- ~~Don't look up a single picture of Ru in Paris, or read a single article about it however tempted or even write this bullet point as it's too depressing~~
- Put up 200 snowflakes

For someone who had run offstage a week ago, I couldn't believe what I was now doing. And that I was wearing my Scottish snowwoman jumper to do it. With tiny lights plaited into my hair. Billy's horse skills had come in most useful.

One by one I moved the miniature reindeer into the

hallway, the snowflakes I'd made dangling everywhere, and stepped outside, the morning air so cold my breath looked like steam. I refreshed what I'd posted last night on the *Sleigh Another Day* official account, my stupid grinning face filling up the whole screen, an elf hat jingling away as I chatted.

"Yup. The rumours are true. I'm Elf Girl. Me, Molly Bell. Or @mollythelolly. Nice to finally meet you. And I'm here to do what elves are meant to do best. Spread some Christmas cheer. Consider it an early Christmas present. Because if you love @SleighAnotherDay we have all the exclusive, behind the scenes prizes you could ever want! Including…"

I jingled some bells

"…giving you the chance to get to meet the cast on a once-in-a-lifetime trip to Lapland! There's no limit to the number of tickets you can buy in this exclusive raffle But be quick as it's only open for forty-eight hours. So, take part, like, share, tell your mates, do whatever you can – because this isn't just an awesome prize, it's the chance to raise money for @TheHollyHospice in Bromster, all in the name of the best Christmas elf there ever was, Grampy G."

I put my hands over my eyes as I watched me awkwardly throw a peace sign to the camera. And for the first time in seven years say the words: "Happy holidays from the cutest little elf in the whole wide world!"

I'd physically folded in embarrassment. I wasn't sure if Grace would see it, but that wasn't the only reason I'd done it. I'd done it because Grace was right – secrets had only ever made things worse so it was time to get it all out in the open. And what better way to do it than by helping Grampy G's fundraiser?

I'd even taken my own profile off private. I was done hiding. The post had had over 13,000 likes already. Yes, I'd had to beg Tim for the Lapland tickets, and had to get Elijah to talk him into letting me put all the other prizes online, but I'd offered to do it along with my elf reveal video and Tim had eventually said yes – I think mainly to get me out of his office. Clearing the posts with them also meant they never needed to know Harry had given me the login details after all. What a guy, risking getting grounded for life, all to support the fundraiser and help me try and make things up to Grace.

Beep, beep, beep.

A loud mechanical noise brought me back to where I was. Watching Elijah in a high-vis jacket, next to Mum, Dad and Billy, aka a turkey, a parsnip and a tiny horse, directing empty trucks into the church car park near our house.

When the trucks started arriving at 6 a.m. the whole village had come out to stare, but two hours later and the whole place was buzzing – all our neighbours bringing tea and biscuits for the crew.

Everywhere was chaos! Would this all be done by half six tonight? That's when I'd asked Grace to be here with her dad, after they'd finished playing minigolf for his birthday. All I'd told her was that I'd planned a big Christmas surprise and I hoped she'd like it. Not that she'd replied.

"I have to give it to you, Molly." Elijah stepped next to me, as we watched my dad manhandle a giant snowman through our garden gate. "You weren't wrong when you said you lived in a village that looked like a Christmas card."

It really did. Last night's snow had settled on the sloping cottage roofs and as more and more of the pieces of the *Sleigh Another Day* set got put in place, the more it looked even better than the film.

"Do you think this will work?"

Elijah rolled his eyes. "I think it has to after I dragged everyone up to Remotesville."

I elbowed him, but we both laughed. We knew full well he wouldn't have done it if he didn't think it was a good idea. Shooting the music video he'd been desperate for. Right here at the home of The Brussel Shouts. In our house crammed with decorations, in our garden that was as bright as Las Vegas, in our village, with all our neighbours at the ready in their Christmas jumpers. Sosig had even had a moustache and beard trim for the occasion. I wasn't going to be in the video, my confession on social media was more than enough elf-ing for me, but this was just what I wanted.

I might have messed up things with Grace, and with Ru, but I didn't have to mess up Grampy G's Grotto. If Elijah wanted a music video, and Tim wanted a big final idea, they could have one. Bigger and better than they'd imagined. And once the cameras stopped rolling, I'd sorted the sets and all the lights staying on for the evening so me and my family could throw the best party Grampy G could ever have imagined. The ultimate Christmas street party. The ultimate Grampy G's Grotto.

We had everything. Snow machines, the igloos, the archways, the trails of baubles, the mechanical robins, all of it. The only thing missing was the giant sleigh pulled by reindeers, but Elijah said London to Bromster was a long way for them to travel when they had the entire globe to do on Christmas Eve next week.

I crossed my fingers. Please let this look good. It was a simple video, The Brussel Shouts performing, a crowd cheering along, lots of hand-held-style filming, Christmas stuff in every direction. I wanted it to be good for SO many reasons, but mainly because Tim and Elijah had agreed that every single stream would raise a tiny bit of money for Grampy G's Grotto fund.

It was so surreal seeing it all here. The night before last I'd sent out an urgent email to all the people who had originally said they were coming to Grampy G's party, telling them it was still on, but that there had been a top secret special change of plan. I hoped at least a few turned up. I'd asked everyone to get here for half five, just in time to record the performance and big crowd scene and then stay for the party to celebrate Grampy G. I'd promised Elijah I could sort a crowd if he sorted everything else, so had invited loads of randoms too – my netball team, people in my year, anyone I could think of, and my family had done the same. I'd even asked Zaiynab and Matt. And Mia, the waitress who had recognized me in the cafe.

But there was really only one person I cared about turning up. Grace. My stomach cramped thinking about her. Grace, who still wasn't speaking to me.

Please let her come. *Please* let her like this.

My eyes moved to the giant poster outside the village shop that I'd helped the art department make to cover up their real signs. A vintage poster of Grampy G as Father Christmas with Grace when she was a little girl, sitting

362

on his lap. I smiled at him. I really hoped this elf was doing OK.

"We'll be on camera in two hours…" Elijah flicked through some papers on his clipboard. "Midday prompt we start rehearsals. Then shoot street and details. Crowd arrive at five thirty p.m. Filming performance at six thirty p.m. Not a lot of time for takes, but rough and ready is the perfect vibe." He peered over at our house. "Very suitable for The Brussel Shouts."

He looked at me – and smiled.

Things with Elijah had changed since we'd had that chat. The last few days he'd worked round the clock to help me pull this off, constantly checking in that I was OK – and as grumpy as he liked to pretend to be, I could see his relief it was working out. He'd even tried to help me smooth things over with Ru.

But when I'd messaged him saying sorry and asking to chat, all I'd got back was, "Sure. When things are less busy." And we both knew with him, things were never less busy. I couldn't really blame him.

"Joseph and Maeve would have *adored* this." Jack came and stood where Elijah had just left. "Shame they're on a plane to Lapland."

It really was. I'd had my chance with Ru. And I'd blown it.

"And one last time…" Jack put his arm around me. All morning he'd been hanging out with Billy, making my mum look super glam (for her tiny bit of face peeping out between the turkey legs), blow-drying Tess's hair and being an absolute hero. "Is there any way I can talk you into making an appearance?" He squeezed my shoulders. "I left a full costume in your room. Because, who knows, in ten years' time you might regret being the only one of your family who's missed out?"

I doubted it. The only thing I'd regretted about the original one was being in it.

"Oh! Little Elf! Little Elf!"

The first line of the song blared out of the speakers so loudly I jumped in the air.

"Positions!" the director yelled. Harry was such a legend for talking his mum into doing this for free, although it was gutting he couldn't come with her. "Ready for rehearsal, please…"

I looked over at the stage. It stretched right across the road from the end of our garden to the pavement opposite. It was glittery and green and looked like a giant cracker had landed in Bromster. There were lights whizzing about all over it and in the middle of it was Billy, trotting around in a reindeer suit, Mum, pinching the bum of a giant parsnip (may potentially need therapy for that image), and

Tess looking like a movie star in a sequinned red-and-green dress, working a mega pout. And behind them all, on our front lawn, was Cara, all lit up. Yup, my family were all absolutely bonkers. But they were *my* bonkers.

And despite everything that had happened, I felt something bubbling up.

Something that felt like excitement. But also, home.

The same feeling I'd got with Grace, Dad and Mr W on the train to Edinburgh.

And singing in Cara with Mum and Billy.

And making silly socks with Tess.

Was *this* what Christmas magic felt like?

I looked at my family onstage. And smiled.

Forget all the flashy events. This year, despite everything, my Christmas spirit had finally come back, and it was all thanks to these guys, to Grace.

And right then, I made up my mind.

It was time to stop watching and go inside.

Thirty minutes later Jack and I walked back out the front door. Billy spotted me first, running over and throwing her arms around me. Mum, Dad and Tess were still onstage rehearsing. I walked up the steps towards them, Bil clinging on to my leg like a koala bear. As I got to the top step she screamed, "LOOOK!!!!"

All three of them stopped dead and gawped. At me. Their middle daughter, head to toe bright green, wearing a stripy dress with jagged pointy red collar and cuffs, big gold buttons down the front, red-and-white stripy socks that came up to my knees and the longest, pointiest green hat with a bell on. I'd even brought my bass guitar out in public for the first time ever.

For a second no one said anything.

But then, in unison, Mum and Dad both ran (well, waddled as quickly as a parsnip and turkey could) and bundled me into a big hug.

"Molly Natasha Bell!" Mum squeezed me so hard one of her drumsticks bashed me on the head. "I have *never* been more proud of you."

Good to know all my studying, my design, all my sports stuff, my kitchen creations, paled into insignificance over dressing as an elf.

Dad rubbed my cheek (although stopped when he realized he was making his hand green). "You, my darling, are the best elf in … all the land…' Uh-oh. Was his voice cracking? "You always were. And…" *sniff*, "look at you now." He gulped. "I'm sorry, Ange. Can you … hold the fort?" He sniffed, his eyes welling up. "I think this is a Christmas present that has tugged a little too hard at this parsnip's heartstrings."

And he ran offstage, to where Jack was already holding out a tissue.

"SNOW MACHINE READY!" Harry's mum yelled. OK. This was happening. "SLATES."

A woman shouted, "'Love Your Elf!' music video. Rehearsal one," and snapped a clapperboard shut. This was just like the movies!

Except…

There was my house. And my still bleary-eyed dad. And Mum and Tess standing back-to-back ready to shimmy. And my furry reindeer little sister clutching Sosig's sleigh bed, with him sitting on it like a throne despite, being dressed as a carrot.

Was I having an "overdone it on the Quality Street" dream?! Or had Hollywood really come to Bromster, with me and my family at the centre of it all?!

WHAT HAD I DONE?

"And … ACTION!"

The song started. My family began jumping about. They looked totally ridiculous!

And I … bounced right over and jumped along with them, pretending to play my bass. Our neighbours were clapping in time, loving it.

It wasn't exactly playing onstage with The POWR, but weirdly, it felt great.

And after a few more run-throughs, it was time to break for an early dinner.

"Back here for half five, then we'll bring on the normals!" Elijah yelled, when we finished.

Lucky my microphone didn't pick up my whimper.

What if no one arrived? The whole video, the whole party, would be a flop!

I sat on the stage drumming my feet against the front of the cracker, bits of glitter shimmering down. It was dark now and with everyone inside grabbing food it was weirdly quiet.

But when five thirty hit, not one person had turned up. I sat staring left, staring right, waiting for a single car, a single new person to appear.

And fifteen minutes later, there was still not one arrival. And less than an hour till I'd asked Grace to come down. I looked at the poster of Grampy G. Please let this work! Please let any of the people I'd invited arrive?! Please let Grace turn up!

But by six p.m. my hope had disappeared and panic had taken its place. My nightmare was coming true. I'd messed up my last chance to save Grampy G's party.

It was time to put Elijah on alert. There was no massive crowd.

Although, where was Cara?!

A loud honk rang out.

IT'S CHRIIIIISSSTTTTTMAAAAASSSSS.

Cara?

I spun round! There she was! Dad behind the wheel, Billy next to him, Cara's lights flashing as she beeped her way down the street. Dad screeched up on to the pavement and jumped out.

"Bit later than planned." He slid the door open. Squished together like sardines, but with loads of grey hair and tinsel, were all of Grampy G's very best friends from Holly Hospice. "Had to stop and get Maude some Baileys. Said George, sorry Grampy G, wouldn't approve without."

Maude waved two bottles in the air, not even flinching at being greeted by an elf. But maybe when you've been driven by a parsnip and a reindeer you stop caring. OH, JINGLE BELLS. Had Dad gone into Tesco dressed as a parsnip?

"Where do you want us to stand?" Maude's hair was shimmering with gold glitter. "Somewhere near the front please. I've got my hopes set on getting a call from that lovely Rock fellow and getting whisked away for some senior shenanigans," she chuckled. "Oh, and my best side is my left."

And out she climbed. Followed by seven more elderly

people, all excitedly chatting away, dressed in the most amount of sparkle – flashing earrings, deeley bopper headbands – you name it, if it was a Christmas accessory, they had it. And a car full of carers had just pulled up to make sure they were safe in their wheelchairs and frames. Michelle, who had been so amazing at looking after Grampy G, was just standing, taking it all in. The set, the poster of Grampy G, the lights, the arches, the cameras, the snow machines. When she saw me she came straight over, putting her hands either side of my face.

"He would have LOVED this, you know. Every bit of it. Finding out it was going ahead after all put *such* a spring in their steps." We looked over to the Holly Hospice crew gathered around the stage, waving their props and even dangling fake mistletoe. "Honestly. With this, and all the money you've raised, you and Grace," she said, her voice breaking, "you just don't know what you've done for us."

And she hugged me. Hard. And as she did, more and more cars started to arrive. And people started tottering in heels down our little village road all ooooohing and and taking photos as they saw the set for the first time.

People WERE coming! This WAS working.

For once, I'd managed to organize something that had actually gone to plan!

Now all I needed was Grace and her dad to turn up.

"Sorry we're late." Dad's friend from aqua aerobics waved at me. "I know you said six, but all the traffic on those country roads? Hope we haven't missed anything."

I'd said SIX? Not half five?!

Yup, I was never organizing anything again.

But there were so many faces I recognized. And … wait…

Was that … Simon?

A really grumpy Simon? Being forced into a Christmas tree suit by Elijah? Yup, I was starting to love that man. Next to him was someone fussing around, brushing down his hair. Brenda, Simon's mum, who worked with Dad. My parents must have invited her, and she must have dragged along Simon. And he was hating every second. How brilliant.

I smiled and waved as Jack clipped on bauble earrings to a protesting Simon. "Remember, more is more, Jack!" I yelled.

"I'm not going to say anything about how evil that laugh was," a voice said behind me, with a very familiar laugh. I turned round.

"You're here?!" I gave Harry the biggest hug.

"Where there's a worried little elf, there's a way…" He grinned, but he was scanning over my shoulder.

"No sign of her yet." I crossed my fingers. "Harry. What if she doesn't show?"

It was only ten minutes till she was due, and Grace was never late.

"She will." I really hoped so. Especially now. Earlier I'd asked Elijah to dangle the largest bunch of mistletoe they could find above the bench where Grace and I always hung out, *just in case* Harry did turn up, and *just in case* Grace took him there. Because just in case she had started to feel different about him, it could be my little helping hand for her own movie-perfect Christmas moment. I'd ruined mine, but I still had hope for hers.

But we were being called into positions, ready for one last rehearsal.

And I finally got a response from Grace.

Grace: *Hi Molly. So you know, we're not going to be able to get to yours*

CHAPTER
27

My stomach twisted. I'd failed. Big time.

It was great we were raising more money for Holly Hospice, but there was no Grampy G's Grotto without Grace and her dad.

I put down my guitar and walked to the edge of the stage. I couldn't do this after all. My phone vibrated again.

Grace: *sorry, pressed send too soon. I meant can't get to yours cos there are too many cars everywhere. Weird. Just walking past the post office now.*

So she WAS coming!

WHOOP!

I punched the air like a cheesy sports coach.

"She's here!!!!" I yelled to anyone – to everyone! "Harry! I'll give you a missed call when we're at the corner and you give the cue."

"Roger," he said with a firm nod. But I was already running down the street.

And when I got round the corner, I spotted Grace and her dad. It was so good to see her, even if we only greeted each other with an awkward wave and "hi".

"Mols." Grace looked at me suspiciously. "I want to say 'you haven't done anything weird, have you?' but the fact you're the colour of a blade of grass is making me worried…"

"My new Christmas look…?" I said, convincing no one. My voice was shaking with nerves. "Anyway, follow me." I started to walk towards my house, my legs trembling. I didn't just want to tell Grace how sorry I was, I wanted to show her. "And happy birthday, Mr W."

"Thank you, Molly. I've had a wonderful birthday with Gracey, so I hope you haven't gone to any trouble." Mr W said softly. But I knew there would have been a big Grampy-G-shaped hole for the both of them.

"All I can say is…" I dialled Harry from my pocket. "I hope you like it. And Grace" – I lowered my voice – "I know how rubbish I've been. And I'm so sorry. But from now on, no more secrets, I promise. From now on everything, EVERYTHING, is quite literally out in the open."

And that's when we turned the corner. And onstage my parents started the biggest cheer, all the crowd joining

374

in. The loudest were Grampy G's hospice friends, who were waving everything they had in the air, even walking sticks with lights twirled round.

"Wha…" Grace came to a stop, completely stunned. Her dad looked even more shocked, and reached for her hand. "W-w-what is this?"

"Seeing as I made such a massive mess with the venue for Grampy G's party, I thought we could do it here instead." I took a deep breath. *Please let them like this. Please!* "I really hope you like it."

"Is that…" Grace stared down the street, taking it all in. The Brussel Shouts on the stage. The wooden chalets from Edinburgh. The Christmas trees lining the pavements. The baubles and archways from the film now decorating the little houses on our street. Harry, who was waving both arms in the air.

"No…" Grace was shaking her head. Did she hate it? Oh no. She hated it! And her dad was just blinking.

Was this yet another mistake?!

"Oh no." I put my hand over my face. "I thought this would be a good idea. They needed a music video and I wanted to save Grampy G's Grotto, and do something that he would love for you guys and…"

But that's when Mr W put his hand up. "Molly. Please, stop." He took a deep breath. "My dad would have

LOVED this." I saw him squeeze Grace's hand. "*We* love this, don't we, Gracey?"

"We … we really do," Grace mouthed, her lips wobbling as a tear rolled down her face. And for the first time in days, she gave me a smile.

Mr W lowered his head. "And we love you, Molly."

And that's when Grace pulled both me and him in for a hug.

"Mol, this is the best Christmas present you could have ever given us." She hugged me again. "Friends?"

And it felt better than any present in the world.

Harry gave the signal and The Brussel Shouts burst into "Winter Wonderland", Grace and her family's favourite song. Mr W threw off his coat, grabbed Grace, and waltzed around the street, the whole crowd immediately joining in. I loved watching their family who had flown down from Newcastle dancing over and surprising them. Grace and her dad only stopped when they spotted the poster of Grampy G, and in amidst all the chaos the two of them stopped, put their arms around each other and smiled. The biggest smile. Just like Grampy G would have wanted. Just like I promised him I'd try and make happen.

That even though he was gone, his family would always carry on finding Christmas magic.

My work here was done.

Well, it would be, if we now didn't have the full music video to film. Argh! This suddenly felt real. Way too real!

But as the director called "action" on our first take, real snow began to fall. And as we sang and bounced round, the crowd joining in, I had one of my weirdest Christmas thoughts yet.

Did I actually quite like "Love Your Elf!"? Because I seemed to be smiling. In fact, I was *loving* singing along. And loving that so many people were singing along with us – including … was that Matt and Zaiynab? And people from the year above who must have heard what was going on and had all turned up in Christmas jumpers, trying to get in on the action. I gave them a big elfy wave. Christmas grudges were so last term.

And as the last take started, and I waved down, a big grin on my face, an even bigger thought snuck in. Was it just the song I liked? Was this how it felt to finally like … me? Just as I was. Bright green, looking ridiculous, laughing my head off.

I hadn't been ready at the end of term show. But I was ready now.

Up here, on this stage, with my family next to me, my house flashing away behind us, my best friend leaping around with Harry, a smile back on her dad's face, I felt the happiest I had done in years.

I was done hiding. I didn't care what anyone else thought. From now on, I cared what I thought.

World. This is who I am. The real Molly Bell. And … I like it.

I just wished I didn't have that niggling feeling that something was missing. And I knew exactly what.

Jay.

I wished I'd had the chance tell him in person how sorry I was. How much I liked him. Really, really liked him.

"CUUUUUUT!" the director yelled, even though we were only midway through the song. She didn't look happy and stood up on her chair, grabbing her megaphone. "THIS PERFORMANCE IS LACKING SOMETHIING."

Uh-oh. I looked over at my dad, who was currently on the floor having just abandoned doing the worm. I wasn't sure we had that much left to give. The director stalked her way over to Elijah. "ANY IDEAS?"

But that's when I noticed she was trying not to smile.

Elijah grabbed the megaphone. "GOOD TOTALLY SPONTANEOUS QUESTION. BECAUSE THIS VIDEO SHOULD REALLY … SLEIGH!"

Ding!

Everyone gasped – as thousands of lights all the way down the street towards the church flicked on.

And wait. What was that noise?! Where was it coming from? The whole crowd shushed as we craned to see.

Was it … bells?

Or was it…

"HORSES!!!!!!!!!" Billy leapt off the stage like a flying squirrel in her fluffy suit. She landed on Grace and Harry. "No! Reindeer!!"

And she was right.

There was a clip-clop of hooves as a light flickered in the dark.

There they were. Some reindeer. Was that Derek? Pulling the sleigh from the film, with Father Christmas and his very own elf holding the reins.

Elijah had got the *Sleigh Another Day* sleigh!

"PLACES!" Harry's mum yelled. "We've only got one take guys. So, from the top…"

My family and I grabbed our instruments and for one last time began to play, the sleigh slowly rolling nearer and nearer to the stage. The crowd, who were all singing along and waving their hats, their lights, whatever they had, parted as it pulled up. Santa was waving, clutching a huge sack of presents. Next to him an elf hopped about ringing a stick with bells on. Finally, an elf more embarrassing than me! As they made their way into the crowd, Father Christmas handed out presents to the Holly Hospice residents. With the snow and everything, it was so magical it almost felt like the real Santa Claus was here.

Grampy G would have loved it.

And as we started the last chorus, Father Christmas and the elf joined us onstage, which soon became one big stage invasion led by Mr W and Grace.

Yes, this last month had all been a shock, but maybe being an elf wasn't so bad after all.

CHAPTER

28

I wasn't sure I was ever going to sing anything ever again with my family, so when my famous last line came, I looked right into the camera, just as the director had asked, and gave it some serious elf-welly.

"Happy holidays from the cutest little elf in the whole wide world!"

I'd done it. We'd done it.

But no one called cut. The cameras kept on filming.

And the other elf stepped up to the mic next to me.

"Don't forget about me!" he sang into the mic, in a truly terrible, squeaky elf voice. What was going on?! The crowd cracked up – whistling, cheering, laughing. What was he doing? And why was he taking off his green elfy beard? His green elfy hat? His black-rimmed glasses with candy canes on?

I should have guessed when I saw beautiful red curls sticking out from under Santa's grey hair. But I hadn't had a clue.

"May I?" my rival elf asked. I could only muster a nod.

But the elf? He held up some mistletoe. Leant in. And kissed my cheek.

What ... the? The crowd went wild. Grace climbed on Harry's shoulders.

Was Joseph D I-Hate-Christmas Chambers dressed as an elf?

Was Joseph D I-Don't-Talk-About-My-Private-Life Chambers kissing me in front of the world?

Was Joseph D I-Should-Be-In-Paris Chambers in Bromster?

Wait. Once more.

Did Joseph D Chambers just kiss me?

"AND THAT'S A WRAP!" Harry's mum yelled. The crowd whooped. But I was in elf-shock. "Great job, guys. Excellent cameos from Joseph and Maeve." *Was Ru really here?* "Parsnip and turkey, I didn't think the twerking was going to work but somehow it did." My dad yelled "turk-ing!", making the crowd giggle. "It's going to look awesome. And Molly – great surprised face! You can stop now though, the cameras are off." *Was Joseph D Chambers here?* "So, let's get some music on and start this party, because I've heard all about Grace's wonderful granddad, and now the boring bit's done, we're all here to party like Grampy George would want us to!" *Had Joseph D Chambers forgiven me?!*

"There'll be raffles and quite a lot of biscuits to buy – so dig deep and raise money for Holly Hospice." The front row whooped! "And, most importantly, have fun!"

And with a big cheer the party kicked off.

But I was still standing at the mic, blinking. I looked down at Grace who was grinning up at me, loving what was happening.

Did Joseph D Chambers just kiss me?

Maeve whipped off her Santa hat and hair and leant over. "All his idea. Told him we'd look ridiculous." She tugged at her beard. "But he said that was the point." She laughed, as next to her the cutest green face smiled at me.

"Just call me Jos-elf." Joseph scrunched his face, embarrassed. "No, that doesn't work, does it."

"And this is where I leave you to it." Maeve gave me a hug and stepped back, waggling her big bushy white eyebrows. "Thanks for getting me out of that red carpet dress, by the way. Total saviour. Now I just have to hope your sister digs girls with serious facial hair…" and she walked off.

My sister? *What?!* But Joseph?! *WHAT EVEN*

MORE?!

And it was just the two of us.

Two elves on a stage. A sleigh in front of us. My house behind us.

It wasn't a surprise I had no idea what to say.

"To be honest, when I heard the music video was actually happening, I worried you might bail on the whole elf thing. So, I thought what's better than doing it by yours-elf?... Doing it by ours-elf-s." He shook his head. "Sorry. Too much elf. I'm nervous, OK?"

He's nervous?!

What about me?! In a daze I walked down off the stage and into the crowd – the few seconds' break allowing me to remember how to speak.

"But … how. What… Who?" OK, maybe not back to fully speaking. "And in case you hadn't worked it out from all the messages. Can I just say, one more time, I'm sorry."

"You can." Ru smiled. "But you don't have to. What matters is that you know who I really am, and not who you think I might be?" He paused. "And that Maeve and I are just…" He laughed. "Maeve and I."

I nodded. Who he was, was someone who had guarded his privacy his whole life. Tried to protect mine. And dressed up as an elf and given me a kiss in public.

Here he was, willing to look a fool in front of all these

people, knowing what the papers would say, giving me a kiss, ending all the Maeve rumours even though he normally kept his private life private, all for me.

"And it matters that you know who I am too," I said. Because he hadn't been the only one hiding things.

He nodded. "Mol, my whole life, things hardly ever felt real. Not until I met you. So, if dressing up as an elf is the way to somehow make you take that seriously," he laughed, "then so be it."

Well, that was the nicest thing he could have said. I needed to say something just as articulate back. Maybe tell him how much I liked him?

But right now words weren't my strong point.

"But you're here. In Bromster. How did you even know? "

Joseph looked to Elijah a few metres away, clutching a clipboard.

Elijah smiled. Guess I'm a romantic after all." He raised an eyebrow. "And don't look so shocked. I *can* do nice surprises too. Hashtag sleigh. Hashtag star-crossed lovers. Hashtag think I'll leave you to it." He stopped. "And yes, this time, no photos. My lips are sealed."

But Ru and I were overdue a chat, so I took him to my and Grace's favourite bench. As I led the way Ru took my hand – it felt amazing. But as we pushed through the crowd I bumped straight into two people who were full on dancing, limbs everywhere. Matt and Zaiynab.

"Mol! That was INCREDIBLE!" Zaiynab hugged me.

"Thanks," I said, awkwardly.

"And before you mention it, can we just say sorry for the radio silence about the band?"

Ru squeezed my hand, the penny dropping. "Hold up. Are you guys The POWR?"

Matt nodded, hardly able to speak. "POWR. Yes."

Zaiynab rolled her eyes. "Ignore him. He's kind of a big fan. But seriously, Mol, we wanted to explain. We went quiet because we were working out what to do; if we needed more people. Not cool, I know. We should have just got in touch."

Yeah, she should have. But I shrugged. "It's OK."

We'd all made mistakes recently.

"But now we just saw we what we saw, we wanted to ask. How would you fancy producing and … playing bass for us?"

What?! "If you'll still have us, that is? We can still all write the material together like we talked about?"

But that would mean being onstage? Not behind the scenes.

"But what if everyone thinks I'm … I dunno … awful. Bad at guitar. Write cheesy songs."

But Ru leant over and softly said, "And what if they don't?"

And he was right. I'd spent too long hiding.

"You know what? Forget that, I'm in!" And just like that, I was officially the final part of The POWR. And what was lovely is that Zaiynab and Matt looked even happier than me.

What a day! But I still needed somewhere private to speak to Ru. We headed to the bench and, trying to ignore the giant bunch of mistletoe above our heads, sat down.

"So, you're not mad at me then?" I paused. "Or in Paris or Lapland, for that matter?"

Ru grinned. Was it wrong to find a green elf sexy?

"Yeah, I'm neither of those things. Lapland flights have been pushed back, and who needs a capital of culture when you have ... Bromster, right?"

I nodded, trying to look as serious. "That's what they say."

"Although..." He looked at his watch. "My train back to London is in about hour, so it's going to be tight to squeeze in a tour?"

He'd done all of this to come and support me for a couple of hours?

"Stay," I said, before I could think of all the reasons not to. "If you want to. Mum and Dad won't mind and we've got air mattresses we can blow up in the lounge. Maeve too." Was I really inviting Hollywood royalty to stay on my floor? To potentially wake up and get licked in the face by Sosig, or worse, see my dad in Lycra on his morning run? To be thrown totally into my bonkers family and even more bonkers house? Yes, I was. "Then you can stay for the party, properly meet everyone, and, y'know..."

"Hang out with you some more?" Ru smiled. OK, I officially fancied an elf. "I'd really like that."

I laughed. "Careful what you wish for. There's a Christmas pudding costume with your name on it. Mum'll have you in it in no time."

But even despite that, he stayed. And partied, posing for selfies with fans, not taking off his ridiculous costume, or the green paint, and he and Maeve even got back onstage to do the auction. In total, with all the online bids, we ended up raising over eight thousand pounds for Holly Hospice, much to the delight of everyone, including the local paper, who turned up to take photos. I don't think they were expecting to see Joseph and Maeve posing with some of the winners, but they probably didn't expect there to be a prize that was "Banjo lesson with the turkey" either.

It was awesome. The whole evening, Mr W was grinning from ear to ear or hugging someone he recognized from the crowd, and by the time the evening ended he was head to toe in Christmas accessories. And Grace and Harry hung out the whole evening – dancing, and drumming up bids. Grace even went onstage to say a few words about Grampy G ... which was amazing. And got even more amazing when, after disappearing for a bit, she came back onstage in a pair of my leggings and baggy Christmas jumper and, with the lights dipped low, a spotlight on her, did the *Nutcracker* dance she'd wanted to do for Grampy G last year. I wasn't sure who cried more. Her dad or mine.

Maybe me and Harry too. I was so glad I'd managed to tell Grace how he'd risked getting in so much trouble to help me get the fundraiser on the official accounts. Not that he'd mentioned any of it to her. He was the opposite of Simon, who, with no one chatting to him, had sloped off as soon as the party started.

The whole evening was perfect. But as it rolled around to midnight, the crew needed to get going and everyone drifted off. And *Sleigh Another Day* got packed up for one last time.

And as I lay in bed that night, Grace on the floor next to me, the entire thing felt like one big, weird dream.

Except, if I was dreaming, then I wouldn't be able to hear Sosig scrabbling at the lounge door trying to get to two of the world's biggest stars asleep on our floor.

Joseph D Chambers was downstairs.

And, ready or not, was only hours away from a Bell family breakfast, in full matching pyjamas.

CHAPTER

29

I wasn't sure what to expect when I went downstairs, but a neatly packed-up airbed and folded mattress, Ru with wet hair playing horse snap with Billy, was not it. I'd left Grace snoring away as she had dance rehearsal soon and last night, after we'd chatted till it was almost light, she'd told me to "do what I needed to do". The only problem was, I had no idea what that was or how to do it.

"Mooornin'," Ru said, totally unfazed as I walked in messy-haired, in my Christmas pudding pyjamas. "I see me and the excellent pyjamas meet again." I grinned. Wet-hair Ru was even better than this morning's advent chocolate. "Your sister is thrashing me. As in, I have zero points right now. Oh, and Maeve says bye and thanks. And something about going to Over Easy?" It was Tess's favourite brunch spot. Tess was wise. She'd cleared her out of the way before the rest of our family descended. I really had no idea the two of them had been messaging. But now I knew why Tess had been so giddy about the new girl she was seeing.

"Did you sleep OK?" I held out an orange juice. Ru was wearing my Edinburgh snowwoman jumper. "Or were you too busy raiding my wardrobe?"

"This old thing?" He pulled the nose off and on. "Is all mine. You inspired me up in Edinburgh." *Edin-in-borooo*. Still made me swoon. "Thought we could be matchy."

Billy was giving him a funny look.

"Why do you say things so weird?" Billy asked. I clobbered her round the head with a cushion.

"Ignore her. She's inhaled so much horse over the years she's forgotten what manners are."

But Ru was smiling. And he was still smiling over breakfast, as we sat through Dad's retelling of the time he fell off the roof while trying to put up Christmas decorations. And he was still smiling when the two of us moved the mini herd of reindeer into the lounge, almost at our tree. And he was still smiling as we headed out, in the biggest snowstorm ever, in matching jumpers, to see the glorious sights of Bromster. The village shop! The pond! The bin that looks slightly like a Dalek!

And he was smiling even more when we walked past Grace's house and spotted a Christmas tree up in their window. Mr W gave us a big happy wave as he whistled away, decorating it. In fact, did he have one in Grace's bedroom and two in the garden?! He must have nabbed them from the set yesterday! I LOVED to see it! And Ru kept on smiling when I told him what Grace had told me last night. That Harry had asked her out on a date and she'd said yes.

And he was still smiling when we headed back to yesterday's bench, to build our very first snow person. And snow dog. Which we called Snowmy and Snowmoo. And Ru confessed he'd hidden a pickle decoration on our tree.

And he was still smiling when I dared him to make a snow angel, which turned into an accidental snow fight.

And he was still smiling when we were sitting on the bench, soggy with melted snow.

The only time we both stopped smiling was the moment I knew Grace had been right all along. And I was wrong.

Because as we kissed on the bench, Ru tasting of gingerbread syrup, I realized that maybe, sometimes, real-life happy endings could be even more magical than in the movies.

LOCAL GIRLS PROVE THEY REALLY CAN
SLEIGH FOR HOLLY HOSPICE

Hollywood came to Bromster last week when Molly Bell and Grace Wright (both 15) pulled off some real-life movie magic – organizing the film crew from the Sleigh Another Day *blockbuster to film the music video for "Love Your Elf!" right here in our home town.*

But that wasn't the only surprise. The two teen heroes made such an impression on the stars of the film that their enthusiastic Sleigh Another Day *auction, with Maeve Murphy as a rousing Father Christmas and the normally serious Joseph D Chambers in character as a naughty elf, ended up going viral, helping the film bounce back to the top of the box office chart just in time for Christmas. The video also prompted an official re-release of "Love Your Elf!" which saw the track rocket straight to number one, with profits going to Bromster's very own Holly Hospice.*

It wasn't just a last-minute prize of some tickets to Lapland that helped the girls raise the crucial cash for the hospice, all in honour of Grace's Christmas-loving granddad, Grampy G (George, pictured right).

The moviemakers were so impressed with the public's reaction to the local fundraiser, they too made a sizeable donation, thanks to executive producers Bry and Cate Chambers.

Elijah Nokes, the newest full-time member on the press team, had this to say about the whirlwind few weeks. "The whole Sleigh Another Day cast and crew were delighted to come to the charming village of Bromster – we couldn't have picked a more Christmassy location to film the video. But, as delighted as we are about Sleigh Another Day hitting the box office top spot, we're even more delighted to have helped the inimitable Molly and Grace raise over £100k for Holly Hospice. Those girls are the true superstars, and it was a real life movie moment when Grace's ticket was drawn out as winner to come with us to Lapland. Christmas magic at its finest."

Holly Hospice has confirmed the funds will be used to build an extensive new social wing dedicated to George Wright. They're hoping to open the new complex with a screening of Still Sleighing, the sequel due to start filming in London this year, with title track again being produced by The Brussel Shouts. Grace was heard saying she was "totally stoked" and "honoured" to be asked to dance at the opening of *the new building when her dad officially declares it open. Molly was also available to comment and wanted to wish all of our readers a Merry Christmas. The familiar face was also keen to remind us that "this Christmas, whoever you are, have an awesome time with your friends and family, and always, always remember to love your elf".*

LOVE YOUR ELF!

Oh! Little Elf! Little Elf!
Ring your jingle bell!
You've come here to make mischief,
And spread havoc this Noel.

Santa sent his elf,
To be his eyes and ears.
From North Pole to our kitchen shelf
Are we good or bad this year?

Creeping down the stairs,
Christmas tree a-twinklin',
But Jingle Bells! Caught unawares,
Not tricks, but joy you're sprinklin'.

Oh! Little Elf! Little Elf!
Ring your jingle bell!
You're bad at making mischief,
But we think you're really swell.

Sugar and salt you switched,
But it made the sprouts taste yum.
Gold glitter you did scatter,
Now the dog looks mighty fun.

Candy canes in bed,
Hidden in the sheets,
But now we smell so minty fresh
And good enough to eat!

Oh! Little Elf! Little Elf!
Ring your jingle bell!
You're bad at causing mayhem,
But we think you're really swell.

Santa said come back,
To his grotto you must head.
But we have got a better idea,
Spend Christmas here instead.

You've made this season great,
We don't want it to end,
Your face is green, your heart is big,
You're our tiny festive friend.

Oh! Little Elf! Little Elf!
Ring your jingle bell!
Please stay with us this Christmas,
And the whole year round as well.

Elf: "Happy holidays from the cutest
little elf in the whole wide world!"

ACKNOWLEDGEMENTS

OK, there's only one page left so I'll keep this quick.

To Yasmin, Sophie and Sarah – thank you for being the dream Jingly team. And for getting Beyoncé stuck in my head for all of the edits (no bad thing). And to the whole Scholastic crew, thank you not just for all your support with this book, but with everything since day one. Special shout-outs to Lauren, Jamie, Harriet, Ruth, all of the Rights, Marketing and PR teams, and Kathy and Jessica too.

Gemma, thanks for being the very best, most supportive (and Christmas loving) agent there is. And to my lovely family – I hope you know how lucky I am to have you in my life. Rose, you rock my world even more than Christmas novelty snacks and that is saying A LOT.

Thanks to my friends too (sorry for making some of you sing Christmas songs in the swimming pool). And a huuuuge thanks to the incredibly talented Elsa – creator and namer of The Brussel Shouts and Rocking Stockings. What a genius. I can't wait to read whatever you write.

And a thank you to you. For reading. I hope Molly, Ru and the crew brought some festive cheer, and in the words of Molly's dad (probably): "Have your elf a very happy holiday!"